THE SAVAGE FORTRESS

SARWAT CHADDA

SCHOLASTIC INC.

No part of this publication may be reproduced, stored in a retrieval system, or transmitted in any form or by any means, electronic, mechanical, photocopying, recording, or otherwise, without written permission of the publisher. For information regarding permission, write to Scholastic Inc., Attention: Permissions Department, 557 Broadway, New York, NY 10012.

ISBN 978-0-545-38517-6

Copyright © 2012 by Sarwat Chadda. All rights reserved. Published by Scholastic Inc. SCHOLASTIC, the LANTERN LOGO, and associated logos are trademarks and/or registered trademarks of Scholastic Inc.

Arthur A. Levine Books hardcover edition designed by Phil Falco, published by Arthur A. Levine Books, an imprint of Scholastic Inc., October 2012.

12 11 10 9 8 7 6 5 4 3 2 1   13 14 15 16 17 18/0

Printed in the U.S.A. 40
First Scholastic paperback printing, October 2013

Half-title and other art by Jason Chan

For my mother

Now I am become Death, the destroyer of worlds.
— *The Bhagavad Gita*

CHAPTER ONE

"That is *so* not a cobra," said Ash. It couldn't be. Weren't cobras endangered? You couldn't have them as pets, not even here in India.

"That so totally *is* a cobra. Look," said his sister, Lucky.

Ash leaned closer to the snake. It swayed in front of him, gently gliding back and forth in tempo with the snake charmer's flute music. The scales, oily green and black, shone in the intense sunlight. It blinked slowly, watching Ash with its bright emerald eyes.

"Trust me, Lucks," said Ash. "That is not a cobra."

The snake revealed its hood.

It was totally a cobra.

"Told you," she said.

If there was anything worse than a smug sister, it was a smug sister three years younger than you.

"What I meant was, of course it's a cobra, but not a real cobra," replied Ash, determined his sister wasn't going to win this argument. "It's been defanged. They all are. Hardly a cobra at all. More like a worm with scales."

Almost as though it had been following the conversation,

the cobra hissed loudly and revealed a pair of long, needle-sharp ivory fangs. Lucky waved at it.

"I wouldn't do that if —"

The cobra darted at Lucky and before Ash knew it, he'd jumped between them. The snake's mouth widened, and he stared at the two crystal drops of venom hanging off its fangs.

"Parvati!" snapped the snake charmer. The cobra stopped an inch from Ash's neck.

Whoa.

The snake charmer tapped the basket with his flute. The cobra, after giving Ash one last look, curled itself back into it, and the lid went on.

Ash started breathing again. He looked at Lucky. "You okay?" She nodded.

"See that? I just saved your life," Ash said. "I practically *hurled* myself between you and that incredibly poisonous snake. Epically brave." And, now that the heart palpitations had subsided, epically stupid, he thought. But protecting his little sister was his duty, in the same way hers was to cause as much trouble as possible.

The snake charmer hopped to his feet. He was an old bundle of bones wrapped in wrinkled, ash-coated dark skin and a saffron loincloth. His only possessions, apart from the snake and his flute, were a shoulder bag made from sackcloth and a long bamboo walking stick. Serpentine dreadlocks hung down to his waist.

A sadhu, a holy man. Varanasi, India's holiest city, was full of them. Legend said that if you died here, you got instant access to heaven, with no worries about the cycles of reincarnation and rebirth. That meant the streets were cluttered with old people, just waiting to live up to the famous saying: *See Varanasi and die*.

Built on the banks of the sacred Ganges River, the city was a living museum with a temple or some dilapidated palace on every street. Ash had loved nothing better than exploring the ancient city. Their first few days here had been an amazing adventure, venturing into the dingy alleys and winding lanes, experiencing the intense, almost overwhelming life of India firsthand.

But now?

Now, two weeks into their trip, Ash felt suffocated by the oppressive temperatures, the stench, the crowds, and the death. It was in your face the moment you woke up. Back home Ash could retreat to his room, to the cool, to the quiet. But India was bedlam.

The narrow, ancient streets shimmered in the July heat. Cars, rickshaws, beggars, merchants, pilgrims, and holy men jammed the lanes and footpaths. A scooter bounced past, its horn crying out like a distressed duck, swerving violently as it dodged around a malnourished-looking cow snoozing in the middle of the road.

"Where is the bloody car?" swore Ash's uncle Vik. He gazed up and down the crowded road, trying to spot the taxi they'd hired to take them to the party. He unfolded a white handkerchief from his breast pocket and wiped the sweat from his shiny bald head.

"The cow's blocking the road," said Ash. "It's just sitting there with its tongue up its nose."

Loose skin hung off the cow's huge shovel-sized hip bones and shoulder blades, and one horn was missing. It sat serene and relaxed while all around it scooters, cars, and irate motorists yelled and swore.

Uncle Vik huffed loudly. "This is very bad. We will be late."

"Why can't I just go back to the house?" Ash asked. "I don't see why I have to go to some boring party."

His aunt Anita sighed. She'd put on her best sari and was struggling to keep it dust-free. "Lord Savage is a most important gentleman," she said. "We have been invited especially."

Lord Savage was some rich English aristocrat who sponsored archaeological digs all over India — all over the world, in fact. Uncle Vik lectured on ancient Indian history at Varanasi University, so sooner or later their paths were going to cross. Ash had heard often that working on one of Savage's projects could do wonders for Uncle Vik's career.

"This is your heritage too, nephew." His uncle's deep brown eyes shone as he put his hand on Ash's shoulder. "This is where we come from."

"I come from West Dulwich, London," Ash answered.

"Why can't you just try and enjoy your time here like Lucky?"

His sister was waving at the cow, trying to get some reaction. It gave her an imperious snort.

"She's enjoying it because she's only ten, and she's stupid."

"I am not stupid!" Lucky poked her elbow into his ribs.

"Oh, was that meant to hurt?" said Ash. "I didn't notice."

"That's because you're so fat."

"I am not fat!" fumed Ash.

"For God's sake, just stop it, both of you," said Aunt Anita. "It's too hot."

Uncle Vik folded his handkerchief away. "I thought coming to India was your idea, Ash."

Ash shut up. Uncle Vik was right.

His room back home was stuffed with books on Indian weaponry and mythology, all from Uncle Vik. There had been endless e-mails and tales via the Internet where his uncle had recounted the grand tales of India's past, stories of maharajahs, tiger hunts, and the legendary wars between heroes and terrible demons.

So when the summer holidays had come around and his parents, both of whom worked full-time, had suggested he and Lucks go over and visit their relatives, Ash had practically packed his bags there and then. Uncle Vik couldn't afford flights to England on his salary, so it was Ash's only chance to meet him and see India for real.

But that had been before the infernal heat, the flies, and the cobras. How was he going to survive another four weeks here?

"There he is. At last." Vik pointed along the road. Through the hazy heat, Ash spotted an old black and yellow Ambassador taxi. But the car couldn't move. Thanks to the cow, the traffic had come to a complete standstill. A couple of men pulled at the rope around its neck, but the white beast remained stubbornly immobile.

The snake charmer ambled up to them, hands cupped.

Uncle Vik handed him a ten-rupee note. "You can have a hundred if you get that cow moving."

The old man nodded his thanks and strolled off toward the cow.

"What's he doing?" said Lucky.

The sadhu swished his bamboo stick back and forth in front of the beast. It blinked, then began to sway its head side to side, watching the stick. The old man swung it wider and wider.

Then he smacked the cow's nose.

The cow bellowed and jumped to its feet. The sadhu smacked it again and the beast stumbled backward. Seconds later engines started up, horns honked, and the traffic got moving.

The holy man came back, grinning broadly.

Vik prodded Ash and put a hundred rupee note in his hand. "Give it to him quickly."

Ash frowned but passed it over to the holy man. Their eyes met and Ash froze. Beneath the thick, bushy eyebrows, the old man's eyes were a startling blue.

The sadhu drew the money from Ash's stiff fingers.

Ash looked back as they clambered into the taxi and saw the old man staring at him, staff resting on his shoulder. Then the crowds spilled on to the now open street and the sadhu disappeared.

Ten minutes later they were out of the city and rolling along the dusty country road. Eyes closed, Ash leaned out of the window, hoping the rushing wind might offer some escape from the furnace-hot temperatures.

Right now his friends would be out and about in London. If he were there too, he, Akbar, and Josh would be holed up in Sean's basement, which, thanks to his dad who was head of IT at some bank, was a gamer's paradise.

All-day gaming sessions. His mates. McDonald's. These were the best things in life.

Oh, and Gemma. Gemma was a new addition to the list.

Ash had to face it, India wasn't for him. The sooner this trip was over, the better. It wasn't worth all the sweat and heat and flies.

No, that wasn't entirely true. He did think the castles were cool. England did castles, but not like India. India's castles could have come straight out of the Lord of the Rings. They were vast and intricate. Halls filled with statues and fountains and gardens of wandering peacocks. The fortresses weren't built for horses but elephants. India didn't do small, intimate, and quiet. From the castles through to the palaces, the Himalayas to the north and the Thar Desert to the west, India was all big-screen cinema, trumpets, and deafening noise.

"You okay?" Ash asked Lucky. She looked pale. "Sit here," he said, and swapped places with her so she could sit next to the window and get some fresh air. She hadn't adjusted to the spicy food the way he had, and all this jumping up and down surely wasn't helping her digestion.

The sun left a bloody smear across the sky as it sank below the horizon. Eddie Singh, their driver, took them off the main road, and they bounced down a winding track. The car seemed to have a supernatural knack for finding the largest rocks and deepest potholes.

"Taxi service and full body massage, no extra charge," laughed Eddie as he wrestled with the steering wheel.

"Is this really necessary?" asked Auntie Anita, struggling to keep her sari in place. "I thought the main road led to the bridge."

"The bridge is down. Loose foundations or something," said Vik. "Lord Savage has made arrangements."

"What arrangements?" asked Ash.

"There." Lucky pointed ahead. ·

Cars lined the river's edge, their drivers chatting and smoking. A woman in a white cotton suit directed guests into a flotilla of row boats, tied up along a rickety wooden platform on the bank. A steady stream of guests were being rowed across the water to the opposite bank, and boys ran back and forth with lanterns. Eddie parked up beside the other cars.

That hurt. Ash stretched as he got out, uncurling his spine and hoping no permanent damage had been done. His bum felt as if the seat springs had left deep impressions in both buttocks.

Brittle leaves rustled in a nearby bush and something moved within it. Lucky grabbed Ash's sleeve as a scrawny vulture, stringy red intestine trailing out of its beak, raised its head out of the bush to watch them.

Ash stepped closer to inspect its feast. A dead water buffalo lay on the muddy bank, its hind legs gone. The vulture dipped its beak into the socket and drew out a plump eyeball. Ash heard it pop as the vulture swallowed.

"That is totally pukey," Lucky said, her nose wrinkling.

"Professor Mistry?"

The woman in white approached them, smiling in greeting. She was Caucasian and very tanned and, despite the oncoming darkness, she still wore a pair of sleek sunglasses. Ivory pins held her thick, unkempt, red-streaked hair loosely in place. She pressed her palms together.

"*Namaste*. I'm Jackie, Lord Savage's personal assistant," she said in a posh accent.

"Vikram Mistry, at your service." He took Aunt Anita's hand. "And this is my wife."

"Namaste, Mrs. Mistry," said Jackie.

"Call me Anita," she replied, smoothing out the creases in her pearly white and silver silk sari. She only wore it for special occasions, like visiting rich aristocrats.

"What a perfectly beautiful child," said Jackie, catching a glimpse of Lucky. She knelt down and stroked Lucky's cheek with a long nail, her smile widening. "Why, you look good enough to eat."

Lucky cringed and took a step behind Ash. Jackie's smile thinned, then she slowly straightened up and faced Uncle Vik.

"Lord Savage is very keen to meet you," Jackie said. "He's a great admirer of your work."

"I am flattered."

Jackie gestured at the boats. "I'm so sorry about this, but I hope you'll be okay. There've been a lot of heavy trucks crossing back and forth because of the excavations. This morning one of them went over the side. A bad business." She snapped her fingers, and a local boy ran up bearing a kerosene lantern.

"Excavations?" asked Vik. "I didn't realize there were any digs in Varanasi."

"In Varanasi and elsewhere," said Jackie. "The Savage family have been staunch supporters of Indian archaeology for many centuries. Lord Savage's weapons collection is one of the finest in the world."

Weapons collection? thought Ash. Maybe tonight wouldn't be a total loss.

"Is this why Lord Savage wants to meet me?" his uncle asked.

"All in good time, Professor."

"What happened there?" said Ash, pointing at the half-devoured buffalo.

"Marsh crocodile. The river has a few," said Jackie. "Not the place for a dip."

Ash couldn't help but notice how her gaze lingered on the dead buffalo. And was she licking her lips? The woman was pure freak show. That's probably what happened to Brits if you stayed out here too long.

Jackie led them to the pier, a rickety row of moldering planks held together by near-rotten rope. The only thing solid about it was the pair of stone pillars that stood at the end. The boat looked like one of the punts Ash had been in during a day trip to Cambridge, shallow and low in the water. Not very crocodile-proof.

"This looks well dodgy," said Ash. "Where are the life jackets?"

"Just get in," said Aunt Anita. "And keep your fingers out of the water."

The boatman pushed them off with his oar and they drifted away from the bank. Ash peered back at the scattered vehicles until the shining headlights dwindled to mere spots in the darkness.

"Look!" Lucky jumped to her feet and the boat rocked perilously.

"Sit down!" snapped Aunt Anita.

A cliff-like mass stood on the opposite bank, rising high straight out of the water. Torches flared, one by one, along its immense, vine-covered battlement walls. Polished marble and the soft egg-curve shape of a roof glistened in the torchlight. Black glass sparkled like ebony diamonds from the balcony windows.

Uncle Vik had told them the building had once belonged to the maharajah of Varanasi but had been abandoned and left to rot for decades. Now the monolithic palace would be grander than it had ever been. It had a new owner and a new name.

The Savage Fortress.

Apart from the castle, the land was empty of any other buildings or life. It was as if the Savage Fortress had devoured everything, leaving only dried-out streams, a few stunted trees, and, in the distance, what looked like a small shantytown of tents and crude hovels. Trucks lined the road, and Ash could see a few big bulldozers, presumably from the excavations Jackie had mentioned.

"Wonder what's out there," said Vik. He wiped his glasses

and cast a critical eye over the wide field. "Whatever he's doing, he's serious about it."

The boat touched the broad steps that led to the water gate. As they ascended the stairs, Ash spotted a stone shield over the arched entrance. The shield was carved with three bulbous flowers and a pair of crossed swords.

"The Savage coat of arms," said Uncle Vik, wiping his glasses to get a better look.

"Are they thistles?" asked Ash.

"No. Poppies. The Savage family made its first fortune during the Opium Wars with China."

"And the motto?" asked Ash, looking at the scroll below the coat of arms. *"Ex dolor adveho opulentia?"*

"From misery comes profit."

Nice.

They clambered up a steep, dank passageway and soon emerged into a crowded courtyard, decorated for a party. Servants, dressed in white and wearing golden turbans and sashes, carried silver trays of drinks and food among a field of color. Silken pavilions dotted the large grass-covered square.

Candelabras and oil lamps lit the area, and moths danced in the glow of the amber flames. Dream-like classical Indian music drifted down from the raised galleries that surrounded the courtyard. There were over a hundred guests, and soon Ash's uncle and aunt lost themselves in the crowd. Lucky spotted a gang of younger kids and ran off to play.

Ash decided to explore.

Marble statues loomed in the corners, and the walls bore

vast carvings of heroes and monsters, many which Ash recognized as images from Indian mythology. One wall was filled with a battle scene taken from the epic tale of the Ramayana — probably the most famous of the Indian legends, and Ash's favorite.

A giant golden warrior dominated the picture, his eyes blazing with fury, his mouth open in a silent roar of rage. He swung a pair of massive swords, reaping men left and right. All around him lay corpses, and behind him stood his army of demons: hideous human-animal hybrids with scales or fur-covered bodies, and tails or wings.

It was Ravana, the demon king.

To the far left of the wall, almost off it, stood a warrior with his bow raised and an arrow pointed at Ravana. The artist had painted the arrow with obvious care, surrounding it with flames and inlaying its center with gold leaf. This wasn't just any arrow. It was an *aastra*, a weapon charged with the power of a god.

The scene caught the demon king's last moment. Any second now the arrow, the aastra, would be launched and penetrate his heart, shattering him. And only one hero could shoot it: the hero Rama.

"What do you think?" said a voice from behind Ash.

A figure stepped out of the shadows under one of the gallery walkways.

"Namaste," he said.

English for sure, the man wore a fine white linen suit with a pale silk shirt, so the only points of color were his blue eyes — two brilliant chips of the coldest ice. He stepped closer and Ash caught his breath as the man came into the glow of a nearby forest of candles.

It was as though his face had been shattered, then crudely recast. Deep irregular grooves covered his waxy skin, revealing a fine network of veins beneath. Limp clumps of white hair hung from his liver-spotted scalp.

His gloved hand tightened around the tiger-headed silver handle of his cane. The ruby eyes of the beast sparkled as they watched Ash. The man inclined his head.

"I am Lord Alexander Savage."

CHAPTER TWO

"Ash Mistry," Ash said.

"Beautiful, isn't he?" said Savage. He drew his fingers over the outline of the demon king's face. "Even with his destruction at hand, defiant to the last."

"He's horrific." Ash wasn't sure if he was talking about the gruesome mural or Savage himself.

"You think so? Why?"

"He was the demon king. He threatened the entire world."

"And the world is such a pleasant place now, is it?"

Ash looked again at the glaring eyes of Ravana. The face seemed alive, a mask of arrogant fury and pure hate. "At least it's not a hell. That's what Ravana wanted, a world fit for demons."

Savage looked at him inquisitively, tapping his walking stick against the flagstone. "Well said, lad, well said."

A woman broke from the crowd and joined them. Dressed in a white silk sari embroidered with spiderwebs, she towered above Ash like a willowy goddess, but close up he saw that the makeup had been laid on heavily; her face was smooth and rigid from a layer of powder, as lifeless as a mannequin's. Eight thick black tresses hung around her cheeks, four on either side. The woman's gaze paused on him and there was a flicker of a condescending smile. Ash saw himself reflected in her big, wraparound sunglasses. He looked small and insignificant.

"Sir, the board of directors is here," she said.

"It's been interesting talking with you," Savage said to Ash. "Enjoy the party." He took the woman's hand and entered the gathering. But even as the sea of people began to swirl and circle around him, Savage briefly looked back at Ash, his smile locked rigidly in place.

"Where's your sister?" Anita appeared beside him.

Ash waved at one of the buildings. "She's probably just gone off to the toilet."

Everyone got some stomach problems when they hit India, the "Delhi Belly" — it was inevitable. Well, everyone but Ash. Vik had joked that Ash could do with a dose as he could afford to lose a few pounds. But Ash wasn't fat. He was just . . . well-covered.

Anita glanced at Vik, who was beckoning her. He was talk-ing to Savage, and clearly needed her.

Ash sighed. "I'll find Lucky."

Weird, wasn't it? Half the time they were arguing and fighting one another, but when it came down to it, he and his sister were close. True, they didn't play much together anymore — he was thirteen, after all — but he had read her all the Harry Potters when she'd been younger. He was the eldest and it was his job to look after his little sister. It was the Indian way.

Anita's wrinkled brow flattened and smoothed. She smiled at him and ruffled his hair. "You are a good boy."

Ash stopped one of the waiters and asked him where the toilets were. The guy, trying to keep a tray of martinis from spilling, just waved over his shoulder, then hurried off.

Ash wandered toward the main building and peered through the half-open doors that led into a dimly lit hallway.

"Lucks?" His voice vanished into the marble-clad hall, bouncing between the walls until it was swallowed by the darkness. Ash proceeded in.

Light shone from within an ancient bronze pendant lantern high above him, its colored glass casting a jigsaw of amber, red, and green over the peeling and broken plaster. Mounted on opposite walls were two huge mirrors with ornate gilt frames. Their backing silver had long since tarnished to black, so the reflections were tainted, dark and faint, like shadowy ghosts.

"Lucks?" Ash's heart beat rapidly in his chest as he crept among the swaying shadows.

Then he spotted the steps, barely visible in the gloom. Had she gone up there?

Climbing up, Ash soon came to a stout, iron-studded door. He turned the door handle and pushed. "Lucks? You in here?"

Oil lamps flickered, spreading warm orange patches of light along the walls. The room was double height, with row upon row of glass cabinets filling the main floor. The upper floor was a balcony with shelves stuffed with books and scrolls. Ash took a deep breath and went in.

He peered at the nearest shelf — and gasped. Shrunken heads, their eyes and mouths sewn shut, sat serenely dumb, blind, and dead within the nearest cabinet. A snake, its skin albino white, floated in a jar beside them, wrapped around and around itself in its yellow liquid. Ash leaned closer.

The snake had a small, utterly human face. A baby's face. Its mouth was half-open, revealing a tiny pair of fangs.

Beyond creepy. Ash backed away, chilly in spite of the day's lingering heat. A shiver crept across his skin as he felt the creature's eyes upon him.

The cabinets were made of dark, highly polished wood, with rows of drawers beneath them. Ash hooked his fingers through an iron ring and opened one.

Knives. Claws. Daggers.

Very cool.

He picked out something that looked like a pair of brass knuckles, but had a row of four steel claws jutting out from it. Ash put it over his fingers and admired the deadly spikes. He read the tag. *BAGH NAKH*: tiger claws. This had to be part of Savage's famous weapons collection.

EXTREMELY cool.

He so wanted the claws, but if he stuffed them in his pocket, they'd tear a hole in his thigh. Reluctantly he put them back and slid the drawer shut.

He wandered around the cabinets, then stopped at a desk that sat in front of a half-open window. He hadn't seen it from the door since it was behind all the displays. A set of moth-eaten velvet curtains hung on either side of the window, their loose threads fluttering in the desert breeze.

A scroll was unrolled over the red leather desktop. Its edges were burned black and much of the writing obscured with soot, but Ash recognized some of the symbols. Didn't Uncle Vik have hundreds of scrolls like this littering the house? He was obsessed with translating Harappan, the ancient language of India. Beneath each line of Harappan pictograms there were another two rows of writing. One set comprised rows of vertical dashes and sloping slashes, and the line beneath that was in Egyptian hieroglyphs. The scroll was held in place by small bronze statues, one standing on each corner. Ash picked one up.

About four inches tall, the statue was of a long-limbed girl, her arms encased in bracelets. Her chin was up, haughty and proud, with wide almond-shaped eyes. Her hand was on her hip, like she was resting after a dance.

Ash put her down and traced his finger lightly over the thin yellow parchment. It felt like the softest leather, old and wrinkled. Then he noticed that the parchment was marked with dark spots, old blemishes like freckles.

Freckles?

Ash froze. He stared at the scroll and suddenly noticed the minute wrinkles and almost invisible cross-hatching. He turned his hand over in the flickering firelight, looking at the similar pattern of lines over the knuckles and fingers.

The scroll was made of human skin.

Footsteps tapped just outside the door. The handle turned and the hinges creaked. Ash darted behind the curtain.

I'm so busted. No one would believe he'd wandered in here looking for the toilets. Ash forced himself to stand utterly still and breathe in the smallest, quietest sips.

"Thank you for accepting my invitation at such short notice, Professor Mistry."

I'm beyond busted. Way beyond.

Ash could picture the rest of his life. Grounded forever. Before he left England, his dad had warned him to be on his best behavior, and breaking and entering did not fall under the heading of "best behavior," no matter how he tried to spin it. But in spite of himself, he wanted to know why his uncle was here. Ash peeked through the gap in the heavy drape.

Uncle Vik entered alongside Savage and someone else. This new guy was a giant, as wide as the doorway. His skin was tough and weathered, deeply grooved like bark, or scales. He was dressed in the same white linen as Savage's servants, but the suit strained over his hugely muscular body. His arms were thicker than Ash's waist, and Ash wasn't slim. A pair of large sunglasses hid his eyes.

"I must admit," said Uncle Vik, "your invitation was a surprise. I wasn't aware you knew of my work."

"Few people have your dedication to ancient Indian history."

The big man went to a cabinet and poured out two big tumblers of whiskey.

Savage picked up the dancing girl statue and gave it to Uncle Vik. "What do you think?"

Uncle Vik stared at it like he'd just been given the Holy Grail. "Is this authentic?"

"Found at the new site, out in Rajasthan." Savage put his hand on Uncle Vik's shoulder and led him to the scroll. Ash's uncle fumbled in his breast pocket for his glasses. He leaned over the desk, his nose just a few inches from the writing.

"As you know, no one has succeeded in translating the Harappan language," said Savage. "The problem is there's no Rosetta stone."

Rosetta stone? Ash remembered seeing it at the British Museum. The Rosetta stone was a big black slab with the same message on it in three languages: Egyptian hieroglyphs, Demotic, and ancient Greek. At the time the Rosetta stone had been discovered, no one knew what Egyptian hieroglyphs meant, but because Greek and Demotic were already understood, the historians were able to compare words and translate the hieroglyphs, turning them from a bunch of mysterious symbols into a language. The stone had been the key to understanding ancient Egypt, and its discovery was one of the greatest events in archaeological history. He leaned closer and listened.

Uncle Vik nodded. "Yes. The only way to translate an unknown language is to have an example of it in another, already-known language. That's why we know almost nothing about the Harappans. We have so much writing from their culture, but no key to unlock it."

"Until now," said Savage. He put his hand down on the scroll. "This is that key. A message in Harappan, Sumerian cuneiform, and Old Kingdom Egyptian. And since we know cuneiform and Egyptian . . ."

"We should be able to translate the Harappan." Vik stared at the scroll. "My God, you're right." He straightened, his face glowing with delight. "Lord Savage, you've achieved a miracle."

"No, Professor Mistry. The miracle will be yours. I would like you to complete the translation."

Uncle Vik brushed the edge of the scroll. "This fire damage is recent. What happened on the dig?"

Ash saw how Savage's gaze cooled as he and the big guy exchanged a brief look. The Englishman stroked his chin before speaking.

"Trouble at the site," Savage said. "Are you a superstitious man, Professor?"

"Why?"

"The local villagers believe the site to be home to evil spirits. There have been several attempts to sabotage the excavations." Savage reached into his jacket and drew out a slip of paper. "Consider my offer."

Uncle Vik took the slip: a check. His eyes widened as he read the figure in the box. Ash squinted — he couldn't make out the number, but there were a lot of zeroes. A lot.

"You're joking. I can't accept this." Vik shook his head and tried to hand the check back. "It's two million pounds."

Oh, my God.

"I am happy to double it." Savage opened his fountain pen.

"No. No." Uncle Vik put his hand on the desk to steady himself.

"We will change the world with this knowledge, Professor Mistry. The Harappans were hundreds of years ahead of their time. What other knowledge did they have that we've lost? The answers are in this scroll," said Savage. "And I'm willing to pay any price to find them."

Savage's eyes shone with desire. A spider of fear crept along Ash's spine and rested its cold legs against his neck as he watched the Englishman lick his lips. He was telling the truth, and it was terrifying. Savage was a man capable of doing anything to achieve his goal.

"Do we have a deal?" Savage carefully peeled off his glove. Wrinkled skin hung loosely around bone and stringy flesh. It was the hand of a dried-out skeleton.

Two million. TWO MILLION. What couldn't the family do with that sort of cash?

But why did it feel so wrong?

No. Don't. Ash wanted to cry out, but couldn't. He was frozen. And the look in Savage's eyes told him that if his uncle refused, Savage would smash his head open with his silver-topped cane.

"A deal." Uncle Vik took Savage's hand.

A feral smile spread over Savage's lips. He shook Uncle Vik's hand, then put his glove back on. The big man handed out the drinks.

"Thank you, Professor." Savage tapped his glass against Uncle Vik's. "I will arrange for all the paperwork to be brought here."

Uncle Vik took two big gulps of the whiskey. "You don't want me out in Rajasthan?"

"No, not yet. The translations refer to some important artifacts buried here in Varanasi." Savage emptied his glass. "Now, if you would return to the party. I have some business to discuss with Mayar."

Oh, no. How long were they going to stay here? Ash wasn't sure he could stand still much longer. If he just ran out to Vik, they couldn't do anything, could they? But before he could act, his uncle left, closing the door behind him.

Savage sighed. "The excavations here are going too slowly, Mayar," he said.

"The men are suspicious. They will not venture near the Seven Queens."

"I do not pay them to be suspicious. See to it tomorrow." Savage walked to the window. He rested his hands on the balcony and looked out, standing only a few inches from Ash. Ash's heart beat so loudly, he was sure Savage would hear it.

"Why not send him to Rajasthan now?" asked Mayar.

"The work there is nearly complete; the Iron Gates have been found. What I want is the key to open them, and the key, my dear Mayar, is buried here in Varanasi. Once the scrolls have been translated, I'll know exactly where." Savage's fingers traced the grooves that crisscrossed his face. "I'm running out of time."

"I will encourage the men to greater efforts."

Ash didn't like the way Mayar said *encourage*. It sounded painful.

"One more thing," said Savage. "What did I tell you about feeding near the fortress?"

Mayar laughed so deeply that the cabinets rocked. It was a laugh full of cruel mockery. "Forgive me, Master," he said, clearly not meaning any of it. "But the buffalo was too tasty to waste. Or would you rather we ate among your guests?"

Savage spun around and smashed his cane into the man's head. Mayar crashed backward, shattering the nearest cabinet. Ash clamped his hand over his mouth as the shrunken heads and the bottles of monsters tumbled across the floor. As Mayar fell, his sunglasses bounced off, landing at Ash's feet.

Oh, no. His feet were visible right at the bottom of the curtain. If they found him now, he was dead. Instinctively he kicked the glasses away.

Oh, please don't see me. Please.

Mayar was big and muscular, far larger and stronger than Savage. But he groveled on the floor as Savage pressed his foot against the man's throat.

"Do not try my patience, *rakshasa*," warned Savage.

Rakshasa? Why did that word ring a bell? And why did it make Ash shiver?

"I . . . meant no disrespect, Master."

Savage lifted his foot. "Get up." He turned and stepped out the door. "And put on your glasses. I don't want you scaring the mortals."

Mortals? What is going on?

Mayar stood up and straightened himself. He muttered something that probably wasn't complimentary about Savage, then picked up his glasses with a grunt.

As he raised them to his face, Ash saw his eyes. They were yellow, and the pupils were a pair of black, vertical slits.

The eyes of a reptile.

Mayar slipped the glasses back in place and the two of them left. Ash suddenly remembered what a rakshasa was. The old Indian legends were full of them, but they had a different name in English.

It was *demon*.

CHAPTER THREE

Ash stayed paralyzed behind the curtain. The formaldehyde from the broken bottles stank up the room, and his eyes watered, but any second now the door would open and Savage — or worse, the rakshasa — would burst back in. No, he couldn't move, too dangerous.

He blinked, staring past the fog that rose from the spilled chemicals. The snake with the baby's head had unraveled from its jar, and Ash saw it had two tiny arms tucked across its chest.

What was going on? Did that man really have those reptile eyes, or had Ash just imagined it? Had Savage called him a rakshasa, or had he misheard? Yes, that must be it. This was the real world. Maybe the man had some sort of disease. There was a lot of that in India. He wasn't a demon. Just a man.

Just a man with crocodile eyes.

Ash slowly drew back the curtain. He held his breath, ears attuned to any noises from outside, then stepped cautiously into the room. He had to get out. There was the door, but what if Savage and Mayar were just outside?

He peered out of the window. Good grief, it was a long way

down. The stones were coarse and weathered. An easy climb. Easy. But as he leaned over, his head swam with vertigo. Yes, easy if you were a ninja.

Think, think, think!

Ash went back to the door. He tried not to panic, tried not to imagine either Mayar or Savage just outside, silently waiting for the thief to emerge. Heart thudding, Ash opened it.

The corridor ahead was dark, silent, and empty.

Thank God.

That was way too close. Ash wiped the sweat off his face with his sleeve as he descended back down into the unlit hallway.

Just get out. That's all. Find the others and get out.

He caught a glimpse of himself in one of the big, dusty mirrors. He looked like death, pale and sweaty, and if his eyes had been any wider they'd have fallen out of their sockets.

Then he saw a man standing right behind him.

Ash screamed as he was spun around and thrown against the mirror. Bony fingers tipped with jagged, talon-like nails dug into his cheeks.

"What have we got here?" the man hissed. "A spy? A thief?"

Tall and exceedingly gaunt, the man was twice Ash's height but so hunchbacked they were face-to-face. The man was bald, utterly hairless in fact, with no eyebrows. His eyes were obscured behind a pair of round, pink-lensed glasses perched on top of a long, hooked nose.

"I was just looking for the toilet," Ash pleaded.

The man shook his head and his skin, two sizes too big for

his body, flapped under his chin. "You're lying, I can see it in your eyes." He pushed his thumbnail into Ash's face until it almost pierced the skin. "Those plump, juicy eyes —"

"Hello? Ash? Are you there?" It was Uncle Vik, appearing around the corner.

The man dropped Ash instantly. Ash ran straight into his uncle's arms. He'd never been happier to see anyone in his entire life.

The bald man cleared his throat. "The poor boy was lost. I was just bringing him to you, Professor Mistry."

"Thank you, mister . . . ?"

"Jat. My name is Jat."

With his uncle beside him, Ash faced the man who'd grabbed him. Why wasn't he surprised he was in a white suit? Another one of Savage's bizarre servants. Ash tightened his hold on Uncle Vik's hand.

"I really want to go home," he said.

Of course Lucky was right there in the courtyard, playing catch with a couple of other kids. Ash and Uncle Vik joined Aunt Anita as she chatted with another guest, a portly man with small, thick Coke-bottled specs.

"We've got to go," Ash said to his aunt. "I feel sick."

It was true. Extremely sick. With fear.

"Very well, Ash." She broke off from the conversation, her eyes bright. "You won't believe what's just happened."

"I've some amazing news," said Uncle Vik. His free hand tapped his breast pocket, where he'd put the check.

"Great. Let's go." Ash glanced back at the doors into the hall. Jat was there, talking to the big man, Mayar, and Jackie.

"Freaks," Ash whispered to himself.

Jackie snapped around and looked straight at him. Had she heard? From way over there? She grinned, then returned to the conversation with the other two.

"No. No. Wait." Uncle Vik carefully drew out the check and, using only his forefingers and thumbs, gently unfolded it. "Look what Lord Savage just gave me."

Up close Ash saw the check was from Coutts bank and a larger size than normal. It would be, wouldn't it? The Queen banked there. Savage's handwriting was copperplate, old-fashioned and elegant, his signature a gracefully drawn series of narrow loops and swirls.

Ash looked toward the doors again. The three were gone. "Can't we talk about this later? I want to go home."

Uncle Vik waved the check in front of Ash. "This is two million pounds, nephew. *Million.*"

"But why? It's not right, is it? He could employ a whole university with that. Why just you?"

"He needs my expertise. You don't understand, Ash. There are some translations that he wants done and I'm the only one who can do them. We'll be making history."

"A man just gives you two million quid. Don't you think that's strange?" Ash checked over his shoulder but none of Savage's white-suited henchmen, or the man himself, were around. "Savage is a freak. He surrounds himself with freaks. Give the money back, Uncle."

"Lord Savage is an . . . unusual man." Vik took off his glasses and turned them over in his hands. "But his reputation, Ash, his reputation is second to none."

"He's a freak! Are you blind or just stupid?" Ash shouted it out and a few guests turned his way. He wanted to shake some sense into his uncle.

Aunt Anita glowered at Ash. "Ashoka Mistry, apologize right now."

Ash was angry and scared. He looked up at Uncle Vik. "That's not what I meant." But it was too late. He'd struck a nerve, and he saw the hurt in his uncle's eyes.

"You don't understand, Ash. This is a golden opportunity for me to prove myself." Uncle Vik nodded as if he were accepting Ash's apology, but he wasn't really listening. "Don't you think we all deserve some recognition? Some small proof that our lives mean something?"

Ash looked down at his Converse sneakers, unable to meet his uncle's gaze.

"My dad thinks a lot of you," said Lucky, taking her uncle's hand. "He's always talking about you and what you did for him."

Uncle Vik cleared his throat. "Lord Savage wants me to start immediately. He'll have our belongings transferred here. Everything will be taken care of."

"Here?" gasped Ash.

Aunt Anita glared at Ash. She certainly hadn't forgiven him for insulting Uncle Vik. "And what exactly is wrong with that?"

"I . . . I just wanted to stay in Varanasi."

"You hate Varanasi."

"No. No, I don't." He had to think quickly. Tell them the truth? That Savage employs demons? *Yeah, right. Like they're going to believe that. Better to lie.* "I'm really interested in looking at the temples. And stuff." Ash smiled at his uncle. "You know, to find out more about my heritage."

Just keep smiling, Ash. Keep smiling.

Aunt Anita looked at Uncle Vik. Uncle Vik looked back at Ash.

They don't believe me. Keep smiling.

"All right," said Uncle Vik, slowly drawing out the word as though testing it. "If you're that keen —"

"I am. Very keen."

"It's not far," Uncle Vik said to Aunt Anita. "I could just drive out here in the morning. Back for dinner. It'll be normal office hours."

"What's he want you to do, exactly?" asked Aunt Anita.

"Translations. He's found parallel texts for the Harappan pictograms. Think about it, Anita." Uncle Vik's voice was high with passion. "A hundred years ago, no one even knew this civilization existed. Now we'll unlock their language, and who knows what we'll find." His eyes shone. "Plus there's a big dig out in Rajasthan."

"Rajasthan? But that's a thousand miles away," said Aunt Anita.

"I suppose I might have to go there sooner or later. But he's got plenty of work for me here first."

That's because Savage is looking for something. Something to do with . . .

"What are the Iron Gates, Uncle?" Ash asked.

Uncle Vik frowned. "No idea. Nothing to do with the Harappans. They were a Bronze Age culture. Iron technology didn't come along until well after they'd gone. Why?"

Ash shook his head but said nothing. Savage had said something about opening the Iron Gates. And a key, buried here in Varanasi.

Two archaeological digs. One way out in the desert, the other right here. Rakshasas. Scrolls written on human skin, and weird servants and serpent babies in jars.

What did it all mean?

"Ash, are you sick?" Anita put her hand against his forehead. "You look pale."

"The boy's not well," said Vik. "Perhaps we should go home."

Ash sighed with relief.

They drove back in silence. Eddie Singh had barely started the engine when Lucky had fallen asleep, her head resting on Anita's lap.

Ash leaned back into the creaking leather, his eyes closed. What an insane evening. He just wanted to get back and leave Savage, his strange henchmen, and tales of Harappans all behind him.

"What do you think?" whispered Uncle Vik. "Do you think the boy is right?"

Ash opened one eye, just a slit. Uncle Vik unfolded the check and held it out to Aunt Anita. She peered at it but seemed afraid to touch it.

"I don't know, Vikram," she said. "It is a lot of money."

"I'm tired of being poor, Anita," said Uncle Vik. "Tired of accepting charity from my younger brother. Tired of all the hard work and having nothing to show for it."

Aunt Anita touched her husband's shoulder. "Sanjay loves you very much."

Ash's ears pricked at the mention of his dad's name. He knew his father sent Uncle Vik money every month, but not as charity — as thanks. They'd lost their parents early on, so Uncle Vik had raised Sanjay. He'd worked from childhood to support him, to make sure his younger brother went to school every morning with a full belly, even if it meant Uncle Vik going hungry.

So Sanjay had ended up with a degree and graduate work in Britain, then a job, family, and life far from the hardships of India. Meanwhile Uncle Vik and Aunt Anita had grown old without children of their own, struggling on a lecturer's wage. Uncle Vik had made huge sacrifices for his younger sibling. Ash's father had often said that was a debt he could never repay.

Ash's gaze fell on Lucky. Could he ever be that sort of brother to her? No, life was too easy nowadays. He'd never been homeless or hungry; he'd never missed a meal in his entire life. Part of him wished he could be better; part of him was pleased he didn't need to be.

Uncle Vik folded the check and put it back in his breast pocket.

The rhythmic rocking and constant drone of the engine was making Ash soporific. His eyelids drooped, and soon he was dreaming of walking crocodiles and broken men.

CHAPTER FOUR

"Ash, you have got to see this."

"Go away. I'm dead."

"No. Get up."

"Go away. Now."

Lucky began cranking open the metal window shutters. Ash groaned as the rusty metal plates screeched.

"A real sister would let her elder brother sleep." He checked his watch. Seven. Seven! "But I suppose you can't help it. Being adopted and all."

"I was not adopted."

"It's true. Found in the trash can. Mum and Dad wanted to sell you to the organ traffickers. I stopped them. You should be grateful. Now go away."

"Look, Ash!" Lucky pulled off his sheet. "Look!"

She never listened to him. She always won. Ash crawled off the bed and joined her at the window.

In the driveway was a car. Which was weird, as they didn't have one. And it wasn't just any car, but a brand-new silver Mercedes S-Class Saloon, gleaming in the sunlight.

"Savage," said Ash.

"Can you believe it?" Lucky was at the door. "Come on."

Uncle Vik had a pink-walled bungalow on the grounds of Varanasi University. It was a staff perk. It was also an insect-infested concrete box with no air-conditioning. As Ash came out, he saw there were dozens of students at the low garden wall, all taking photos of it with their cell phones. Most of the lecturers still rode bicycles, and here was a bank-breaking Mercedes.

"It's amazing," said Uncle Vik from the driver's seat. The dashboard was all walnut trim with a 3-D map display, multimedia system, all the bells and whistles. Any more gadgets and it would have had a NASA logo on it. "It was here when I woke up."

Ash tensed. "Did . . . did you see anyone?"

"No. But the guard said it was an Englishwoman who dropped it off."

Jackie.

"Isn't this all too much?" said Aunt Anita, worriedly. "Maybe you should give this back, Vikram."

"The only way they'll get this off me" — Uncle Vik's grip tightened around the steering wheel — "is from my cold, dead hands."

Lucky opened the rear passenger door and started bouncing on the white leather seats.

"Ash, what's wrong?" asked Uncle Vik.

This wasn't right. The car. All that money. Savage had bought his uncle. It made him sick. "I just want some breakfast."

Back in the kitchen, Ash poured out some cornflakes while Aunt Anita put on the kettle and toast.

"He's dying, you know that?" said Uncle Vik as he packed papers into his briefcase.

Ash paused, the spoon an inch from his mouth. "Who?"

"Lord Savage. A skin disease. Cancer. I spoke to one of the other guests about it last night."

Aunt Anita filled up the white china teapot. "You think this business has something to do with his illness?"

"He wants to leave a legacy. See something done in his name." Uncle Vik clicked his briefcase shut. "He can't take it with him, can he?"

"Still, two million pounds, Vikram. It's not normal."

Uncle Vik kissed his wife's forehead. "Who knows what is normal to a man like him? Lord Savage wants immortality. If these excavations are a success, he'll have it. He'll be the one who unlocked the secrets of an entire culture. Two million doesn't seem much for immortality."

"And you'll be rich and famous too, Uncle," said Lucky. She shook her head at the toast and picked a banana from the fruit bowl. "Can I have a pony?"

Uncle Vik laughed. "What's mine is yours. We're family."

"What about those freaks he has working for him?" asked Ash. "They aren't normal."

"Bodyguards," said Vik. "Lord Savage is immensely rich, and India is not like London, Ash. He needs protection."

That made sense. But things were clearly not right with Savage. Ash chewed his cornflakes as he went over last night. Memories of rakshasas and men with reptile eyes didn't last long in the sunlight. If Jat was a bodyguard, maybe it was his job to scare intruders. That didn't mean he really wanted to eat their eyeballs. Savage had called Mayar a demon, but Uncle

Vik often called Lucky his little monkey. That didn't mean she had a tail.

Perhaps his mum was right and he should cut down on all those computer games. They were giving him an overactive imagination.

What was real? Believable? That Lord Savage was a terminally ill man with strange servants living in a run-down fortress, trying to get his name in the history books — or that he was an evil fiend, served by demons?

Get a grip, Ash. Next thing you know you'll be checking for monsters under the bed.

After breakfast, Ash followed his uncle to the car. Vik popped open the trunk and dropped in his briefcase, ready for his first day working for Savage.

"Be careful." Despite everything, Ash couldn't get rid of the fear he'd felt last night. "You know. Drive carefully."

"You think I'm going to risk a dent on this beautiful car?" Uncle Vik slid on a pair of driving gloves. "Our luck's changing, Ash."

"Put this on," said Aunt Anita, handing Ash some sunblock as he came back in.

"We're going out? Where?"

"We've just been given two million pounds." Anita smiled. "We're going shopping."

While Aunt Anita was busy buying up the entire stock of the silk emporium, Ash and Lucky settled in at the Cyber Café to surf the Web and catch up on e-mails.

The emporium was a grand old government office built by the Victorians, now divided up into a hundred private stalls. Ash got himself a booth open to the outside where the traffic and pedestrians formed a continuous, noisy stream.

Ash Googled *Lord Alexander Savage* and came up with a long list of charities, business ventures, and offices all over the subcontinent and the Far East. There was a photo of the current Lord Savage having tea with the Dalai Lama. Ash even found a portrait of the first Savage: a pirate, drug dealer, slave trader, and member of a group called the Hellfire Club. The original mad, bad, and dangerous to know. The ice-cold blue eyes stared at Ash from all those centuries ago, filled with cruel indifference and contempt.

Ash picked up messages from Josh, Sean, and Akbar. They'd had an all night multi-gamer and were wondering if he wanted to hook up when he got home. A big fat yes to that. If Lucky was getting a pony, then he was getting all the gaming hardware now that money was no object. Like Uncle Vik had said, they were family, and Ash's uncle was eager, desperate even, to pay his brother back for all the support he had received. He seemed a new man, raised by Savage's patronage. Maybe he was right: Their luck was changing.

Ash could picture his room now. New console. Huge flat-screen. Cinema surround-sound system. The guys would go nuts.

Josh added that he'd bumped into Gemma at the pool. Ash should have seen her, he wrote, all tanned and in a flower-patterned bikini. Josh, as Ash's best friend and on his behalf, had admitted to her that Ash had a total crush on her. Josh also added that she hadn't been violently sick when he'd told her. So that was good.

Gemma. In a bikini. Ash couldn't think about that without blushing. She was going to the top of his "Things I Like" list. Josh was going on his "To Be Killed as a Matter of Urgency" list.

Ash didn't venture much near any swimming pools. He was worried some Japanese fisherman might mistake him for a whale and harpoon him.

Lucky nudged him.

"What?"

"That girl. She's so totally checking you out." Lucky stuck her tongue out the side of her mouth, pointing in what she thought was a discreet manner.

"Shut up."

"No, she is. Honestly."

Ash glanced over his shoulder. "Which one?"

"Green."

He turned around and looked for someone in —

Wow.

An Indian girl in a green top and trousers sat at the edge of the café — tall, slim, and ultra-cool. She was about the same age as him, maybe a year or two older. Her long black hair was spread over her shoulders, shimmering like oil on water, and her lips glistened with pale gloss. She rested her pointy chin on her fist, and it did seem like she was looking straight at Ash, but her eyes were hidden behind a pair of big sunglasses, so he couldn't be sure. She could be asleep for all he knew.

"She's not looking at me," Ash said.

"Go and say something." Lucky nudged him again. "Go on."

"She's not looking at me," he repeated.

"Your loss. She's going, anyway."

Ash spun around. The stool was empty. He caught a glimpse of green silk entering the busy crowd, then the girl disappeared into the ever-moving river of people.

He could have said something.

Ash turned back to his computer again. And said what? Nothing. Girls like that weren't interested in guys like him.

Over the next few days, the mood in the house changed. Uncle Vik was busy and excited by the translations and reckoned he'd be finished within two weeks. There was talk of a new house, holidays abroad, even a pony for Lucky. Everyone was happy.

Except Ash.

Something still niggled at him. It was like a mosquito bite just under the skin. He could scratch all he liked, but it wouldn't go away.

"Ashoka!" Aunt Anita called from the front door.

"What?"

"You coming or not?"

Drat. He'd forgotten they were going to meet Uncle Vik near the Savage Fortress for a picnic. He'd planned to do some research online down at the Cyber Café. Check out prices for the best computer hardware. And she might be there, the girl in green. But that wasn't why he was going. Honestly. Just research. He slipped into his Nike T-shirt and checked himself again. It was his lucky T-shirt, and if he held his stomach in a bit, it wouldn't sit over his belly like a tent.

And if she did just happened to be there, this time he'd speak to her. See if she wanted to hang out or something. But not a date. Definitely not a date.

Ash went to the door. "I've got stuff to do. I'll go next time."

Anita glanced at her watch. "The taxi's waiting. You'll be okay?"

"He's going to look for his girlfriend, I know he is," said Lucky, sucking on a curly straw.

"You have a girlfriend?"

"No. Lucky's being an idiot. As usual."

"Then why are you wearing the Nike shirt?" Lucky turned to her aunt. "He thinks it makes him look athletic. As if."

"What's her name?" asked Aunt Anita.

"I don't have a girlfriend."

The taxi horn honked outside and Aunt Anita picked up a large wicker basket. "Well, I hope you are not mixing with bad girls, Ashoka. I'm sure when the time comes your mother will pick a most suitable girl for you from a good, respectable family."

Lucky made smooching motions from behind Aunt Anita's back. Ash glowered but forced himself to keep quiet.

You just wait, Lucks.

He went back to his room and picked up his wallet. He should just face it; the girl in green wasn't going to be there at the café. He tossed it aside.

He didn't want to go with them, and there was only one reason why: He was scared. Scared of Mayar, Savage, all of them. Even now, days later, when his uncle had been back and forth and everything was great, all Ash wanted to do was hide.

What was he afraid of? Rakshasas that didn't exist?

Stupid. You're being stupid.

And why would any girl want to go out with a guy who couldn't even leave his house? Best deal with it now.

Ash ran back out. "Hold on!" he shouted. "I'm coming!"

Uncle Vik was waiting for them on the riverbank, collecting a lantern from the trunk of the Mercedes.

"The bridge still down?" asked Aunt Anita as she saw the rowing boat up on the bank.

"Welcome to India," said Uncle Vik.

Ash looked at the boat, then at his uncle. "You can row?"

"Just get in." Uncle Vik called out to Eddie, the taxi driver: "You go. I will bring them home."

Vik pushed off with the oar and, after a few seconds of faffing, found his rhythm and took them across the Ganges. The far bank was about half a mile away, but the river flowed at a languid speed, like it knew it was too hot to hurry. Ash peered into the water and watched his face ripple and part in the oily dark waters.

"See anything?" asked his uncle.

"Just me." Ash leaned back. "How can anyone be so ridiculously good-looking?"

"So modest also," said Uncle Vik mockingly. "Just like your father."

"What's that?" Lucky pointed at something upstream.

It looked like a half-submerged log, wrapped up in cloth. The current brought it closer and Ash swung the lantern toward it.

A woman's face gazed at him. Her mouth was partially open and filled with weeds. The skin was sallow and waxy, her eyes misty, and a damp thread of white hair hung over her ancient, wrinkled skin. She'd been wrapped in a rice sack: Ash recognized the elephant logo of the Varanasi Best Rice Company.

Anita covered Lucky's eyes, but Ash just stared, in spite of the tightening of his throat and the accelerated beating of his heart.

"Why didn't they cremate her?" Ash asked. His uncle grunted as he strained with his strokes, eager to get them away from the dead woman.

Vik sighed. "Not everyone can afford the wood, Ash."

So they just dumped her in the river. He watched the woman float away until she was lost in the darkness.

The boat bumped against the bank. Trousers rolled up, Ash helped his uncle haul it out of the water. Uncle Vik pointed up the slope. "We'll head up to the Seven Queens. It's a good place for a picnic. You'll have a great view over the countryside."

Ash stopped as a sudden rush of coldness spread over him. "The Seven Queens?" What had Savage said about them?

"You'll see," said Uncle Vik.

They clambered up the slope and onto the flat terrace of fields. The countryside was divided by shallow dried-out river-beds that would only fill during the monsoon. A few bare trees dotted the landscape, and ahead were huts and tents, with a few parked Humvees bearing the poppies-and-crossed-swords emblem of the Savage Foundation.

"There's the Seven Queens," said Uncle Vik.

A row of seven white marble platforms glowed like pale bone in the bright moonlight. Over each stood a gently sloping marble canopy held up by slim columns.

"They're beautiful," said Aunt Anita. She stroked the marble with her fingertips. "Why are they called the Seven Queens?"

Uncle Vik gestured downriver, toward the fortress. "They were the wives of the old maharajah. This marks the spot where they were cremated."

"You do pick the most romantic places, Vikram."

CHAPTER FIVE

"What are you working on, Uncle?" asked Lucky. "And when can I have my pony?"

"We'll see about that," said Aunt Anita.

"I want a black-and-white one."

"Lucky . . ."

Uncle Vik took something from his pocket. As he held out his hand, Ash saw the glimmer of what looked like small silver and gold coins.

"Have a look," said Uncle Vik. He handed over a large magnifying glass.

Using the glass, Ash inspected the minute images stamped on the coins: long-horned cattle, bearded men, lithe women, and shapes that seemed either distorted or a weird combination of human and animal.

"These are seals from a new dig out in Rajasthan," Uncle Vik said.

"Where, exactly?"

"Savage is keeping most quiet about that, but I suspect it's near Jaisalmer, in the Thar Desert. There've been a few similar finds out there recently."

"What finds?" Lucky asked as she arranged the seals on the floor, inspecting each with the big lens.

Vik took off his glasses and rubbed them with his shirt. He coughed as he put them on, going into professor mode.

"The Harappans were an incredibly advanced civilization that prospered between six and four thousand years ago. They traded with the other civilizations of the age, the Old Kingdom Egyptians and the Mesopotamians. Then overnight" — Vik snapped his fingers — "they disappeared."

"Disappeared?" Lucky put the seals down and wrapped her arms around her knees, her attention now on her uncle's story.

Vik continued. "It was like they wanted to be forgotten. India went from being a great kingdom with links to all corners of the world to a cluster of illiterate villages, just like that. The cities were consumed by the sands within a few decades. Uncanny."

"War, then?" said Ash.

"No," said Uncle Vik. "From the places we've excavated, we've found no signs of weapons, burned buildings, or broken walls, the usual signs of military conquest. The Harappans simply vanished from history. It's only in the last hundred years that we've started uncovering their cities. Now Savage believes he's found the capital." His smile broadened. "Think what we might find there."

"Maybe more treasure?" said Lucky.

Ash laughed to himself. She was no doubt hoping there would be an entire stable of ponies on offer if there were.

"To be sure, there will be palaces, libraries, royal tombs, and temples. Treasures in gold and in knowledge. The city hasn't been disturbed for thousands of years. Whatever was buried there still remains." He picked up one of the seals. "I'll probably go out there once I've finished Savage's translations."

"What are you translating?" Ash asked.

"Some ancient royal treasury list," said Uncle Vik. "Savage believes there's treasure buried here too, near Varanasi. It has some connection to the works out in Rajasthan. I just don't quite know what yet."

Aunt Anita opened a box of pastries, handing one out to each of them. Uncle Vik fiddled with his old radio. The soft chords of a sitar strummed out, rising above the crackle of static and the whispers in the wind.

"Come on, Lucks." Ash got up, brushing pastry crumbs off his lap. He picked up one of the spare flashlights and flicked it on. "Let's have a nose around."

"Ash —"

"We'll be careful, Uncle."

They climbed about the ruins that dotted the northern fields of the old fortress grounds. The walls were in poor condition. Local people had been steadily pilfering the bricks over the years to help assemble their own houses. There were rows of excavation pits too, each neatly marked out with red string. Vik had told them how sites were searched: Each area was divided into twenty-foot-square packages and dug to an agreed depth, usually around ten feet. Picks, shovels, and trowels were neatly stacked up against the various huts and temporary offices, little more than awnings, with light and power fed by thick black electric cables that branched out from a rusty generator like a network of tentacles.

No one's here, Ash realized. That was strange. Uncle Vik had said that once word got out there was a dig going on, amateur treasure hunters and thieves would creep over the site at night, hoping for some gold or artifacts to sell on the black market. So why no guards?

And no workers either. There were tents, cooking equipment, and all the signs of a large workforce, but no one around. They must commute in every day. That too was unusual. What was it about this place that frightened everyone?

And what was Savage looking for?

He couldn't get the worry out of his head. There was more to this than merely translating the Harappan language and opening some ancient tomb.

"Listen, Ash." Lucky had a stick and was poking it under a rock. "I can hear something." She put her foot against the stone and heaved. The big lump rocked a bit, and then some more as Lucky worked it back and forth.

"Lucks, I wouldn't —"

It tipped over and cracked in two.

Scorpions poured out.

Shiny and black, they scuttled rapidly out of their now exposed hole under the rock. Lucky screamed and jumped back on to one of the yellow transformers. Ash backed away, kicking sand at the cluster of black shapes spilling over the ground toward him.

"Ash! Look out!"

Twine caught the back of his leg. Ash lurched and spun his arms as he tried to keep upright. The cord tangled around his ankles as he tottered on the edge of one of the excavation pits.

Lucky reached out, but she was too far away. Ash fell backward as the sandy earth beneath his feet collapsed.

CHAPTER SIX

Ash hit the bottom hard, backside over elbow, banging the back of his head. A supernova of stars erupted behind his eyes as he lay there, coughing in the dust.

"Ash, are you okay?"

He winced as he touched the scratches on his face.

"Ash, say something. Please," she said.

"This is all your fault."

Lucky by name, lucky by nature. She had upset the scorpions, but he was lying at the bottom of the pit.

Scorpions. Oh, crap.

"Where are the scorpions?" He didn't dare move. They could be sitting on him right now. In fact, he could feel something there — oh, God, were they all over him? "Can you see them?"

"Dunno. I think they ran away." But she didn't sound that sure. "You don't have any down there, do you?"

"Let's hope not."

Cautiously Ash pushed himself up to his feet, expecting a sharp stab in his back and the sudden injection of hot poison into his body at any moment. But nothing. He waited for the dizziness to pass. Then he looked around his hole. The pit was over ten feet deep. But when he tried to clamber up the sides, the soft, sandy walls crumbled under his fingers.

"Can you see a ladder or anything?" he asked.

"No." Lucky knelt over the edge. "I'm so sorry, Ash."

"Just go and get Uncle Vik."

"Okay." She stood up. "Don't go anywhere." Then she ran off, shouting.

Ash brushed himself down. Apart from the lump on the back of his head, he just had a few bruises, scratches, and a soft spot on his butt where he'd landed. He found the flashlight and, with a shake, a dim glow rose from the bulb. He searched the rest of the pit, finding a pick and a plastic water bottle filled with a yellow liquid that probably wasn't lemonade.

"Lucks?"

Nothing. He couldn't even hear her shouting. How far had they wandered? No idea. Would Lucky even recognize his hole? There were hundreds. He could be down here ages!

Ash lifted the pick. Maybe if he jammed it into the wall halfway, he could use it like a step. He drew it over his head and swung with all his might. Dust and chunks cracked and fell after a few hefty wallops.

What's this? He put his finger against a piece of rubble. The corners were square and even. It was a brick. He saw that behind a few inches of the compact, hard sand was a brick wall, definitely manmade. He tapped it — it gave a dull, hollow sound.

That means there's an open space on the other side. He lifted up the pick and struck the wall, his muscles reinvigorated with excitement. He hit it again and again, breaking up the earth.

Each blow sent a bone-jarring tremor right through him. A brick fell back with a sharp crack. Then another fell away until he was deafened by an avalanche of dust and sandstone.

Coughing harshly, Ash waved his arm at the dense cloud of dust until it cleared enough for him to see what had happened.

The wall had collapsed, revealing a chamber beyond. Even in the weak light Ash sensed the space was large. He dropped the pick and stepped through the hole, flashlight in hand. He had to duck; the ceiling was dangerously bowed by the weight of the sand upon it. The ground above groaned and dust showered down over him. Not good.

As he swept the beam of light across the rectangular room, it fell on a dusty, cobweb-covered statue.

Ash pulled away the handful of webs and saw the statue was bronze and of a muscular, blue-skinned man, roughly life-sized. In his right hand he held a curved bow, in his left an arrow.

Rama. India's greatest mythological hero.

Light shone off the arrow in his hand, attracting Ash's gaze. The shaft was ivory and the fletching white. But the light came from the arrowhead, a broad shining triangle.

It looked like gold. Real gold.

Ash touched it with trembling fingers.

The ivory shaft crumbled. The arrowhead fell away, and instinctively Ash grabbed it.

"Ouch!"

He felt a splinter go into his thumb. The tip of the

arrowhead had broken off, only a few millimeters of metal, and lodged itself deep in his flesh. It stung like a scorpion.

How could it hurt so much? His head throbbed like there was a drum behind his eyes. The statue seemed to sway, to come alive. Rama's chest rose as he took a deep breath and he tore the cobwebs off his face.

Ash's blood went cold. The face was his own.

Thud. Thud. Thud. The pounding threatened to split his skull. Ash sank to his knees, clutching his head, as waves of nausea engulfed him. The drumbeat grew louder and louder until he could hear nothing more. He closed his eyes and screamed, but his cries vanished in the echo of the drum.

CHAPTER SEVEN

"Rama!"

He blinks. The pain in his head recedes, but his vision is blurred, and all he sees is a vague shadow standing over him.

Rama? Why do they call him Rama? His name isn't Rama. It's . . .

He shakes his head. It is full of sand, obscuring his thoughts and memories. What is his name? He lies on the ground, armored warriors looming over him, their shadowed faces marked by fear and concern. He tries to rise, scraping his fingers over the hard, dusty earth. No, it is not dust that covers the earth.

"Ash . . ." he mutters. Why is that so familiar? The word cries up from a distant place, from a deep cavern. Is it some forgotten memory?

Ash. Is he Ash? Or is he —

"Rama." A hand reaches down and touches his shoulder. "My brother."

Brother? He doesn't have a brother. Does he? He turns his attention to the man above him. The face is slim, handsome but careworn. He wears armor, ornate, princely, but battered and covered with patches of dried blood. The man's brown eyes are bright with love, with worry. It is a face he recognizes.

"Lakshmana, is it you?"

"Aye, brother." Lakshmana tightens his grip and puffs hard as he lifts him back on to his feet.

Rama rises. He sways momentarily, but steadies himself. Beside him stand a few of his generals and he smiles to them. Their relief is clear. If Rama had died, then all hope would be lost.

"You fell, my prince," says Neela, his most dedicated general. The old warrior passes him a skin filled with lukewarm water. Rama guzzles it down, then pours the remainder over his head and torso. The armor steams as the water evaporates on the burning metal plates.

"You have been fighting seven days without sleep. You must rest," says Lakshmana.

Rama — yes, he is Rama — breathes deeply, settling the whirling confusion in his head.

There was a pit, and a chamber beyond. He couldn't see clearly: It was dark. He closes his eyes, trying to recall the details, but the harder he tries, the vaguer the memory becomes. All he remembers is he hurt his thumb.

He looks down at his thumb, but sees nothing. What was that name? He has forgotten already as he brushes the ash off his fingertips. No matter. He is Rama, prince of Ayodhya, and he is here.

At war.

The sky blazes red, as though the clouds themselves are on fire. The four winds howl across the endless battlefield, adding their cries to the shouts of a million soldiers, to the din of clashing blades and battered shields, the screams of the rakshasas.

The world is aflame, and Rama stands in the heart of the inferno.

"Look!" cries Neela. Neela has stood and fought beside him in countless battles, proved his courage and bravery a thousand times over, but Rama sees fear in the old warrior's eyes, hears how the voice trembles.

Rama's heart quickens and his breath is hotter than the desert wind. He looks out across a sea of blood and death at the thing that terrifies even the heroic Neela.

A giant, made of gold, plows through Rama's army. In each fist he carries a bronze sword, and he laughs as he swings them back and forth across the battalions, reaping the lives of dozens of men with each stroke. His armor bristles with spears, arrows, and broken swords. Any mortal creature would be dead a hundred times over from such injuries, but he is anything but mortal.

Behind him, his army roars with glee and savage delight. A hundred thousand rakshasas follow on the heels of their king. He is beautiful, golden-skinned and shining like the midday sun; bright flames lick his body, and he radiates such light it hurts to look upon him. Brightest of all is the brand upon his forehead, the circle of ten heads, glowing like a third eye. The mark proclaims his mastery of the ten forms of sorcery, his mastery over reality. He has such power that even the gods are afraid.

"Ravana," whispers Rama. The demon king.

How many years have they fought? How many lives have been lost in this war? It comes down to this. Rama gazes across the field of death, stares at the white-limbed corpses of friends, cousins, countrymen, tangled in their death throes with the demonic forms of the rakshasas, with their tusks, claws, and hideous, sharklike teeth. A black emptiness swells in Rama's breast, a despair. So much death. Is this to be his kingdom? A land of broken men, of widows and fatherless children?

But even that world is better than the one Ravana seeks to build.

"The Carnival of Flesh," whispers Neela, his voice almost gone by the horror of what approaches.

Men, what were once men, parade and gibber, driven by the whips and howls of the rakshasas. These were the ones who surrendered to Ravana, who broke under his threats and who thought to make treaties with the demon king and live under his rule.

Some drag themselves forward on stumps, blind eyes staring wildly, wailing in endless torment. The skin has flayed from their bodies, their bones exposed and organs trailing through the dirt and filth, yet they are still alive and suffering. Some scavenge about the dead, tearing flesh off corpses and lapping up the blood of the dying. They have been driven beyond mere insanity by the tortures they've suffered.

Creations more monstrous than any rakshasa trample across the fields: huge, lumbering giants built from whole populations, tumbling creatures of hundreds of arms, legs, and screaming mouths. Each is still alive, but forever trapped in a waking nightmare by Ravana's magic.

Neela's hands tighten around his sword. "How can such things exist?"

"Ravana is the master of reality," says Rama. "He can make anything possible." But how can he, a mere mortal, defeat him? Rama steps back.

"Steady yourself, brother." Lakshmana grips his arm, meeting his gaze with determination. "You can end this. Only you."

Tears fill his eyes, and Rama's knees weaken. All strength pours from him, and but for Lakshmana's support, he would fall. He stares at the golden warrior, bright as a funeral pyre, the center of the carnage.

"How?" he asks. "How?"

"It is your destiny, Rama. What can you do but follow?"

It takes all his remaining energy to make his lips curl into a smile. He sees himself reflected in the breastplate of his brother. It is not the smile of a living man, but the rictus grin of the dead. Yet all men die. Better here, surrounded by his generals, beside his brother, fighting the greatest evil the world will ever know.

Today is a good day to die.

"Give me my bow."

Rama holds out his hand. The weapon is as tall as he, and only he is capable of bending it. Brilliant white, the bow is engraved with the blessings of all the gods. He plucks the string.

The air trembles with its vibration. The winds fall silent. The storms still, and each man lowers his sword and looks toward Rama. Even the rakshasas falter in their charge.

Ravana, his golden armor covered in blood and gore, looks at him, grinning.

"Surrender, Prince Rama." He does not shout, but his words carry across the battlefield. "And I will be generous."

Rama's hands tighten around the bow and he feels the hot rush of blood pounding in his temples. He conquers his fear, burying it deep under a mountain of rage. "My aastras, where are they?" he says to his generals.

Each of the gods has armed Rama for this battle. Each has given him a divine weapon, an aastra, to use in this final conflict.

But how many has he already cast against the armies of rakshasas? How many swords has he broken on the endless sea of demons Ravana sent before him?

"My lord," says Lakshmana. "There are but two left."

Rama takes the two arrows, one tipped with silver, the other with gold: aastras of the greater gods. Ravana roars and the earth shakes as he charges. Rama's generals run ahead to protect him but they fall like wheat beneath the scything blades of the demon king.

He has time for only one shot. Rama raises his bow.

But which arrow?

The first was a gift from his patron god, Vishnu. He gazes at the bright arrowhead of silver with a shaft of deepest ebony. Each aastra demands a sacrifice of its wielder to awaken its power. To Vishnu, he will offer his crown, his mortal power. He will serve Vishnu till the end of his days, and will serve willingly.

But the other aastra?

The second arrowhead is of the brightest gold, the shaft bone white. It hums in his fingers. The power within slumbers, and there is only one way to wake it.

"Use it," urges Lakshmana. "I am ready, my brother."

To awaken this aastra, the highest price must be paid, greater than any kingdom or crown. Rama looks into his brother's eyes. "No, I cannot."

"I am ready," repeats Lakshmana. He unbuckles his breastplate and pulls open his silk shirt. "Strike now. Awaken the aastra."

"I cannot," Rama says again. The price is too high, even for him. And what would he become if he paid it?

A monster. A creature more terrible even than the demon king. One that would devour the universe. No, the price is too high.

He tosses the gold arrow, the second aastra, into the blood-soaked sand.

Rama notches the Vishnu-aastra and draws the bowstring. He peers along the ebony shaft at the demon king. Their eyes meet across the battlefield.

"My Lord Vishnu," whispers Rama. "I am yours."

He releases the aastra.

CHAPTER EIGHT

"Ash!"

Ash tried to move, but he was pinned face down to the ground. Dirt stuffed his mouth and clogged his ears.

"Here, I'm here," he groaned. Spots of light slid over the rubble.

He glanced around him, half-expecting to be surrounded with dismembered demons. The ground trembled, and he gulped. Ravana's footsteps? No. It was just his heart, running overtime.

It had been so real. The war. The slaughter. He closed his eyes again and out of the blackness he saw him, Ravana, the demon king. Ash knew how the story ended. Rama fired the aastra and destroyed Ravana. The story. End of.

And demons. They weren't real, none of it was. But still . . .

He'd *been* Rama. He'd felt the hot wind, he'd smelled the awful stench of war and death. It had seemed so real. More than a dream: a vision. Or a memory.

I am not Rama. I am Ash Mistry. I am thirteen, and this is turning out to be the worst day of my life.

"I see him!" Feet scrabbled over the collapsed chamber roof and Ash tried again to move, but the fallen ceiling had him pinned. His breath came in shallow pants; he felt trapped in a giant's fist. He ached all over, but it was his left hand, his thumb, which felt like it had been dipped in acid. It was as if that splinter was burrowing itself deeper into his flesh.

Ash saw his uncle climb down toward him, white with fear. Then a flashlight blinded him.

"Get that out of his eyes," Uncle Vik snapped. He brushed the dust from his face. "Are you hurt, Ash?"

Nothing felt broken and he could still wiggle his toes. That was a good sign, wasn't it? "I'm fine. I think."

"You men take hold of the slab. On three we'll lift." A figure moved across the beam, taking command. Ash caught a glimpse of a pair of highly polished black shoes. Lord Savage put a hand on Uncle Vik's shoulder. "When we lift, Professor, you'll draw the young lad out."

Uncle Vik nodded and took hold of Ash's wrists.

"One. Two." The slab across Ash shed some loose dirt and sand. "Three!"

Men groaned and stone scraped against stone. Ash took a deep breath and kicked with his feet. Uncle Vik pulled hard. Ash's knees tore across the hard clay-packed floor, but he didn't care. He kicked again and slid free.

"Drop it!"

Uncle Vik clung to Ash as the three men released their grip on the heavy stone. It smashed down, breaking into four huge lumps.

"Ash . . ." Uncle Vik was crushing him more than the collapsed ceiling. Then he stepped back to look him over. "Ash, are you all right? Anything broken? Pain anywhere?"

"I'm okay." Ash coughed again and someone handed him a water bottle. He poured half the lukewarm water down his throat. The rest he tipped over his head.

People with flashlights clustered all around him. He was half-pulled, half-carried out of the collapsed pit. Head still spinning, Ash could see that the chamber he'd been in had fallen in on itself. Maybe he shouldn't have bashed a hole through a supporting wall.

Ash clambered up a short ladder and found himself in a small semicircle of people. They were just dark shadows, but one stepped forward and entered the crisscrossing beams.

"The boy looks fine to me," said Lord Savage.

Ash turned away. Where was his uncle? In the flashlight, the men around him didn't seem human, but grotesque distortions of man and beast, and . . . something else. The teeth were too large, the eyes too big, the smiles too hungry. He stumbled back, his heart pounding with panic. Was it the dream still?

No, no, no. He covered his face. The rakshasas weren't real. Still, even with his eyes closed, a smell lingered, stuffing his nostrils. Blood and sweat.

"Maybe we should take him back to the palace?" Mayar came forward, wearing a new pair of black sunglasses. "We could take care of him."

"Uncle?" Ash said.

His heartbeat doubled as Jackie, the Englishwoman, blocked his way. In the semidarkness her hair seemed denser, like a mane or a pelt of fur. "Poor boy," she said with mocking sympathy. "He looks dead to the world."

"Uncle?" *Where is he?*

"Yes, Lord Savage," said the tall, hook-nosed man, Jat, as he tapped his nails together. "Let us deal with this boy." Was it Ash's imagination or had those nails grown? They looked like the curved talons of some hideous bird.

Hands grabbed Ash's shoulders, and he almost screamed. But it was only Uncle Vik. He smiled and drew Ash close beside him.

"I think we should go home," Uncle Vik said.

"Really, Professor Mistry, I don't think that's necessary." Savage snapped his fingers. "I'll have my staff prepare a place for the boy to rest and have one of my doctors visit him here. Far easier than traveling all the way back to Varanasi."

"Mr. Savage, I know how to look after my nephew."

"*Lord* Savage, if you don't mind, Mistry," said Jackie.

"That's *Professor* Mistry, if you don't mind," replied his uncle.

Savage waved his hand. "No, it's fine. Professor Mistry is just a bit upset." He set his gaze on the two of them. "Be sensible, Professor. It's a long way back to Varanasi and the roads can be . . . unsafe. Stay here."

"Are you ordering me, Lord Savage?"

"If that's how you want to put it, yes, I am." Savage licked his dry, cracked lips and reached out for Ash. "The boy will remain with us."

Uncle Vik stepped between them. "Ash is going home, with me."

Savage thrust his tiger cane into Uncle Vik's chest. "I've

paid good money for you, Professor Mistry. I expect obedience. I *demand* obedience."

Uncle Vik knocked the cane away. "I am not a slave, Lord Savage."

Savage wiped dripping saliva from his lips. "You want more, is that it? I know what you Indians are like. Always begging. Very well. I will have another check drawn up in the morning." He looked Uncle Vik up and down, making no attempt to hide his contempt. It was the same look Ash had seen in that portrait of the first Lord Savage, arrogant, superior, and cruel. "Do we understand one another, Mistry?"

Uncle Vik lowered his gaze. "I understand, Lord Savage. Perfectly."

Savage smiled and summoned Mayar. The huge servant lumbered over, the ground shaking with each footfall. "Prepare the spare rooms —"

Uncle Vik pulled out a folded piece of paper: Savage's check. He hadn't banked it. He slowly tore it in half, then in half again. He gazed up at Savage. "Thank you for your hospitality, but I must decline it."

Ash gasped as Uncle Vik threw the pieces into the air and two million pounds fluttered away in the desert wind. This was all of Uncle Vik's dreams. This was flashy cars, big houses, exotic holidays, the respect of being his own man at last. It was all that anyone could ever want.

But Uncle Vik squeezed his hand.

No. It was only money. Those things didn't matter like family. Ash had been so wrong about his uncle; he'd thought him weak and a bit pathetic. Now he understood what guts it took to put family first. He saw the man his father admired and loved.

Thank God. Ash's heart lifted with sheer relief. He just wanted to get as far from here as possible and never, ever, come back.

Together, Ash and Uncle Vik walked toward the Seven Queens and found Aunt Anita and Lucky waiting. Lucky gave him a sympathetic smile, but Aunt Anita glowered at him. "Do you want to give me a heart attack?" Then she crushed him in a hug and kissed his head. She looked inquisitively at Uncle Vik. He just gave a weary shake.

"It's over, Anita. Let's go home."

"But what about our things?" she said. "The picnic's still —"

"I'll collect it tomorrow," said Uncle Vik.

Ash turned to his sister. "You're going to get such a slap when we get back," he whispered.

"Just try it." She touched his fingers. "You okay?"

"Yeah. Let's just get home."

"What's that?" said Lucky, pointing at Ash's left fist.

He stared down at his hand. His grip was frozen around something, and he had to force his fingers to uncurl to see what it was.

It was the golden arrowhead.

CHAPTER NINE

By the time they'd rowed back across, Uncle Vik had explained everything. Only Lucky had a question.

"No pony?" she asked.

Aunt Anita stroked her cheek. "No pony."

They got in the car, and the engine purred to life. Ash sat in the front passenger seat beside Uncle Vik while Aunt Anita and Lucky dropped down in the back.

Uncle Vik sighed deeply. "Well, if they put a price on love, I've just paid it," he said. "Two million pounds, that's what you cost me, nephew."

"Sorry." He felt wretched, having just destroyed his uncle's hopes and dreams for a better future. Ash wished there was a better, bigger word than just *sorry*.

"I'll ask your father for a refund." He ran his fingers over the steering wheel. "Let's get home before Savage confiscates this and has us hitching home on the back of a buffalo cart."

Ash slipped the arrowhead out of his trouser pocket. The golden object glistened as he cupped it in his hands. It was a narrow triangle about two inches long with two long edges ending in a needle-thin point. But the tip was missing, a sliver a few millimeters in length, barely noticeable unless you looked very closely. He checked his thumb, unable to see the splinter. Maybe it had fallen out by now. It certainly didn't hurt as much, just throbbed a bit.

He hadn't even realized he'd taken it. And he'd almost died getting it, so it was his now. Maybe they could sell it? If it was real gold, it had to be worth something. It might go a little way in making up for all that money Uncle Vik had just lost.

Ash rolled down the window and let the cold air rush over his face. The desert smelled of age, of time; not like a living thing but of sand, rock, and wind. Eternal things.

"You were right, Ash, about the money," Uncle Vik murmured. "It was too much. I knew it wasn't right. That's why I couldn't cash it."

"Savage wanted to buy you," said Ash. "The guy's hideous."

"You can't blame him for his illness," said Aunt Anita.

"It's more than that." Ash closed his eyes, trying to search his memory, check the facts. Mayar with the reptile eyes. Jackie's freakish fur. Savage's words and the things in his study. What bit of that was normal? Normal people didn't have jars with human snakes sloshing around in them.

"It'll all seem better in the morning." Uncle Vik said. "Come on, nephew. You've had a bit of a rough evening. You'll be fine once we're home."

"India is not my home," said Ash. Suddenly he was shaking. All the night's events, the dreams of Rama, the collapsed tomb, and Savage and his hideous henchmen crowded his memories. "I hate India," he snapped. "It was stupid of us to come here and it was stupid for you to work for Savage."

"You think your uncle's stupid?" said Aunt Anita, accusingly.

"That's not what I —"

But she was too angry to hear him. "Ashoka Mistry, you apologize to your uncle right now."

Ash glanced up at the rearview mirror and saw Aunt Anita staring back at him, her lips locked in a thin, firm line.

"Well?" she asked.

Anger buzzed around his head — anger at them, anger at himself. And fear: He'd thought he was going to die, first buried under the rock, then when he'd been surrounded by Savage's people. Even now it left a sickening dread in the pit of his belly.

"Right," his aunt said. "I am going to count to three, and if you don't apologize, you're grounded for the rest of this trip, and there will be no Internet and no gaming. You understand?"

Ash knew he was being unfair. His uncle was a good man; he was trying his best. But he clamped his mouth shut.

"One . . ."

He heard the noise of machinery, just buried under the whistling wind and the steady rumble of the Mercedes. He leaned against the passenger door window, staring out.

"Two . . ."

Ash caught a glimpse of metal in the side mirror. He peered closer at the reflection. Was that another car?

"Look out!" he screamed as headlights burst to life, flooding the interior of the car with an explosion of brilliant, blinding whiteness. Another vehicle rammed into the rear of the Mercedes, hurling them forward. The car swung out wildly, and Ash was deafened by the sound of tearing metal and Lucky's screams. He caught a glimpse of their attacker: a white Humvee. One of Savage's vehicles.

The Humvee plowed its chunky crash bars into the side of their car. Tires shredded on the crude road as it was pushed along, locked to the giant SUV.

We're going to die. Blank terror seized him as he was thrown against the door. He was inches from the Humvee — all he could see was the bright chrome, and he felt the dragon-breath blowing heat off its giant radiator.

Then the Humvee spun around again in a tire-melting handbrake turn, tearing itself free of the Mercedes. Ash's door, trapped in the crash bars, was ripped off like it was made of paper. The car slid along the road, the metal screaming, and sparks erupted along the steel undercarriage.

Ash sat there, gasping. He couldn't move. Blood dripped from his face, and he touched his cheek. A small cut from the shattered windshield. Broken squares of glass covered his lap, sparkling like a scattering of diamonds.

"Ash, Ash . . ." His uncle grabbed his arm.

"I'm okay."

The Humvee paused like a huge white bull, its engine growling, a hundred yards away. The Mercedes had spun all the way around so the two vehicles were facing each other. The Humvee began to creep forward, slowly picking up speed.

"Open the bloody doors!" shouted his aunt. She was twisting the handle, but the doorframe had buckled, locking them in.

Ash fumbled with his seatbelt and it clicked open. He stared at his uncle as Uncle Vik struggled to undo his seatbelt.

"Get out, Ash. Get out," said Uncle Vik.

"Let me help." If he pulled they could both —

"Get out!"

The Humvee roared and the stark headlights glared down at them like the eyes of demons.

Ash scrabbled out and began pulling at his aunt's door behind him. The air stank of burning rubber as the Humvee accelerated toward them. The driver of the vehicle grinned at him, and Ash's blood turned to ice. Jackie was hunched over the wheel, and beside her Mayar licked his lips.

Aunt Anita hoisted Lucky on to her lap, and Ash grabbed his sister and hauled her through the broken window. Lucky sobbed as she clambered out, then Ash turned back to his aunt.

"C'mon!" He pulled at the door handle, but his palms were slick with sweat and the door wouldn't budge. He pulled and pulled until his arms ached.

Tears streamed down his aunt's face, the mascara leaving big black tracks down her cheeks. Her mouth seemed caught between a frown and smile. She just shook her head and met his gaze. "Look after your sister," she said. Then she shoved Ash out of the way as hard as she could.

The car crumpled like an accordion as the vehicles collided, and the Mercedes tore through the thorny bushes along the shoulder of the road and tumbled down the steep slope. Ash's screams were drowned out by the sounds of grinding metal and shattering glass. The noise seemed to go on forever as the car turned over and over, plowing a deep furrow through the hard-baked earth. Ash stared at the black skid marks and the shiny black oil that lay like a trail of blood along the ruined path.

The Humvee spun once, and howls of joy burst from the driver and her passenger. The front of the big SUV was smashed, a headlight dangling out of its broken socket, and Ash's door still hung off the mangled crash bars. Steam hissed out of a dent in the radiator. Jackie stared at Ash through the cracked windshield, a big, eager smile across her face.

She revved the engine once more, and the vehicle rolled forward.

Ash looked around. He was in the center of the road. Lucky knelt sobbing a few yards away. There was no escape.

The Humvee accelerated.

CHAPTER TEN

Ash dragged his sister to her feet and started running. The terrible growl of the Humvee's engine filled the night, drowning out everything but total fear. Ash stared at his long shadow running ahead of him, cast by the glaring eyes of the mechanical monster that had already killed Uncle Vik and Aunt Anita. If only they could get off the road and down the slope, they might live. But there was no gap through the spiky bushes that lined the shoulder. The ground trembled as the car descended on them.

We're not going to make it. Heart pounding and his lungs burning with desperate gasps, he ran anyway, hand in hand with Lucky.

Don't look back. Even though the headlights bathed them both and the stench of burning gasoline filled the air, he kept his head and ran.

"Boy."

Rough hands grabbed him and lifted Ash off his feet. Blindly he swung his fists at the stranger, then stopped.

He dangled before a pair of intense blue eyes, almost lost under a forest of thick dreadlocks. It was the blue-eyed sadhu.

The guy who'd hit the cow back in Varanasi. Ash stared at him, speechless with disbelief. What was he doing out here?

"Behind me," the man commanded as he dropped Ash to the ground, and Ash scrambled to put the man between himself and the Humvee, dragging Lucky with him.

The skinny brown man stood in the path of the thundering Humvee, his hands resting on his bamboo stick. His matted white and gray hair hung loose about him, the thick vine-like tresses whipped about by the rushing wind. He was chanting something, but the words were lost in the cry of the oncoming vehicle.

How was the old man going to make any difference? They were facing a three-ton vehicle, not some lazy cow. Ash clung to Lucky. Death rushed toward them. Any second now all three of them were going to be red smears on the road.

"Ash . . ." Lucky whispered.

Lucky's long, straight black hair was rising. The air about them hummed. The old man's eyes shone with radiant blue light. Sparks of electric power ran over his body as a storm of lightning erupted along his staff and sharp, jagged bolts flew off in all directions.

The Humvee was a heartbeat away.

The sadhu swung the stick high over his head and slammed it down on the accelerating vehicle just as it reached him. Thunder exploded, and the SUV stopped dead. The windshield erupted and an ear-piercing wail rose out of the grinding gears and engine parts as they were utterly flattened. It was as though a giant fist had punched down on the hood, driving the car into the ground. The earth rippled, hurling Ash backward.

He lay sprawled on the broken road, his ears ringing. He struggled to his feet, gasping, and swayed side to side, muscles and bones rocked by the battering. He stepped forward, arms out, blindly reaching into a dense cloud of smoke and dust. All he knew was that it had fallen quiet, but for an evil hissing coming from . . . somewhere.

What had happened to the car?

Oh, God. Where was his sister?

"Lucks?"

A sudden breeze dispersed the worst of the cloud, revealing the old man. The sadhu stood in the center of the crater with the flattened car. His head was lowered and his stick raised horizontally, high over his head. His finger joints clicked as he adjusted his grip on his weapon.

Two other figures prowled through the wreckage as well. Jackie and Mayar moved to either side of the motionless holy man. They looked bloodied and dishevelled, not seriously injured but definitely *wrong*. Jackie stalked closer on all fours, her face elongated and covered in reddish brown hair. A row of slavering fangs dripped saliva from her ever-widening grin, and her arms were now forepaws, each one tipped with wicked, yellow claws.

Mayar pulled off his white jacket, revealing a torso covered in dense green scales. Heavy lumps encrusted his snout-like jaw, lined with jagged crocodile teeth. He too lowered himself down to all fours, and a long thick tail tore itself out from his trouser seat.

Ash felt a slick bubble of vomit tremble in his throat but held it down. He blinked again, hoping the creatures would vanish and be replaced by something normal, something believable. But they were sickeningly, grotesquely real. He stepped back, panting in short, weak gasps, staring at the two monsters. *Monsters.*

Rakshasas.

"The boy is ours, Rishi," Jackie growled. She crept forward, just outside the reach of the old man's stick. "He has stolen from our master."

"Then take him, if you can," answered the old man.

Ash stared at him, still bewildered that the skinny guy had crushed a car with his stick. If he could do that, what else could he do? The two rakshasas kept a wary distance; despite their huge size and all their fangs and claws, they seemed reluctant to make the first move against the sadhu.

Jackie threw back her head as she laughed at the moon. It was a high-pitched and cruel noise, half-human and half-beast, the cry of something that fed on the dead. A jackal's laugh.

Mayar snapped his jaws. Spittle dripped from his mouth and there was hunger in his eyes. He looked toward his demon companion.

Then at the same moment, Jackie leaped high and Mayar rushed in low. The sadhu jumped over Mayar and slammed his stick across Jackie's chest, catapulting her high into the air. Mayar's eyes blazed and he opened his jaws wide. Ash stumbled a few paces backward and the crocodile was upon him, so close that he could see down the monster's red throat and almost count every dagger-like tooth.

Mayar roared as he crashed to a halt, barely a handsbreadth from Ash. Discarding his stick, the old man had grabbed the crocodile by the tail. Mayar turned and snapped at him, but the sadhu just hopped backward, dragging the thrashing monster with him.

"Ash!" shouted Lucky.

Ash spun around as a gigantic vulture swooped out of the darkness. The wings were fifteen feet wide and attached to the body of a tall man: Jat, the third of Savage's henchmen. His hooked nose was now transformed into a curved beak, and his feet had become long talons. Ash threw himself to the ground, and the talons tore the back of his shirt. Jat screeched in anger.

Then Lucky screamed as Jat went after her instead.

She fought hard, but the scaly talons locked around her arms. Ash ran toward them but Lucky was rising away, Jat flapping furiously to get some lift with the additional weight.

Ash leaped up, arms straining as far as they would stretch. His fingers closed around nothing as, with a sudden jerk and cry of triumph, the vulture monster rose into the night sky and out of reach, Lucky dangling from his taloned feet.

The sadhu ran in a strange bowlegged way and leaped into one of the trees that stood alongside the road. His big hands hooked around a branch and he swung upward, launching himself into the air. He turned over and over, a tight ball of leathery muscle, at the last moment thrusting out his large feet and slamming into Jat's chest. The vulture man was knocked backward and Lucky fell from his grip.

Ash dived for his sister, leaping farther than he'd thought possible, and she crashed into his arms. They bounced a few yards, Ash trying to let her land on top of him. He cried out as they skidded along the broken tarmac, a layer of skin tearing off his back.

With barely a sound, the sadhu landed on the ground. He flicked his staff into the air with his toes and caught it.

Jat circled overhead, but the sadhu raised his staff and bolts of blue energy crackled along it. Jat screamed in frustration, obviously afraid to get within range of the old man. With one mighty sweep of his wings, he rose away into the sky.

Ash lay on his back, staring into the night. The other two monsters had fled, but black dread still swirled in his belly. He must be sick. Delirious. This couldn't be happening.

"Lucks?" he said. "You okay?"

Lucky rolled off him. She nodded her head. Her arms bled from Jat's claws, but the cuts weren't deep.

"Where are they?" she asked. "Where's Uncle Vik and Auntie?"

He gritted his teeth as he peeled himself off the ground. His back was hot and sticky, and not with sweat, while his spine felt stiff and ready to break.

"Wait here, Lucks."

He ran past the ruined Humvee in the crater, steam rising out of the radiator and small pockets of fire glowing from where the gas and sparks had met. Silhouetted against the swaying firelight was the sadhu.

"Are you hurt?" asked the old man.

Ash rushed past him to the edge of the road. The long black skid marks and the torn-up foliage showed where the Mercedes had gone. He peered over, his heart hammering and his throat dry.

The Mercedes lay at the bottom of the slope, its wheels torn away and the roof completely caved in. Steam hissed from the mangled engine. Ash clambered down the slope littered with broken metal and rubber torn from the tires.

Maybe they were alive. They could be. His heartbeat rose rapidly and he was panting hard as he skidded down the slope. He could hear something. Yes, there it was again. Tapping. Someone was tapping. They were alive. He'd get them out and everything was going to be okay. Everything would be normal like it had been five minutes ago.

He was at the car now. The engine groaned and there was the *plink, plink, plink* of oil dripping onto metal. The air stank of gas fumes. But he could hear tapping. Someone was alive.

"Uncle Vik?" Ash looked into the car.

His uncle leaned back in his seat. His eyes stared blankly ahead, unblinking. Blood dribbled from the puncture wound in his forehead.

"Uncle?"

His uncle blindly watched the windshield wipers slide back and forth. Each time the wipers reached their zenith, they hit the bent roof, tapping the metal at each pass.

Aunt Anita lay asleep, so it seemed, in the backseat. Only the crookedness of her neck betrayed that she was never going to wake.

Ash stared, empty-eyed. His palms scraped along the broken glass, but he barely noticed. Something stuck painfully in his throat. The temperature was warm, even now, but he shivered. He took his aunt's hands in his own.

"Please." He put his cheek against her cold palm. "Please." All he wanted was the smallest sign. Just a little movement. Trembling, he shook his aunt. "Please wake up!"

"Boy?"

Ash slowly turned and saw the old man squatting some yards away. His stick lay across his arms, but he waited patiently.

"Please help," Ash said. He'd seen the man do amazing things. Miraculous things. Couldn't he help them?

"I am sorry." The sadhu stood up and looked around. "We must go."

"No," Ash said through gritted teeth. "I'm staying here." He couldn't help but think of the angry words he'd thrown at his aunt and uncle just minutes ago. Words he'd never be able to take back. "I didn't mean what I said," he whispered.

The old man gazed at him from under his bushy gray brows. "They are dead, boy." He put his hand on Ash's shoulder. "Come. Before the rakshasas return."

Ash wiped his face. He started up the slope and saw Lucky kneeling there. She looked at him, eyes filled with tears, but silent. She took hold of his outstretched hand as he reached the top and he squeezed her warm fingers, determined not to let go. They'd almost got her too. He wouldn't let that happen. Not ever.

"Why?" he asked the old man. Only a few days ago, Savage had given Uncle Vik millions. It didn't make any sense.

The sadhu joined them, picking up a sackcloth bag lying behind a bush.

"They want the aastra," he said.

"Aastra? What aastra?"

The old man stuck out a long, bony finger and pointed at Ash's pocket. Ash slowly reached in and pulled out the golden arrowhead. It glowed faintly in the darkness.

"The aastra," said the sadhu.

CHAPTER ELEVEN

"Where are we going, Ash?" asked Lucky.

"Away."

Lucky looked back across the flat, featureless landscape they'd spent the night crossing and Ash knew what she was thinking: Their uncle and aunt were dead back there.

"We had to leave them, Lucks." Even as he said it, his chest tightened — *abandon them*, more like. But as the wind moaned through the stiff branches of the trees, Ash thought he heard the flapping of giant wings and glanced skyward, afraid. A vulture? Jat? He searched the star-blazed sky but saw nothing. "We need to keep moving."

Lucky dropped to the ground. "I want Auntie Anita back. And Uncle Vik."

"I know." Ash checked for the sadhu. The old man waited ahead of them on a shallow ridge, leaning on his staff but eyes focused on the horizon.

Ash knelt down beside his sister. What could he say? The golden arrowhead was heavy in his pocket, the edges biting into his thigh. Had he brought this on them? The guilt wrapped heavy around his heart, a dragging weight that wanted to pull him to the ground, to make him lie in the dirt and give up.

But not yet, not yet.

He wouldn't give up while Lucky was counting on him. He had to look after her. He had to get them both home. That was what he focused on to lift him back up, to stop him from despairing.

Ash smiled down at her. "Your hair's a mess." He dragged his fingers through the dusty tangles.

Lucky blinked at him through red and puffy eyes. She wiped her nose. "What are we going to do?"

"Keep moving." Ash fought back his own tears. "C'mon. Those monsters might still be after us."

Lucky turned white. Her big, frightened eyes stared hard at him and she bit her lip. "Okay, Ash."

He helped her up. The sadhu waited until they were level with him.

"We will find somewhere safe," he said.

"We need to go to the police," said Ash. Savage and his monsters were murderers. The police had to know. He'd make sure Savage went to prison for a million years.

"That will do no good. Men like Savage own the police."

"Then what? Just hide?" said Ash. "What about my uncle and aunt?"

"What do you want, boy?"

Wasn't it obvious? "I want Savage to pay." A black pain stabbed through him, one of anger, of hate. "Revenge."

"Revenge is a dark path."

"I don't care. We're just going to let Savage get away with this?"

"We will deal with Savage." The sadhu glanced at Lucky. "But first look to the living. To those who still need you."

Yes, he was right. Who was Ash kidding anyway? He wasn't a fighter.

"Who are you?" he asked.

"I am called Rishi." The old man raised his eyebrows. "And your name?"

"Ash. It's short for Ashoka." His dad had named him after the first Indian emperor. Some name to live up to. It was like being called Napoleon.

"A hero's name."

Ash laughed bitterly. A hero would have saved his aunt and uncle. A hero wouldn't be sniveling with fear. "I'm not a hero."

Rishi put his hand on Ash's chin, turning it up so they were eye to eye. "Then we will make you one, Ashoka," he said as he released him. "And your name, little daughter?"

"Lakshmi. But everyone calls me Lucky."

"Come then."

Ash and Lucky took a few steps up the shallow ridge. The Ganges River lay before them. On the far bank rose Varanasi, ethereal as it floated upon a pale mist. Over the still air came the distant sounds of temple bells. Rishi wandered down to the river's edge, then squatted on his haunches, resting his staff across his shoulder. He glanced up at the gently brightening sky, still dark but tinged with pale lavender in the east.

"We must get back to Varanasi. I have friends there who will help us."

"What sort of friends?" Ash asked. "Someone who can stop Savage? How?"

"With training, with knowledge, with the aastra," said Rishi. "We will find a way to defeat Savage, and discover why he is so eager to get his hands on it. That Savage is searching for an aastra disturbs me greatly."

Ash dropped on to the sandy mud, sinking his head into his hands. He didn't want any of this. The world was insane. He closed his eyes but couldn't stop the tears from falling. Lucky sat down beside him and put her small hand on his shoulder.

"I just want to go home," Ash whispered.

"Home?" asked Rishi.

"London. This sort of thing would never happen in London."

"It happens everywhere, Ashoka. Demons, and creatures far worse, lurk in the shadows all over the world. But wherever there is such evil, there are also those who oppose it. Even in London."

"In London? Who?"

"An ancient order of knights. Warriors dedicated to fighting what they call the Unholy. They are the —"

"Rishi! Master!" A voice cried out from the thick morning fog. Ash took hold of Lucky's hand.

Rishi pointed at a dark shadow floating on the river. "There." He waved his stick and a boat appeared. Nets hung along its sides and a wiry-looking fisherman, dressed only in a dirty white loincloth, waved back.

Varanasi at dawn. Gossamer mist rose off the waters as the heat descended. The sun, just a red disk on the horizon, peered through the gray haze and promised another baking day.

It was a long, slow journey back upriver. Lucky slept, but Ash couldn't. Each splash of the oar or bird cry had him twitching, staring everywhere, clutching the boat's old wooden frame with stiff fingers. His heart raced, expecting the monsters to burst out of the water or swoop down at any moment. Rishi, the sadhu, just sat cross-legged, staff across his lap, eyes closed.

What could they do? If he could just call Dad, tell him what had happened, he'd come and sort it out. If the Indian police couldn't touch Savage, the English police could. Things were normal in England. He just wanted to be back there. The pain of longing twisted his guts. Home. That was all that mattered now.

A dog barked as they approached the southern edge of the city. Two women stood knee-deep in the water, washing clothes. One attacked a shirt with a brick-sized lump of soap while another thrashed a rolled-up sheet against a stone slab, knocking out all the dirt. The dog, skinny and small, barked again, wanting attention, wanting a few scraps. One woman flicked the shirt at it, showering its face with soapy water, and it ran off. She laughed and got back to work.

His life had changed so much in the last twelve hours, but for the rest of the world it was another normal day. Demons didn't exist in their lives.

Ash couldn't get Savage out of his mind. He pulled the aastra from his pocket. "If Savage wants this, could I use it against him?"

"Be careful with that." Rishi spoke quietly. "It was forged by a god."

"This?" He turned the arrowhead over in his palm. "How does it work? Just fire it at Savage?"

"No, it has no power yet," said the sadhu. "An aastra must be awakened, charged with energy. You must make an offering to the god who made it and then they will fill it with their power."

"What sort of offering?"

"Each aastra is attuned to the power of the one who made it. One constructed by Agni, the god of fire, would have powers over that element. Place it in a fire, and the energy from the flames would be absorbed by the aastra. The greater the fire, the more powerful the aastra would become. You would be able to create infernos, burn entire buildings with a glance, immolate armies, and, with a snap of your fingers, extinguish the fiercest firestorms." Rishi looked down at the water. "Or if it was made by the river goddess Ganga, you would immerse it in water, and it would take the energy of the water itself." He scratched his beard. "And this one. Who gave it to you?"

No one. He found it. In a buried chamber he wished he'd never entered. He wished he'd stayed in the pit and waited. Not gone through the wall and stolen the arrow from the hand of the statue.

"Rama was holding it."

"That narrows it down. Rama was a great hero. He would have been armed with only the most powerful of aastras."

"So what does this do?" How could he use it to beat Savage and his rakshasas?

"Rama was a warrior, so what else could it be? It is a death bringer."

"Aren't all weapons?"

"All other weapons are mere shadows of what you hold in your hands."

Brahma. Vishnu. Shiva. Ganesha. Yama. Durga. The list of Hindu gods was endless. He didn't know much about the gods, had never taken them seriously. Sure, he went to temple, but that was just going through the motions. This was *real*.

"You said if the aastra was made by the river goddess, water would awaken it," said Ash. "So if I dip it in here, I'll be able to command the rivers, right?" He held the golden arrowhead over the edge of the boat. If this worked, he'd summon up a tidal wave to drown the Savage Fortress and everyone in it.

"Just don't drop it," warned Rishi.

Arrowhead in his fist, Ash put his hand under the water. And waited.

"How do you feel?" asked Rishi.

"Nothing." Not a tingle. No sudden surge of superstrength. No feeling that he'd be able to leap tall buildings in a single bound.

"So it is not an aastra of the goddess Ganga," said Rishi.

"How did Rama awaken his aastra, the Vishnu-aastra?"

asked Ash. Maybe there was a connection between that aastra Rama had fired at Ravana and this golden one.

"He pledged his crown to Vishnu."

Ash frowned. "But didn't he become king?"

"Yes, a ruler with no will of his own. Everything he did was for the good of his people. That was why Rama is considered the perfect king. He kept nothing for himself. Not even Sita."

"Sita? His wife?" Ash knew the story. The entire war between Rama and the demon king was over Sita. Ravana had fallen in love with Rama's wife and kidnapped her, keeping her imprisoned in his kingdom of Lanka. "Didn't he get her back?"

Rishi looked sadly into the waters. "Not for long. You see, she'd been Ravana's prisoner for years, and people questioned her faithfulness. Had she succumbed to Ravana's advances? The rumors never died down, and if a king does not have the respect of his subjects, he has nothing. So Rama banished his own wife. After all he had done, all he'd suffered, after the millions who'd died, he could not have her.

"That was the price he paid for his crown. The price he paid to awaken the Vishnu-aastra. He gained a kingdom, but Rama himself lost everything dear to him."

Ash looked at the golden arrowhead. Rama lost the woman he loved, yet he knew the golden arrowhead's price was even higher. Suddenly it felt cold and heavy in his palm. He'd only had the thing for a few hours, and two people had already died. "You take it."

Rishi gazed at the arrowhead long and hard. His fingers tightened around the staff so the wood creaked under the strain. "I am a priest. I am not permitted to bear weapons."

Ash tucked it away.

On the bank, pilgrims came down the *ghats* — the stone steps that ran the entire length of Varanasi and offered easy access to the riverside. People emerged from the temples, ashrams, and old palaces that lined the bank. The grand buildings had seen better days, better centuries, but that was India. The ancient never died. The palace walls bore ads about local cafés or restaurants, or some doctor or other service. One building of pink stone had been covered with garish portraits of the gods. Krishna, blue-skinned and playing the flute. Elephant-headed Ganesha. And Shiva, his arms spread out and foot raised, poised to dance.

Rishi followed Ash's gaze. "Music would awaken an aastra of Krishna's; the more beautiful the tune, the greater would be the power bestowed to it. Dancing would count as an offering to Shiva."

"Let's hope it's not one of Shiva's, then," Ash said. "I dance like a three-legged hippo." Then he caught sight of another figure, lurking in a shadow. "And her?"

There in the corner of the building stood a stone statue, ten feet tall and partially hidden, as though it was a thing best suited to darkness. The body was that of an emaciated skeleton, a woman, her black skin tightly stretched so each rib stood out against it. Around her neck dangled a skull necklace, and her skirt was made of severed arms.

"The goddess Kali," said Rishi. "What pleases her most is death."

Kali's ten arms were outspread, almost all of them carrying a weapon: a spear, sword, ax, noose, an immense bow, a sheaf of long arrows. In one hand she grasped a decapitated head by its hair, and hideous rakshasas writhed in terror beneath her feet. She glared, her red tongue hanging out, hungry for blood. Ash felt her gaze upon him as they drifted past.

Men drew cups of water from the river, pouring libations to the gods, while others laid garlands of flowers upon its surface. Farther along Ash watched an old man dive under again and again, washing away his sins.

Smoke rose out of a pile of ash and charred logs on the banks of the river. Ash peered at the crumbling stack. That was what all pilgrims strived for — to die here and be cremated on the banks of the Ganges.

Among the smoldering logs were the remains of a person. Had some family just left after cremating their father? Grandmother?

But at least they'd said good-bye. If only he'd been able to say good-bye to Uncle Vik and Aunt Anita. Maybe that would fill up the hole in his chest.

"They are not gone, Ashoka," said Rishi. His intensely blue eyes glistened behind barely-open eyelids.

Had Rishi read his mind? What other powers did the sadhu have? "They're dead," said Ash. "They couldn't be more gone."

"They will come back. We all come back." Rishi's eyes shimmered. "Some more often than others." He stiffened as if to say something more, but instead directed the boatman toward the steps. "Time to get out."

Ash nudged his sister. Lucky opened her eyes instantly, her body tense. Then she saw him and slowly relaxed.

"Where are we?" she asked.

Rishi hopped off the boat and held out his hand for her. "The old city. You will be safe here."

As they came up the steps, Ash looked up at the building before him. Overlooking the water was a great, crumbling palace of red sandstone. The fifty-foot walls were lined with battlements and domed watchtowers. Washing lines crisscrossed the roof, so it looked as though a battalion of warriors waited above, their banners gently fluttering in the breeze. Balconies lined the three stories; most had clothing slung over them, while others were partially collapsed and held up with bamboo scaffolding. The only sound was the cooing of pigeons.

A minute later they stopped at a stout door with a heavy iron knocker in the shape of an elephant's head.

"Ujba?" called Rishi, banging the door.

Nothing.

"Ujba!"

A face appeared at a window above them, and a few more people gathered on an old crumbling balcony nearby, all children. Some were younger than Lucky, others older and bigger than Ash. One boy, maybe sixteen or so, pushed his way through the crowd and hopped on to the balcony edge, squatting there to eat an apple. He didn't seem to be bothered by the long drop.

"What do you want, old fool?" he shouted. A few children

behind him giggled. Some peered down at Ash and Lucky, curious.

"Where's your *guru*?" Rishi used the old word for *master* or *teacher*.

Was this some school? Ash stepped back. It didn't look like a school.

"Come back tonight," the older boy shouted. "He's out."

"Let me in or I'll blow the door down."

Rishi spoke quietly, but the power in his voice frightened a flock of birds. They launched themselves away, wheeling overhead before scattering in all directions. The door opened. A young child gazed at Rishi with undisguised terror. As Rishi stepped in, the boy immediately bent and touched his feet: a show of respect, one tainted by fear. He scurried away, leaving Rishi, Ash, and Lucky in a dark, shadow-cast hall.

The building was cold and gloomy, the only light coming from the internal courtyard beyond and the few small high windows that were mostly roosts for the pigeons.

"The maharajah of Rajasthan built this three centuries ago," said Rishi. He touched the mildewy walls. "It's called the Lalgur, the Red House."

The children came out of all corners and formed a wary crowd. The sixteen-year-old appeared — he obviously ran things when Ujba wasn't around. Even in the gloom, Ash could see he wasn't to be messed with. Taut, lean muscles slid under his glossy, dark skin. Faint, healed-up scars marked his arms and his bare chest. His hair was long and slick, loose over his shoulders, and beneath the bangs gazed out a pair of hawkish eyes. He wore a pair of loose cotton trousers and was barefoot like the others. A red sash covered his waist and something metal glinted among the folds. The boy's hand rested on it.

A *katar*. An Indian punch dagger. Ash had seen one just like it in Savage's study. But Savage's had been gold and studded with gems, while this was plain and simple, designed for killing and nothing else.

"Give these two food and a room to rest in," ordered Rishi.

"No way I'm staying here," said Ash. "I want a phone."

"Do not think of venturing outside these walls. Savage will have his demons scouring the city for you. He has spies everywhere." Rishi turned to leave. "I have some business to attend to."

"Wait!" Ash grabbed his arm. "You can't just leave us." The other kids had a hungry, feral look about them. He leaned closer and whispered, "I don't trust them."

"They will not harm you."

"How can you be so sure?"

"Otherwise they will answer to me," said Rishi, "and I don't think anyone here is foolish enough to want that." He faced the boy with the dagger, who scowled but took a step back. Rishi drew Ash closer and whispered, "But the aastra, keep that to yourself, for now."

Once Rishi had gone, the gang of street kids gathered around Ash and Lucky. Ash turned to the boy with the dagger. Whatever issues the guy had with Rishi were nothing to do with him. "My name is Ash. This is Lucky. We're here —"

"I don't care why you're here or what your names are." The boy grabbed one of the other kids. "Give them a room."

"Which one, Hakim?"

Hakim. So that's his name. The one to watch out for.

Hakim kicked the boy's butt. "Just do it."

Rubbing his sore behind, the other boy beckoned to Ash and Lucky and gave them the once-over. "Come on, then."

They followed him up a narrow spiral staircase, and eventually they came out on to a flat roof that was covered with clotheslines and drying clothes. But among the walls of bright cloth fluttering in the wind was a small room, a box, sitting alone on the roof and overlooking the river. The walls were carved stone latticework, and the triple-domed roof would have been pure white, except it was covered in pigeon droppings. Tons of them.

"The maharajah would rest here," said the boy, "when it was hot and when he wanted to watch the sun rise."

"I'm Ash," Ash started again. "This is my sister —"

"Lucky. I heard the first time," said the boy. He was still rubbing his rear. That must have been one sharp kick. He pulled back the bolt on the wooden door of the latticework room. "I'll get some food brought up."

"What's your name?"

"John."

"John?" That wasn't very Indian.

"Ujba found me outside the Church of St. John," he replied. "Can't remember what I was called before that."

Ash gazed about him. "What is this place?"

"It's where we live. With the master. We train here too."

"Train? To do what?"

John paused like this was the most stupid thing he'd ever

heard. Seeing Ash's confusion, he gave a small, sly smile. "You'll find out."

"You all live here? What about your homes? Your families?"

John shook his head. Second stupid question. "Think we'd be here if we had families? We're here 'cause we're orphans." He pushed open the door and revealed a square, breezy room with a couple of wooden-framed beds. "Just like you."

"We're not orphans," snapped Ash as he and Lucky entered the room. But right now his parents, his home in London, seemed as far away as the moon.

John shrugged. "Whatever. You're here now."

When John left, Ash shut the door.

"I don't like it here," said Lucky.

"Me neither."

"Then let's go."

Ash nodded. He was sure Rishi was right; Savage would be hunting for them. They'd have to be careful. But Varanasi was one big labyrinth of alleyways; it should be easy to hide. "We'll wait until tonight." He picked up a pile of sheets off the rickety table and began unfolding them over the beds. "We'll eat and rest here for a couple of hours, then sneak out and get a message to Dad."

And tell him Aunt Anita and Uncle Vik are dead.

So much had happened, Ash couldn't believe that this time yesterday they were all alive and happy. Yes, happy. He hated how he'd moaned and fussed over things that seemed so stupid now. His constant complaining. There were things he should have said to his uncle and aunt, that he appreciated them, that he loved them.

But it was too late for anything but regrets.

Lucky gazed morosely at the wall. She was trying not to cry, but her shoulders shook.

"It'll be okay, Lucks. I promise."

"You can't promise those sorts of things."

He said nothing, because she was right. They had no power, no friends. Then he drew out the aastra, watching the sunlight catch its edges.

No power? Maybe that wasn't totally true.

"Just rest, Lucks. You'll see."

CHAPTER TWELVE

Ash opened his eyes a few hours later and found himself face-to-face with a rat. An unbelievably big rat. An unbelievably *huge* rat. It sat on the bedpost, rubbing its nose, staring at him with black beady eyes.

"Get lost," snapped Ash. He flicked his foot, and the rat jumped down and ran off through a crack in the wall.

The sun was high and the air oven-hot. He shielded his eyes against the blinding intensity of the sunlight shimmering on the whitewashed roofs around them.

Ash and Lucky got up and scooped water over their faces and heads from a bucket. John stood in the shade of the doorway. Ash wondered if he'd been there all morning, making sure they didn't make a run for it.

"Is Rishi back?" Ash asked. He touched the cold metal arrowhead dangling from his neck, pressing the metal against his skin. Last night he'd smeared it with some dirt and bound it up with twine, turning it into a crude, cheap-looking amulet . . . nothing anyone would notice or want.

"No."

"Then when?"

John shrugged. "Who knows? There's lunch downstairs."

Not good. Not good at all. The old man was the only protection they had and now he was gone. Maybe he had realized it was hopeless and split. Rishi had been lucky last night, taking those rakshasas by surprise. They were bad enough, but Ash had seen Mayar grovel at Savage's feet, so Savage had to be way, way worse. Maybe he was out of Rishi's league, and Rishi had run, abandoning them. It was the only thing that made sense.

Fine. Ash would look after himself and Lucky both. *But how?*

His stomach rumbled loudly. *First things first. Get some food in you, then make a plan.*

Ash looked at Lucky. Her eyes were dark and tired, her face drawn. He took her hand and they followed John down from the roof into the cool shadows of the Lalgur, the Red House.

The derelict palace was built around a central internal courtyard designed to keep the dust, heat, and noise of the city out. There were three floors, each guarded by a balcony that ran around the courtyard's edge. The balcony walls had collapsed in places, but none had been repaired. Ropes crisscrossed the empty space above the courtyard floor.

Children walked along the ropes, slowly crossing from one side of the courtyard to the other. They bustled in an impatient line as one child after the next made his or her way across. Even the lowest rope was twelve feet above the stone floor, and there was no safety net. Ash watched a girl no older than Lucky walk across, blindfolded. She held a cup of water in each hand and seemed more focused on not spilling any than staying upright and alive.

On the first floor, other children jumped and tumbled and juggled and bent their bodies into impossible shapes, contorting spines and limbs like they were made of rubber.

"Ujba runs a circus?" Ash asked John. Not what he'd expected, but that did explain how they made their living.

And this is what Rishi wants for us? How is juggling going to turn me into a "hero"?

"Think that's easy?" said John, pointing up at the kid performing the high-wire act far above them. "You need balance and courage. Ujba teaches us to master our bodies, our minds, our emotions. That's just for starters; wait 'til you see what happens in the basement."

Lucky let go of Ash's hand and went to sit against the wall, watching the others. A girl came up and offered her a small toy, a broken doll. Lucky, usually the first one to spring up and join in, just stared blankly. The girl shrugged and left.

Lucky seemed like a broken doll herself.

But what could he say? *There, there, it'll be okay. Don't worry, Lucks, it'll be fine.*

It would never be fine, ever again. People were dead. The only family they had was thousands of miles away. They were being hunted by demons.

Ash closed his eyes and a sudden, clear memory of his aunt came flooding back. It hit him so hard he stumbled back, slumping against the wall. Her final words.

Look after your sister.

Yes, whatever else, he would take care of her. He would keep Lucky safe.

And to do that, they needed to get out of here. Ash sat down beside his sister.

He was taking a sip out of a tin cup, thinking about escape, when a foot darted past and kicked it out of his hand.

"Who are you, English?" Hakim, the older boy, stood over Ash, his fingertips resting on the punch dagger tucked into his waistband.

Ash peered up. "My name is Ash."

"We don't like English here."

"I'm not English."

Hakim sniffed. "Smell like English." He poked his toe into Ash's ribs. "Feel like English: soft and weak. Like a sack of puke."

The other children went quiet. Ash knew no one was going to come to his rescue. He'd faced guys like Hakim all his school life. They were the sporty ones, the cool, good-looking ones. The ones who pushed him around in the gym and classrooms. They'd kicked the back of his chair and stolen his lunch money.

Ash gazed at the bigger boy. That was then.

He stood up.

Hakim's fingers tightened around the dagger and drew it out. Ash didn't blink.

"Well, English?" The blade was an inch from his eye.

"Sorry, are you expecting me to be scared?" Ash replied.

Yes, he should be scared, but he wasn't. Last night his entire world had collapsed, and now the threats of a school bully just didn't amount to much. What could Hakim do that was worse than what had already happened?

"If you're going to use the knife, then use it." Ash's jaw stiffened as he snarled. "Otherwise get that thing out of my face and let me finish my meal."

The katar was poised in the space between them. Hakim's eyes narrowed. Then he pushed Ash's head against the wall and stalked off.

John scurried over. "You must have a death wish." He poured Ash a fresh cup of water. "But that was seriously cool. No one stands up to Hakim. You're lucky he didn't slice you."

"Thanks for the backup," Ash said sarcastically.

John scratched his head. "Listen, you don't live here. You don't know the rules. Come with me. We'll eat somewhere with a bit of privacy."

He took them into a small room on the first floor. There was a low wooden bed, a table, and some Bollywood posters on the wall.

Ash looked at John as he perched himself on the bed. He was smaller than Lucky, though probably close to Ash in age. Years of malnourishment had given him a small frame and little muscle. His jaw seemed too big and his eyes too large, sitting in a head that was all angular cheekbones and cavernous sockets.

"Don't look at me like that," said John. "That 'poor Indian' look. You Westerners all have it."

"That obvious?" said Ash. "What are you doing here, John?"

"Don't know." John winced. "Mum left me here a few years ago."

"Your mum abandoned you?"

"Dad died. Simple as that." John spoke plainly, like it was

hardly news at all. "Mum couldn't afford to keep us. It's better here. I earn my own keep, enough to pay for food and a bed. It could be a lot worse."

"How'd you earn money?"

"I'm a fully qualified doctor, of course. Can't you tell?" John said, grinning. "I steal. Pick pockets, open locks. Climb up a drainpipe and onto people's roofs. They don't expect that. Sneaking in is easy when you're this size."

"What do you take?"

"Wallets. Cameras. Cell phones. Anything some tourist might put down for a second and look away. We all do it. It's better than begging."

Cell phones. That was it. "Call home," Lucky whispered, guessing exactly what he was thinking.

"Look, John, I need your help," Ash said. "I need to get a cell."

"You think Ujba lets me hang on to them? The moment we get anything, Hakim takes it off us to give to the guru. If he caught me hiding a phone, he'd beat my brains out. Forget it."

"John, just listen. What would you give to be with your mum again?"

"She left me. Why would I want to be back with her?"

"You said so yourself; she couldn't afford to feed you. You help me and my dad will give you a reward, all the money you could ever want. You could be with your mum tomorrow, easy."

A flash of pain shot through John's eyes. Ash felt guilty, playing on the boy's weakness, on what must be his secret dreams, things he wouldn't allow himself to acknowledge.

"We're all alone here, John." A lump rose in Ash's throat and he choked out the words. "But my dad will come and get us. I just need to call him. Please, get me a cell."

John met his gaze, biting his lip with indecision. Then, abruptly, he shook his head.

"No. Sorry. I çan't."

"Lucks. Get up. We're leaving."

Lucky opened her eyes instantly. She sprung up and checked the door, making sure no one was around. "What's the plan?" she asked.

"The plan is to get the heck out of here. Good enough?"

"Certainly is."

Night had come. They'd rested and eaten and were now ready. No one had bothered to check on them for the last few hours. If John wasn't going to help them and Rishi had run off, then they couldn't count on anyone, not anymore. It was a bitter thought, but he and Lucky were getting out tonight.

Ash tied his shoelaces together and hung his Converse All Stars around his neck. No point making any more noise than totally necessary.

In the distance the temple bells chimed, and somewhere nearby dogs barked and fought. The chatter of Varanasi drifted up from the crowded streets of the old city.

"Come on."

Ash dragged the door open. They'd head down into the streets. There were loads of Internet cafés. They'd call Dad from there, get out of India, and put this nightmare behind them. His hand rested on the door handle. They'd deal with Savage. But first they needed to leave.

Lucky grabbed Ash's arm.

A living line slithered across the roof. The moonlight shone on its dark green scales, glistening like oil. Two green eyes blinked in the darkness.

Ash moved back as the snake came closer. It curled up in the doorway, blocking their exit, then rose. Its tongue flickered between its ivory fangs. Its hood spread as it swayed.

A cobra.

Lucky stepped up on to the bed, pulling the sheet up.

"Don't move," Ash whispered. *Now what?* He reached for the door again, but the snake hissed loudly, its head weaving toward his hand.

"Ash . . ."

"Shh." The snake's eyes focused on him.

Suddenly Lucky pushed Ash aside and threw the sheet. The snake whipped forward, but not before the cloth covered it. It struggled and thrashed under the cotton, and Lucky leaped off the bed, grabbing Ash's shoes from around his neck.

"Hit it!"

The snake thrust its head forward under the sheet, but Lucky whacked it sideways. If they could get it halfway through the door, they might squash it. Ash shoved it with his foot and the serpent snapped toward him, batting its head against his ankle but unable to bite through the sheet. But it still blocked the door, and taking out a live cobra wasn't easy with just a shoe.

Still under the sheet, the snake coiled into a lump, flicked its tail, and went limp.

"Think you got it, Lucks."

Its body rippled with a shiver and a small, broken sigh whispered out.

Hold on, wasn't it bigger now?

Ash stepped back as the sheet rose. It was as if the snake was growing. The sheet hung now over a curved back. Long green-tinged nails poked out from the cloth.

Ash pushed himself against the wall. The door was on the far side of the room. If he shouted for help, the snake would attack the next person in. He reached over for the lamp.

Limbs took shape under the sheet, and the creature that had just been a cobra now stood up on two legs. The sheet fell away from the head, and glossy black hair shone in the darkness. The creature straightened its neck and stretched out its arms. Then fingers curled around the sheet and drew it tightly around itself. The creature faced Ash.

It was a girl. An Indian girl of similar height and age to Ash, long-limbed and elegantly graceful — inhumanly so. Her eyes were almond-shaped, with green irises slit by black, vertical pupils. Her features were elongated, with highly arched eyebrows.

Features he recognized.

"Hold on. I know you," said Ash. "You were at the Cyber Café."

Her serpent tongue flickered, then retreated behind sharp teeth.

A rakshasa. He couldn't believe it. He'd been planning to ask her out!

The girl blinked slowly, then snatched the All Stars from

Lucky. "That. Hurt," she whispered. With a flick of her wrist, the shoes flew over the side of the building.

"Hey!" shouted Ash. "Those were my Doctor Who specials!"

"Reality check, Ash," said Lucky. "Demon at twelve o'clock."

"Yeah, right. Sorry." He turned back to the problem at hand. The snake-girl blinked again and her eyes shone with a green light. She slowly opened her jaws, and Ash stared, mesmerized, at the two wet, venom-coated fangs.

"You're scaring them, Parvati." Rishi crossed the flat roof, swinging a small lantern. "And put some clothes on."

Thank God. Rishi was here.

The rakshasa flicked her hair away from her face and smoothed it down. Then with one more scowl, she pulled up the sheet and skillfully wove it around her body. In seconds she'd arranged it into a crude sari. "She hit me," muttered the rakshasa girl.

"Her?" Rishi pointed at Lucky. He patted Ash's sister on the back. "Good for you."

Rishi and the rakshasa? The old man knew her? Ash realized he was still holding his breath. He let it out and wiped the sweat off his face.

"She's a demon," he said.

"Rakshasa, if you don't mind," said the girl.

Oh, great, he'd hurt the demon's feelings. Demon. Rakshasa. Or whatever she was. She began to plait her hair, but kept her weird snake eyes on them.

So Rishi was in league with the rakshasas too. How could Ash trust anyone?

Rishi nodded. "Yes, she is. But she is on our side. Rakshasas are like people. Some good. Some evil." He glanced back at the girl, who pretended to ignore him. "Some a bit of both."

"You were the cobra in the basket, weren't you?" said Ash. "You tried to bite me!"

"Oh, please," Parvati replied. "If I'd wanted to bite you, you'd be dead."

"So you were spying on us even then?"

Rishi shrugged his shoulders in a sort of but not quite apology. "I needed to know what Savage wanted with your family."

"Oh. That's okay, then." Ash took his sister's hand. "We're leaving. Good-bye."

He pushed past Rishi and kept well away from the rakshasa. Lucky scurried beside him and Ash didn't look back. He and his sister got to the top of the steps. He could hear people below — the street kids were already up and about.

"Wait, Ashoka." Rishi stepped up beside them. He had his stick, but it didn't buzz with power now, and his eyes were plain blue. "Where would you go? You are safe here."

"For how long? We can't stay here forever."

He put his hand on Ash's shoulder. "Long enough to be trained. I will help you, Ash, but you must learn —"

"— the ways of the Force?" Ash pushed Rishi's hand away. "I'm sorry, but who died and made you Obi-Wan Kenobi?"

"Wait until I find out what Savage is planning." The old man squatted down, leaning his stick over his shoulder. The lantern went on the floor in front of him. The rakshasa, Parvati, stayed a few yards back, just out of the light. But the moon shone on her jet-black hair and her skin glowed dimly, like a ghost's.

"Let's talk," Rishi said.

"About what?"

"You. Savage. Why he hired your uncle." He crossed his arms, leaning forward attentively. "Tell me everything."

Ash sat down and crossed his legs. He told Rishi about the Savage Fortress, the study, and the two million pounds Savage had offered his uncle to translate the Harappan scrolls. Then the underground shrine, the rakshasas. The car crash. His voice cracked as he remembered seeing his uncle and aunt for the last time.

Rishi sat silently after Ash had finished. "Savage did it for the aastra," he said finally. "But to use it how?"

Ash tugged it off his neck and tossed it on the ground. He hated the thing. "Savage was looking for a key," he said, remembering that conversation he'd overheard in Savage's study.

"You believe the aastra is a key?" asked Rishi. "To what?"

"Savage said he needed it to open the Iron Gates," said Ash. "Mean anything to you?"

Rishi scowled. "Savage has robbed many places in India in his search for treasures and power. But one with iron gates?"

"Fire melts iron, if you have enough of it," said Ash. "Could the arrowhead be the aastra of the fire god?"

"Agni? Perhaps," answered Rishi. "There are so many gods. But whoever's aastra it is, it will have to be very powerful to open iron gates. Iron resists magic."

"Magic?"

Rishi stared out over the city — south, toward the Savage Fortress. "What do you know of Savage?"

"He's evil."

"And he's been like that for the last three hundred years," said Parvati.

"What?"

Rishi drew his fingers jaggedly across his face. "He came to India in the eighteenth century. Back then he was little more than a pirate. He robbed and destroyed many palaces and temples in his quest for power and wealth." He sighed. "And power and wealth he found."

Parvati came into the edge of the lantern light. "He . . . acquired scrolls of sorcery. Studying them, he gained immense magical power."

Rishi spoke again. "You must endure great, great hardship to acquire the power to alter reality. And there is a price. There is always a price."

Ash nodded. The old legends always went on about wise men living for hundreds of years in meditation, surviving on a single raindrop. Eventually through such austerities, they gained magical powers. The most powerful could create their own universes and were even feared by the gods. Ash thought of the painting he'd seen on the Internet of the first Lord Savage.

"You're telling me this guy is the same one who came here all those centuries ago?"

"Yes," said Rishi. "He vanished in the 1940s. We believed his sorcery had finally destroyed him, but it turned out he was traveling the Far East, looking for ways to extend his lifespan even further. Now he's back."

"And looking worse than ever," said Ash.

"Yes. He is very corrupted by all his power. He rarely uses magic because bit by bit, it consumes him. He relies on his rakshasa servants nowadays."

"Does he think the aastra will heal him?"

"I have heard there are aastras that can repair all injuries, even raise the dead, but Rama would have been given a weapon, not something that heals. I believe Savage is after whatever lies behind these Iron Gates. We must stop him at all costs. He is desperate, and desperate men make dangerous choices." Rishi stood up, slowly stretching himself straight, each bone and joint creaking and popping. "Did Savage say where these gates were?"

"My uncle said Savage had uncovered a big city out in Rajasthan."

Rishi looked at Ash. "We need your help if we are to stop the Englishman."

"Me? What can I do?"

"More than you can imagine," whispered Rishi.

Ash stared at the arrowhead on the floor. He wanted Savage stopped; he wanted him to pay for what he'd done. Of course he did. But he was just an ordinary boy, and they were talking about demons, immortals, and black magic. Rishi had said he'd turn him into a hero, but being heroic would only get him killed, and then he'd be no good to anyone. His job was to look after Lucky, and that meant getting back home.

Ash heard footsteps on the stairs and John appeared. Rishi put his foot over the arrowhead, hiding it. The boy glanced at Parvati and kept a wary distance, but approached Rishi with a bow.

"Yes?" asked Rishi.

John pointed down the steps. "Ujba has arrived." He bowed again and, with a final glance at Parvati, scurried back downstairs.

So, they know what she is, and have seen her before. But they certainly don't like her. How could they? Despite Rishi's protestations, she was a demon. One of *them.*

Rishi moved his foot. "This is your choice, Ash. There is only one way to stop Savage and you know it."

So you say. But for now, until he could get a phone or get out to an Internet café, he had best play along. Ash picked up the arrowhead.

Rishi took him by the shoulder. "Remember what I said about keeping the aastra secret?"

"Yes." Ash rehung it about his neck. But as he looked at the old man, he could see Rishi was worried. "This Ujba. What will he teach me?"

"The Americans have a most appropriate phrase." Rishi headed down the steps. "He will teach you how to kick butt."

CHAPTER THIRTEEN

They made their way to the ground floor. The rakshasa girl followed a few paces behind, and Ash couldn't shake a burning sensation of her gaze stabbing him square between his shoulder blades. Rishi led them to a corner room of the palace.

A single candle flickered in the gloom.

"Ujba, I have some new students," said Rishi.

A man stood in the darkness, his back to them. His legs were the size and strength of solid marble columns, and his chest was wider than the door they'd come through. He leaned over a bowl, and a flash of steel shone in his fist. A small mirror faced him, and Ash saw a pair of dark, cold eyes peering at him in the reflection.

"My school is full." The steel razor tapped the bowl, then the man drew it steadily over his scalp. The blade crackled against the stiff bristles.

Rishi rummaged in his shoulder sack and out came a small cloth purse. "I don't expect you to train them out of the kindness of your heart. I will pay."

He held up a diamond as big as Ash's thumb. He'd never seen a gem that big, except in the Crown Jewels.

Ujba stopped shaving. Rishi flicked the diamond at him and Ujba snatched it out of the air. He inspected it, then tucked it away. He clicked shut his cutthroat razor and turned to face them.

Gold earrings hung from his ears and a thick mustache, its ends curled, covered his upper lip. A heavy brow hung like a cliff over his intense, cruel black eyes. He wore only a white loincloth and a thin yellow cotton scarf, loose over his massive shoulders.

"You want me to teach them to juggle? Maybe to sing a song?" he asked.

Rishi laughed. "The girl, the healing arts. The boy . . ." He glanced at Ash, checking his resolve. "The path of battle. We must make this one a warrior."

Ujba towered over Ash and laid his palm on the boy's head. The fingers flexed and covered the top of his skull, ear to ear. He turned him side to side.

With a sharp twist he could snap my neck.

"Impossible. He does not have it in him."

"Come now, I thought the great Ujba could teach even a mouse to defeat a lion."

"A mouse, yes," said Ujba. "But this is a flea."

Ash slapped Ujba's hand away. Glaring at the big man, he replied, "I'm not some dumb animal."

Rishi gave a snort of a laugh. "This flea bites."

Ujba paused, and Ash saw the big man's fingers clench into a fist. Ash stood firm. He was sick of being bullied, even if it meant he was about to get punched through the wall.

Then Ujba grunted and turned away. "John, take the girl to

the apothecary," he said. "Come, boy," he added, addressing Ash. Ujba picked up the candle.

Rishi put his hand on Ash's shoulder, and for once Ash was glad the old man was around. Lucky squeezed his hand before she went, and Ujba pushed open a stout wooden door, invisible in the darkness.

Parvati, who'd been leaning against the doorpost, took a step toward them.

"The rakshasa cannot come," said Ujba. His distaste was clear.

"Parvati, wait here," said Rishi.

Parvati leaned back against the post, her cold gaze passing over Ujba as he walked past.

They descended more steps, but these were narrow and damp. The walls were slick with green algae and the only light came from Ujba's candle. Ash heard shouts and the clang of steel.

They emerged into a low-ceilinged chamber. Weapons lined the walls: spears, daggers, swords, and shields, all arranged neatly on wooden racks. The center had been excavated to create a six-foot-deep pit of hard-packed red earth that filled almost the entire floor, leaving only a narrow walkway around its edge.

A dozen boys fought in the pit, some in pairs, others in larger groups. They wore nothing but tightly bound white loincloths or their underpants, and their bodies shone with sweat. Two of them, older than the rest, fought with real weapons. Hakim was one, and he wove the katar through the air as though it was lightning, not steel. His opponent fought with two batons, the air whirring as he spun and parried and thrust.

"*Kalaripayit*," whispered Rishi. "The world's oldest martial art."

Ash spotted a young man approaching a shrine in the corner of the training hall. He went through an extravagant series of moves, high kicks, low bows, and spins, finally ending with a prayer to the statue, a black-skinned skeleton. Its bloodred eyes glared at the martial artist as though it was watching every movement, waiting to devour him if he displeased it.

"Kali," said Ash. The goddess of death.

"She frightens you, doesn't she?" asked Rishi.

"She's evil." Ash had never seen anything so monstrous. Not even the rakshasas.

Rishi shook his head. "She is beyond good and evil. She is a goddess. She is terrifying, yes, but she's also the greatest protection humanity has. Kali is the one who fights the rakshasas, so she must take a form that is more frightening than theirs."

"But you said she loves death. Isn't that evil?"

"Is death evil?" said Rishi. "Ask the old. Or the sick. Death frees them from suffering. And think of those who would do evil. Death brings an end to their actions, does it not?"

"Enough," commanded Ujba. One by one, the fighting pairs stopped. The boys stood, panting, watching their master. Only Hakim and his opponent continued.

They want to kill each other, Ash thought. It seemed like any second now the dagger would spurt red, or the baton would smash a skull and Hakim's brains would burst out of his ears.

But somehow the blows made no contact. Hakim jabbed but his katar was caught between the sticks. His hand slipped free and his fist drove square into the other boy's face. The boy blinked and his attention wavered, just for an instant. Hakim sprang into the air and his knee smashed into the boy's jaw, lifting him clean off his feet. The boy crashed to the ground, arms splayed out, unconscious.

"I said enough," repeated Ujba.

Hakim pressed his palms together. "Forgive me, master." Then his gaze fell on Ash. Confusion flickered there for a second, turning to anger. He opened his mouth to speak, then slowly shut it.

The boys cleared the space, two of them dragging Hakim's unconscious victim. Ujba picked up the discarded katar. He wiped it clean, then handed it to Ash.

"Hakim," said Ujba. Hakim sprang forward, touching his master's feet. He then looked at Ash and smiled.

Ash's fingers tightened around the weapon. It was way cool. The handle was in the form of an H, so he gripped the crossbar, with the two long bars on either side acting as forearm guards. The blade was a long triangle of steel sticking straight forward in front of the fist. He had read that the tip was especially hardened so it could break through plate armor. There was no other weapon like it in the world. Ash moved it from one hand to the other before settling it into his right.

Ujba pointed at Hakim. "Kill him."

"What?" replied Ash. "I can't do that."

"Yes. I am sure you can't. But I want you to try."

"No," said Ash. He looked at Rishi, but the old man merely squatted at the edge of the hall, watching intently.

Ujba sighed. "Motivate him, Hakim."

Hakim walked up to Ash. Nothing flashy, just straight and direct. He opened his right fist into a flat palm and hit Ash — hard.

Ash's ears rang and he fell. His cheek was on fire. He hadn't even seen Hakim strike — the slap had been that blindingly fast. Ash's fingers groped for the katar, and the steel settled into his hand.

He had just gotten to his feet when he collapsed again, this time on his front. His chin bashed against the hard, compacted ground and tears bubbled in his eyes. The back of his head throbbed. Hakim had punched him again before he was ready!

Ash gritted his teeth, staring at Hakim. "You scum," he whispered. But this time as he stood, he kept his eyes on the older boy. Hakim stepped forward. He'd cut him, just once. Just draw a little line of blood and teach Hakim a lesson. Ash thrust forward.

Hakim kicked his hand away and the katar scuttled into the corner. He twisted Ash's arm tightly behind his back, locking his own forearm across Ash's throat. He squeezed, shoving Ash's Adam's apple into his neck.

Stop. But he couldn't speak; his windpipe was blocked. All he could do was flail with his legs. His eyes bulged and blood pounded in his ears. He couldn't breathe.

Stop.

He reached behind him and with his free hand grabbed a fistful of Hakim's hair. But Hakim jerked back, out of reach.

Stop.

Black clouds swelled in Ash's eyes and his legs turned to jelly, twitching but powerless.

"Stop," said Ujba.

Ash slumped to the floor. When he gasped, it felt like he was swallowing razor blades. Each breath was a shot of pure agony.

Rishi helped him up. Ash coughed and retched. His head swam and the ground swayed like a ship in a storm. Rishi led him to the side of the chamber and put him gently against the wall. Ash hung on to it, pushing his fingers into the cracks to hold himself upright.

"You didn't help me," he said with a gasping croak.

"It was not my fight."

"He almost killed me."

"It is the way of battle. The way you must learn, Ashoka. This is your life, now."

Ash stared at the gecko on the ceiling. It hadn't moved for a couple of hours and neither had he. Lucky murmured as she slept in the next bed. While he'd spent the rest of the evening down in the training hall, she'd been with Ujba's healers, working hard with the pestle and mortar to make medicine. Pilgrims and locals who couldn't afford Western doctors came to the healers. Some paid with a sack of rice; others offered

Ujba a day's work, or information. The old city was a tightly woven network of whispers and prying eyes, and Ujba sat at the heart of it. Nothing happened in Varanasi without him hearing.

By the time they'd finished, Ash and Lucky were too exhausted to do anything but drop into their beds. Now, hours later, she slept and Ash watched the gecko. The small lizard clung to the underside of the ceiling, eyes on the flies and insects humming in the room.

Ash's fingers rested on the aastra, flat on his chest. What had he got himself into? Demons. Weapons made by gods. Ancient martial arts. His body was exhausted from the pummeling he'd gotten while training, but his mind wouldn't rest. His life seemed a jigsaw, broken into pieces without a pattern by the deaths two nights ago.

Despair and doubts whispered to him. Who did he think he was? He was in way over his head. Could he trust Rishi? The old man wanted Ash to become a warrior. He must be insane. Ash winced as he flexed his biceps and blasts of pain ran along his arms.

Some warrior. Some hero.

Silently Ash got to his feet. He checked that Lucky was fast asleep, then crept out of the room. He reached the edge of the roof and leaned over the balcony. The river was a dozen yards from the building. He pulled off the aastra. One good swing and it would be lost forever. Let it be someone else's problem. He'd have no reason to fight Savage, and he and Lucky could leave. He dangled the arrowhead from his fist.

"What are you doing?"

Parvati glided out of the darkness, moving with preternatural grace. Her dark green clothes shimmered — a light pair of silken trousers and a sleeveless top with serpents embroidered across it. Her hair was as smooth and as black as oil. She could be any girl, but her eyes remained those of a cobra — utterly inhuman.

"None of your business." Ash still had the aastra in his hand, ready to throw. "What are *you* doing here?"

"Keeping an eye on you. Making sure you don't do anything stupid."

"So you're Rishi's spy?"

She shrugged her slim shoulders. "That. And your bodyguard."

"And I'll be safe with you?" *A rakshasa?*

Parvati said nothing. She sat on the edge of the balcony, watching him. Around her neck was a silver locket that she turned idly with her fingers.

Ash knotted the aastra back around his neck, uncomfortable under her intense gaze. "I suppose it's magic. It'll turn up in my breakfast if I try to chuck it, right?"

"Depends on what you have for breakfast."

Parvati swung her legs back and forth. Ash watched as she drew her long fingers through her veil of black hair, turning a strand around and around her index finger. The nails were green. She was a rakshasa, a demon, but she acted just like a regular girl. She caught him looking at her. Ash blushed and rubbed the back of his neck.

"How long have you known Rishi?" he asked.

"On and off for about four and a half thousand years."

Ash glanced back at her. That wasn't possible, was it?

Parvati must have read the doubt. "I'm an immortal, Ash. I've been around a while."

"And Rishi?"

"He's human, like you. He's destined to be reincarnated. Not that he remembers any of his past lives."

"What about me?" The question blurted out before he'd even registered it. "You've met me before?"

Parvati laughed. Her voice rang like crystals chiming, and Ash felt the vibration of the sound travel deep through him.

"Yes, of course I have." She raised her hand to stop his next question. "And you are the same each time. It's as though your destiny is to repeat the same mistakes."

"What mistakes? If you tell me what I do wrong, I could fix them now."

"It would make no difference, Ash."

"What about Rishi? He makes the same mistakes too?"

"Oh, yes. He always has too much faith in you."

Ash stood back, wondering what she meant. How could he be responsible for previous lives? That didn't seem fair. He was him, and him alone. Not these other ghosts of the past.

But the thought made his head swim: All that had happened before, he'd been part of it. Him, Parvati, and Rishi.

"After I found the aastra, I had a dream — kind of like a vision," said Ash. "I was on an endless battlefield. I was Rama, and I was fighting Ravana, the demon king, who wielded two huge swords. Everywhere he struck, men died." He faced Parvati. "Was I Rama? Once?"

"You've been many, many people," she replied. "Right here,

right now, you are Ashoka Mistry. And that is all that matters."

"So it's my destiny to always fight? Lifetime after lifetime?" he said, really to himself.

"An eternal warrior. But you're not the only one, Ashoka Mistry." Parvati gave him a narrow-eyed look and her brow wrinkled with indecision. Then, abruptly, she spoke. "Some souls have been chosen, I don't know why, to face evil. I've met them over the centuries. Some fail, some join the very forces they are meant to oppose, some are victorious. But all of them, *all of them*, change the world in profound ways."

"I'm one of those?" said Ash. "So, no pressure, then." He gazed down at his bruised knuckles. "Why can't you get one of these other 'eternal warriors' to deal with Savage?"

"We have you. We don't need anyone else."

"Is that a joke? I can't fight."

"A joke? How typically human to make a joke of serious business."

"What? Demons have no sense of humor?"

She just stayed silent and gave him one of her creepy slow blinks. It was like she was deciding whether to let his comment pass or finish him with one quick bite. Now Ash knew what a mouse must feel like.

This was way too big a subject. Never-ending battles. Eternal warriors. Fate-of-the-world stuff. He couldn't deal with all that responsibility. No one could. Ash wished he'd never asked about it now. He changed the subject.

"When did you first meet Rishi?" he asked.

"In Lanka."

"Ravana's home city." That was straight out of Indian mythology, like someone saying they'd been at the battle of Troy. "You were there?"

"It was my home too." Parvati's eyes darkened. "It was filled with beautiful palaces made of glass. Perfumed gardens. Lakes the most perfect, clearest blue." She rubbed her eyes, like she was trying to get rid of a painful vision. "Or at least, that's how it looked."

"What do you mean?"

"Ravana was a great sorcerer, so great that reality itself bent around him. He could make anything seem real. He could raise mountains from valleys, turn desert into orchards," said Parvati. "Alter your mind, your emotions. He could make you hate the person you loved, make you kill them — and you'd laugh as you did it.

"Rakshasas can adapt to such ever-evolving surroundings, but humans suffer in mind and body. They are changed in ways you cannot imagine, even in your worst nightmares. Lanka was a realm of insanity."

Ash could imagine. "The Carnival of Flesh."

Parvati gasped. "You've seen it?"

"In my dream. Vision. Whatever."

"Then believe me when I tell you those he used in the Carnival were the lucky ones."

Ash could see the pain on the girl's face: Her brow furrowed and the demon eyes filled with tears. But she caught him looking at her and wiped her cheeks. Ash decided to change the subject again.

"What about Rishi?"

"Back then he was a general in Rama's army."

"And now you serve him?"

"After Ravana was killed, Rama declared an amnesty for all rakshasas who'd fought against him. But some needed special watching, those who might start a rebellion against him."

"And you were one of those?" Ash couldn't understand it. She wasn't nearly as terrifying as the three rakshasas who served Savage. "Why?"

"Ravana is my father."

She might as well have hit him in the chest with a train. He stared, dumbfounded.

"I was the last of his children, born of a mortal mother, so I'm not considered rakshasa royalty," Parvati continued. "But of all his offspring, even if I say so myself, I was his favorite." There was a hint of pride in her voice.

"So you and he hung out and did lots of father-daughter stuff. What, like playing catch and stories at bedtime?"

"Hardly. He taught me to kill. My venom is fatal to *every-thing,* you see. No mortal, no rakshasa, can survive it. I think he loved me most because he was afraid of me." Parvati dug her nails into the wall. When she spoke, her voice filled with cold hate. "He was evil, Ashoka. The purest evil. My mother was a human princess. He kidnapped her and kept her prisoner for many years. He . . . altered her so that by the time I was born, she could barely be recognized as a human, let alone the princess she once was. He did that to all his prisoners, sooner or later. It amused him to hold some royals for ransom, then when the treasure was paid he'd return them, hideous beyond description, twisted in all ways. My mother's single day of happiness was the day she killed herself. It was the only way to escape Ravana and his madness."

Ash leaned his elbows on the battlements, watching the dark river. A trail of glowing candles floated upon the shimmering surface, a hundred glowing spirits. He looked obliquely at Parvati. She was too lost in her thoughts to notice him.

She had such rage inside her. It was both frightening and, he had to admit, pretty cool. He didn't have many female friends, and girls he fancied, like Gemma, were way out of his league — so far out he got tongue-tied as soon as they came anywhere near. Yet here he was with a demon princess. His heart beat faster as he watched strands of her hair float in the breeze. She touched the locket again, gently rubbing it. It was beautifully engraved, and Ash reckoned it must be pretty important.

A boat drifted in out of the darkness and he saw a couple of the kids on the riverbank run toward it. Light streamed out from below as the door to the Lalgur opened and out came Rishi.

"Where's he going?" asked Ash. Why was he leaving? He couldn't. He had to stay here with them. Ash's voice trembled with anxiety. "He can't go."

Parvati took his hand. It was such a strange, unexpected gesture that he just blinked and stared at it.

"I'll protect you," she said. She flexed her long fingers and looked into his eyes. Ash could have been swallowed up in them, they were so deep and dark and hypnotic. She closed them slowly and shook her head. And then she left.

What was that all about?

"Ash and Parvati sitting in a tree," said Lucky, her face peering through the stone lattice wall of their room. "K-I-S-S-I-N-G."

"Shut up, Lucks."

CHAPTER FOURTEEN

Days passed, and after a while a routine fell into place. Hakim's friend Monk beat Ash up at breakfast. Hakim's other friend Rajiv took a turn at lunchtime, and Hakim himself did the honors just before bedtime. All Ujba did was make sure they didn't actually kill him.

Every inch of Ash's body was bruised and battered. But, after a while, he discovered something he'd never known about himself: He could take it. Still couldn't dish it out, not yet; he hadn't landed a single punch on any of them. But with his feet planted firmly and body tensed, he fell less and less, though the blows still hurt. And when he got knocked down, he always got back up.

Parvati lurked in the shadows and doorways, watching. She'd appear suddenly when he'd sit down for food and disappear within an eye-blink. But even when he couldn't see her, Ash felt her eyes upon him. The only place Parvati wasn't permitted was the training hall in the basement.

It was suffocating down there. The underground chamber had no real ventilation except for a few missing bricks high up in the walls. With thirty-plus boys sweating away, all day, every day, it was like living in a sauna. The first day he'd fought in his trousers and T-shirt, but by day two he'd put his embarrassment aside and stripped down to his underpants like everyone else.

Now Ash slumped in a corner of the chamber, gasping for breath after a solid thump in his guts, delivered with undisguised glee by Monk. John poured out a cup of water, and Ash emptied it with a swallow. He held it out for refilling. "I think I've broken something," he said as he felt along his ribs.

But John wasn't listening; his eyes were on Hakim. Hakim moved with a dancer's lightness and grace, every move executed with machine-like precision combined with devastating power. Ujba scolded him, beat him, but Hakim didn't flinch under the hardest of blows. He seemed immune to fear. Dripping in sweat and covered in bleeding cuts, he just moved faster and fought harder.

The rumor among the boys was that Ujba was teaching Hakim *marma-adi*, the 108 kill points. The Chinese called it *Dim Mak*, or the Death Touch. It was believed the body contained channels of energy, life force, and a master of the art could see these points as glowing spots of light, brightest at the most vulnerable locations. By attacking these, a warrior could bring about crippling pain and death with the lightest of blows. To master marma-adi was to master the art of death.

Ash had asked John about it, but John had scoffed. Marma-adi was a myth, he said. He'd seen Ujba at work fighting, and the guru was a skillful bruiser, nothing more.

John refilled the cup. "He's testing you."

"Hakim?"

"No. Ujba. He never puts beginners against his best," said John. "You're very lucky."

"Oh, yes. That's what I tell myself every morning. How lucky I am." Ash lightly touched the bruise on his chin, courtesy of Hakim. "Why does Hakim hate me?"

John shrugged. "You're the new boy. He wants to establish the order of things, to put you in your place. Doesn't help you being English."

"I'm not English." Ash pinched his dark skin. "I'm Indian."

"No. You're a coconut," replied John. "Brown on the outside, white on the inside."

Funny. Back in Britain he was too Indian, too Asian, to really be British, and out here he was too British to be Indian. So what was he?

Lost.

Ash groaned as he leaned up against the wall, trying to find some position that didn't ache. And failing.

"Ash." John nudged him. "You all right?"

"I'm just reflecting on the total suckiness of my life." He needed to escape, just for a minute. He closed his eyes and tried to summon memories of London and his parents. They must know about Anita and Vik. They must be worried sick. What were they doing right now? Waiting by the phone? Wondering what had happened? If he could just call them, just for a minute. Tell them he and Lucky were alive at least.

But they never left the Lalgur. Each time Ash had wandered down to the front door there was someone standing there on guard, and Parvati in his shadow. Apparently Rishi had left strict instructions that they should be kept within the boundaries of the old palace. But there had been no word from the sadhu since he'd gone.

"Hey, English." One of the boys, Monk, tossed a folded sheet of paper at him. "You're famous."

Ash opened it up and John leaned over to have a look. It was a poster with photos of Ash and Lucky. The text mentioned a car crash and two missing children. Lord Savage, out of the goodness of his heart, was urging everyone to look for them, and giving a hefty reward of ten thousand rupees to the person who found them.

"They're all over the city," said John.

"And you didn't tell me?"

"That Savage is after you? Don't you know that already? Isn't that why you're hiding here?"

Ash ripped up the sheet. They were totally trapped if the entire city was looking for them. And what about the Lalgur? He wondered if there wasn't some traitor here, looking to get some easy cash.

"What's wrong?" asked the Indian boy.

"Everything." Ash groaned. "Still, I suppose it can't get any worse."

Ujba crossed the hall, Hakim next to him, and dropped a pair of swords on the floor.

"Weapons practice for the rest of the day," said the guru. He turned to Ash. "First pair, Hakim and English."

John slapped Ash's back. "I think it just has."

CHAPTER FIFTEEN

"Honor Kali," said Ujba as the boys gathered in the basement training hall every morning. Ash looked toward the black, gruesome statue in the corner. He never took his eyes off her as he completed the ritual, an elaborate series of high kicks, low lunges, strikes, and jumps. Did it please the goddess how much sharper his moves were now than at the beginning of his time at the Lalgur? How much leaner he was? The endless training and the basic diet meant the excess blubber was being sweated out, changing Ash both physically and mentally. His head was clearer, reactions faster, limbs quicker, and there was hard muscle forming under his dark skin. To lose weight, he just needed to diet and exercise. Who knew?

Three weeks they'd been here now, the routine unchanged. And still imprisoned in the Lalgur. No news from Rishi. Was he even alive? But Ash could do nothing but wait, and fight.

Ash came down just before dawn for another breakfast of cold lentils and rice. The kids descended on the large steel pots, using elbows, knees, and hair-pulling to jockey for space as they scooped up as much as they could with their bowls.

Ujba was nowhere to be seen. The only adult was an old woman who did the cooking. She squatted over a small fire, rolling dough out into thin, flat discs before flipping them on to her pan. After a few seconds the dough would inflate into a *chapatti* and off it would go, on to the pile with the others.

John scurried in and out of the kitchen carrying an iron teapot. There were only a handful of glasses, so they were passed around from one mouth to the next.

Ash dug out two bowlfuls of rice, added a big scoop of lentils to each, and wandered off into a corner, handing one to Lucky.

"You okay?" he asked.

Lucky nodded, but Ash could see the fight was dying in her. She studied with the physicians, but her eyes were always tired, empty. He put his arm around her.

"We'll get home, Lucks, you'll see."

"Okay, Ash." She didn't sound like she believed him.

John nudged Ash. "Look who's coming," he said before retreating into a group of the other kids.

Parvati gestured to the vacant floor space beside Ash. "May I?"

"All yours."

Ash squashed the mixture of rice and lentils into a rough ball and popped it into his mouth. One of the other kids, hands trembling, offered a full bowl to Parvati, but she brushed it away.

"Not hungry?" Ash asked.

Parvati smiled and put her finger to her lips.

Ash listened. There: a noise. A scratching.

Parvati's hand blurred and there was a surprised squeak. She pulled a struggling rat from a crack in the wall. The brown rodent thrashed in her grasp, and she tightened her fingers. Shivering in terror, it twisted frantically as she dangled it from its tail. She held it above her head.

"Oh, no, you're not . . ." said Ash.

"Oh, yes, I am," said Parvati as she opened her mouth.

The rat stared into her eyes. It seemed paralyzed. But as its head disappeared into her mouth, it scrabbled with its tiny clawed feet, its tail whipping wildly. Parvati's throat bulged, the skin thinning as it stretched to accommodate the animal. The tail flicked back and forth before it too vanished through her lips like a string of spaghetti.

"That was truly disgusting," said Ash.

Lucky stood up. She looked green. "Excuse me," she said. "I'm just going over there to puke."

A shiver suddenly ran along Ash, as though someone had pressed ice against his spine, but it was over the moment it had begun.

"How are you feeling?" asked Parvati.

"Fine. How was your meal?"

"Delicious. Varanasi rats are the best. Free range, you see."

"I'll remember that next time I'm at the supermarket."

Parvati stood up and stretched, almost bending double, backward. She clicked her neck joints, turning her head side to side. "I've a few errands to run. I'll see you later."

Ash watched her step over the crouching children and make

her way out. He looked at his half-empty bowl, his appetite completely gone.

Hakim sat leaning up against a column, eyes on Ash. He didn't need to fight over food; a couple of the kids acted as his servants and brought it to him. Hakim held out a glass and John poured him tea. John followed Hakim's gaze and looked at Ash as well.

Suddenly Hakim swore as the scalding hot tea splashed over his hand. He leapt up and swung his fist straight into John's face. The boy fell with a cry.

"That is out of order," Ash snarled.

Hakim kicked John in the guts, again and again. All John could do was curl up as blows rained down.

Ash was across the floor before he knew it. Hakim spun around just as Ash reached him.

"It was an accident," said Ash.

Hakim's eyes narrowed. "Servants must be beaten or they don't learn."

Ignoring him, Ash looked down at John. "Come on, get up."

Hakim shoved Ash against the wall. "It looks like you need to be taught a lesson too," he growled.

"Is that a threat?" Ash laughed. "You'll need a better line than that. Seriously, it's like you've been watching way too many bad gangster movies."

"I'll break every tooth in your face, fat boy." Hakim raised his fist.

Fat boy? Yeah, back in the day, but not now. Ash lacked Hakim's lean, hard edges, but he was more muscle than flab.

And he was sick of being pushed around. "I'm way past caring."

Hakim's fist shot forward and Ash moved — not consciously, but on pure reflex. Hakim cried out as his knuckles cracked hard into the stone wall. His eyes widened in shock, surprise, and anger.

How did that happen?

Ash brought his knee up and blocked Hakim's kick with time to spare. He ducked as Hakim swung again. It was if he could predict every move and knew what was —

Snake-strike next.

Hakim's fingers, locked and ridged, jabbed at his throat. Ash trapped his opponent's hand in his own and twisted sharply. Hakim's wrist snapped.

Hakim screamed. He glared at Ash, then, cradling his broken wrist, he stumbled away.

As soon as he had gone, John, nursing his bleeding lip, stood up next to Ash. "That was amazing. How did you do that?" All around Ash, the kids were staring at him in silent disbelief.

"Honestly? I have no idea." Ash caught a small movement above. Looking up, he saw Ujba leaning over the highest balcony, watching him. How long had he been up there? What had he seen?

"I cannot believe it," said John.

Ash looked at his friend. "Me neither." There was no way he should have done that, not against Hakim.

What was happening?

CHAPTER SIXTEEN

Ash noticed how the other boys watched him as he came down into the training hall that evening. Everyone in the Lalgur was talking about the fight, and for the first time Hakim wasn't there. If it bothered Ujba, he didn't show it. It was business as usual.

And after five minutes, Ash was sweating, bruised, and lying in the dust.

It didn't make any sense. He'd beaten Hakim, been able to predict his actions and react like lightning, and yet now? Now he was back to normal, somewhere between completely hopeless and a bit pathetic.

What was his malfunction?

After an hour of blood, sweat, and tears, mostly his, Ash dropped down in a corner, trying to catch his breath. John handed him a cup of water. "What's wrong? One minute you're fighting like Spartacus and the next more like Santa Claus."

"Don't remind me."

"Hey," John said. "I've got something that'll cheer you up."

"Later. Can't you see I'm feeling sorry for myself?" Wow, how could he ache so badly? Even his hair ached.

A sigh. "All right. I'll put the cell right back, then."

Ash's eyes snapped open. "This better not be a joke."

John tilted his head toward the door. "In my room."

A cell. In an instant all Ash's weariness vanished. He wanted to run and grab the phone, but he forced himself to sit still. Ujba was sitting opposite, and the guy missed nothing.

Breathe slow and steady. Calm down. Be cool.

John tapped the edge of the water bucket and stood up. He glanced toward Ujba. "Master, the bucket needs filling."

Ujba barely acknowledged him.

"Come and help me," John said to Ash.

Ash nodded and got up. John walked to the door and put his foot on the step.

"Stop," said Ujba.

He can hear my heart beating. The whole class must be able to hear it. Ash kept going.

"Did you hear me, boy?"

Ash's legs trembled. Every instinct warned him to run to John's room and call Dad. He just wanted to speak to him, hear his voice. Tell him that he and Lucky were here, tell him to come and get them. It would take just one minute.

He turned on his heels and looked at Ujba.

Ujba tossed him a clay jug. Ash barely caught it. A couple of the kids laughed.

"Make sure it's cold. Get some ice from the kitchen," said Ujba. Then he shifted his attention back to the fighting.

"Come on, Ash," urged John.

Minutes later they were in John's small room. Ash closed

the door while John pried a brick out of the wall. He drew out an object wrapped in plastic and handed it over.

"I stole it a few hours ago."

"I thought Ujba collected all the takings as soon as you came in." Ujba or Hakim personally checked all the kids to make sure no one was hanging on to anything they shouldn't. That especially included things like cell phones.

"Ujba was still patching up Hakim's broken wrist when I came back." He switched it on. "It's still got a few credits on it. Enough for a call to England."

Ash cradled the cell as if it was the most precious thing he'd ever owned. He wiped his hands on the bedsheet before dialing, not able to trust his slippery fingers to get the numbers right.

It rang and rang.

Please, please pick up.

Voices called from outside, demanding to know who'd left the water bucket on the stairs.

It kept ringing.

Click.

"Hello?"

A woman's voice, worn and tired, a little bit scared too. His mum. He'd imagined this so many thousands of times over the last few weeks, and now, actually hearing her, it was as though his voice had been stolen. His mum.

"Hello?" she said again.

Fists pounded the door. "Oi, Johnny! This is your jug!"

It was going to be okay. At last, it was going to be okay.

"Fine!" Someone whacked the jug against the wooden door. "If it gets broken, it's your fault."

"Just get lost!" shouted John.

"Mum," said Ash. He bit down on his lip to stop it from quivering. "It's me."

His mum sobbed. "Thank God. Thank God. We've waited so long. But we knew, we *knew* you were alive."

"Lucks is fine, we're both fine." Tears filled his eyes. "I'm here in Varanasi."

"So's your dad. He's been looking for you everywhere. That Englishman, Savage, he's been helping."

Of course. Savage would have known Ash would contact his parents sooner or later.

"Listen, Mum, you need to speak with Dad, but not tell Savage anything. Do you understand?"

"What's going on, Ash? You sound so different."

"A lot's happened, Mum."

"Where are you? I'll call Dad right now and tell him to come and get you."

John slapped his hand over the cell. "Not here. Not here. Meet him somewhere else."

Ash blinked, but understood. Ujba wouldn't take kindly to some stranger turning up, demanding to be let in and take them from him — and Ujba was dangerous.

"We need to meet," said Ash. "We'll come to Dad."

"The Good View Hotel, know it?"

Ash glanced at John, who shook his head. "Half the hotels on the riverfront are called the Good View. Ask her for the nearest ghat."

"Which ghat, Mum? We'll meet him there."

"The Manikarnika ghat," she said.

"We'll be there at two in the morning," Ash promised. That would be late enough to make sure everyone else in the Lalgur was asleep.

"I love you, Ash. Tell Lucky I miss her so much. Be quick, my darling. Be quick and we'll have you home tomorrow."

"I love you, Mum." He switched off the cell and threw it to John to hide back behind the brick.

Ash wiped his eyes; he had to act totally normal. But his mum! He'd spoken to his mum! He could picture her so clearly. With her voice still echoing in his head, Ash realized how much he'd missed her and Dad. Now that he'd spoken to her, he had to get back. Nothing else mattered. Tomorrow they'd be on their way home. He couldn't help grinning: They were going home! He opened the door.

And found Parvati waiting outside.

"What's with the stupid smile?" Parvati looked around the room, an eyebrow raised. "What are you both doing in here, anyway?"

John looked at Ash. Ash looked at John. Both blushed. Here was a beautiful girl and they were both still in their underpants.

Parvati sighed. "Never mind. What you two boys get up to in private is your own business. But save it 'til later."

Ash gasped. "It's nothing like that!"

Parvati smiled. "No, of course not."

John stood there speechless until she'd gone. Then he

grabbed the jug and swung it at Ash. "Well, we certainly fooled her, didn't we?"

"Thanks, John. I owe you big time."

"So? Where are you going to meet your dad?"

"Manikarnika ghat. You know it?"

John stared at him. "Of course." He didn't look happy. "It's the main ghat. It's where you go to burn."

That night, Ash walked up the steps to the roof. He couldn't disguise his excitement. Their dad was here. Just wait 'til he told Lucky; she'd go insane with happiness. They were going home. The nightmare was almost over.

"You're looking very pleased with yourself."

Parvati slinked out of the darkness. Her skin seemed to glisten with a greenish hue under the weak lamplight.

Ash said nothing, only watched her. How could he not?

"You're up to something, aren't you? Now what might that be?" Parvati's vertical pupils dilated. Her bright eyes almost filled the gloomy staircase with an emerald light. Her voice, barely above a whisper, dipped into his mind.

"Tell me."

He wanted to. So badly. He wanted to explain the cell, the phone call, and how Dad was waiting at the ghat. Those green eyes grew larger and larger until they were all he could see.

"I . . ." Sweat broke out across Ash's forehead. He wanted to tell her, but a small part of him fought back. His head wouldn't move. He couldn't even blink.

"Tell me, Ashoka."

His aunt used to call him Ashoka; she was old-fashioned that way. No one else had the right to call him Ashoka — only her. Sadness, loss, and anger burned in his chest, freeing him, and Ash snarled, "I've nothing to say."

The green light died. Parvati was just a girl, standing on the steps. "I'm sorry. I shouldn't have done that."

Ash let out a deep breath and rubbed his temples to clear the confusion that hung like a cloud in his head. "What was that? Magic?"

"Hardly. It's just what I can do. Sometimes."

Ash sank down and rested against the wall. Parvati sat down too, a few steps above. She idly fiddled with the silver locket.

"What is that?" asked Ash. She was always playing with it. "Something important?"

Parvati's eyes narrowed, then she slowly lifted it over her head and handed it to him. "It's best that you know."

The locket was old, that was for sure, and it must have had gems studded into it once, as there was a series of small holes and catches in the surface. The chain was thin and delicate, almost as fine as silken thread. Someone had put in a lot of effort into making this.

Ash nudged the locket open. He met the gaze of two people, portraits no more than an inch high. The left-hand portrait had been scratched out so all that could be seen was a blur of blue and yellow paint, tinged green where the colors had merged. The right-hand portrait was of a young Indian woman in her early twenties. She wore a silken scarf and leaned her head on a bejeweled hand. A diamond stud shone on the side of her nostril as she gazed languidly at him with her big green eyes.

"That's you," said Ash. But there was ten years difference between the girl in front of him and the one in the portrait. "How is that possible?"

Parvati took the locket back and clicked it shut. "I am half-human, Ash. I age just like you."

"But she's older than you are now. You age backward?"

"No, I age like any human until I'm an old woman. When I die, I'm instantly reborn." She sounded weary, even sad. "Like all rakshasas."

"It doesn't sound so bad." What would he give to be able to do that? What any mortal would give, to live forever.

"When you've done it as long as I have, you will realize it's a curse." She sighed. "Even death is no escape."

"Why not?"

"I think I'm human, at least to begin with. Then my rak-shasa soul manifests itself in my early teens, and with it come the nightmares and my old memories. The first sign is these." She pointed at her eyes. "They change from human to serpent. I have to leave my home because I become a danger to those I love. I am a monster, Ash. A monster living among humans."

Ash watched her silently. So that was her life, to be feared and shunned by all she knew, forever. Parvati slipped the locket back over her neck.

"And who was the other portrait?"

"Savage."

"What?" How could it be Savage? Ash shot forward, unable to disguise or control his rage. "You knew Savage?" He felt totally betrayed. Of all the people to carry in her locket, Savage!

"It was a long time ago, Ash."

"And how well did you know him, exactly?"

Parvati responded with icy coldness. "I don't see how that's any business of yours."

"You've got his portrait in your locket," said Ash, still hot with rage. "That's usually reserved for 'extra special friends,' isn't it?"

"Listen to me, Ash." Parvati took his hand. "Listen to me."

It took a few minutes for Ash to calm down, but eventually he sat down and leaned against the wall. Still, all he could think of was the portrait in the locket.

"I hate Savage more than you could possibly imagine," Parvati said, sitting down next to Ash. "We have the same enemy, you and I. And I promise you this — I will do everything I can to help you avenge yourself against him."

That was the truth. He could hear the cold, ancient hate in her tone.

"What happened?"

"I was in the court of the maharajah of Lahore, back in the mid-nineteenth century. I helped keep his rivals in line."

"How?"

"I am the daughter of Ravana. I was born to end men's lives." Parvati frowned. "I served the maharajah as his assassin, Ash."

An assassin. How insanely cool. "So how did you meet Savage?"

"Savage was part of a diplomatic mission sent by the English to make a peace deal with the maharajah."

"Did they?"

"The treaty was signed, but I was sent to spy on them. I discovered Savage was a magician, a good one. Nothing big, and nothing a thousand sadhus couldn't do. But he interested me. And he made me an offer."

"What?"

"To make me wholly human."

Ash nodded. The way she spoke about her past life, her hatred for her father and sadness toward what had happened to her mother, it was clear Parvati was conflicted; the demon versus the human. He wondered what she was capable of if she gave in to her demon side. As she had said: She was Ravana's daughter, and Ravana had terrorized the gods.

Parvati continued. "But he needed my father's scrolls of magic, scrolls I'd salvaged from the destruction of Lanka. Savage wanted to master the ten sorceries, like my father. He said he'd use them to cure me." Her eyes darkened and there was a grimness there. "And like a trusting fool I gave them to him. But the scrolls were incomplete, so he only acquired a few simple magics, like immortality."

"Immortality doesn't sound so simple to me."

"There are spells that can alter time itself, Ash. Be thankful Savage never learned those." She sighed. "But you're right, it is not simple. Savage ages, but cannot die. So now he's little more than a grotesque, living skeleton."

"So he took the scrolls and fled?"

She sank her head. "Yes. Something like that."

"I'm sorry."

"It was not your fault, but mine." Parvati snarled. For a second the demon took control of the girl. "I made Savage. If it hadn't been for me, he would be long dead. But with my father's scrolls, he became a powerful sorcerer. The other rakshasas gathered around him. If they couldn't have my father back, then Savage was the next best thing. All he's done since, I could have stopped, if I hadn't been so desperate to be something I'm not."

She stood up and walked away down the stairs without even looking at Ash, obviously lost in her own guilt and mistakes.

Revenge. Pure and simple. That's what motivated her now.

But Savage had done much worse to Ash. He'd taken not just some scrolls, but his uncle and aunt. Ash sat there, feeling the hole inside his heart swallow more of him.

His hand went to the aastra around his neck. Parvati and Rishi thought he was the weapon they could use to defeat Savage once and for all. But they were wrong. He touched one of the big bruises on his torso. If Parvati couldn't beat Savage, what chance did he have, even with this magic arrowhead? He didn't even know how it worked.

Ash felt pity for Parvati, but all of this was way too big a problem for a thirteen-year-old boy. This was a war between gods and monsters, and kids like him had no part in it.

"Sorry, Parvati," he whispered. He'd spoken to his mum and that was that. His job was to get himself and Lucky home. Back to his parents. Back where they belonged.

Ash got to his feet. In an ideal world he'd be a hero and go off to fight Savage and have his revenge. But this wasn't that sort of world. He wasn't that sort of hero.

Tonight he'd take Lucky and sneak out of the Lalgur. They'd find Dad and go back to England. They would leave India, Savage, Parvati. They would leave everything.

Forever.

CHAPTER SEVENTEEN

"You've got five minutes," said John. "Rajiv's on door duty, but I told him I'd cover for him while he sneaked off to see Padmi."

"Let's go, Lucks."

John went down the stairs first, Lucky next and Ash behind. It was one o'clock, and pretty much everyone in the Lalgur was asleep. The door was open to one of the larger rooms, where a whole bunch of kids slept, sprawled over the floor on thin mattresses. A rusty old fan cranked in the corner. If the other kids could sleep through that, then Ash's soft footsteps weren't going to wake them. But in a building with about fifty people in it, there was always a chance someone was wandering off to the toilet or to find a midnight snack.

A mat lay beside the door, a half-finished bowl of plain rice on top of it. Otherwise the small lobby was empty.

Ash pulled back the heavy iron bolt. The metal screamed. He stopped dead.

"Shut up!" hissed Lucky, thumping him on the arm. "Why not just bang a gong and tell everyone we're going?"

"Sorry."

They listened in fearful silence, waiting for the sound of feet on flagstones and expecting Rajiv or, worse, Ujba, to come running in.

But nothing. Hardly daring to breathe, Ash twisted the bolt farther. It squeaked as the metal worked its way against the stone. Then, with a final cry of protest, the door opened.

The air was fresh and cool, rising straight off the Ganges and carried by a soft night breeze. The sky was clear, but the route John had explained to them would keep them in the alleyways, hidden from the stark eye of the moon.

"You want to come?" asked Ash.

John shrugged. "And what then? This is my home." He smiled. It was sort of sad. "Good-bye, English."

"You'll get in trouble, you know that."

"Not as much as you if they catch you standing around here."

Lucky embraced John. "Thanks," she said with tears in her eyes. Then she scurried out into the alleyway.

"Anything for Parvati?" asked John.

Ash grinned. "Yes. Give her a huge kiss on the lips. Don't hold back."

"I do that and she'll tear my face off."

Ash hugged the small boy. "Thanks, mate. I owe you."

He wanted to tell him that he'd been a good friend, a great one. The boy was taking a big, big risk in helping them escape. He wouldn't be treated gently when their disappearance was discovered. John deserved more than just thanks. He was saving their lives. But before Ash could speak, the door behind him closed and the little light that had spilled through vanished.

He took Lucky's hand. Though the last few weeks had been hard, there was something about the Lalgur. The simple food, the harsh, brutal training. A strange magic had been worked upon him. He was sharper, tougher than he'd ever been. He felt . . . awake. India had awakened him.

Lucky's fingers tightened around his.

"Dad's waiting," she said.

Varanasi never truly slept. Even though dawn was hours away, sweepers brushed up rotten vegetables, plastic litter, and animal dung in the streets. Ash saw the priests at work in the temples. He caught the gaze of one of the holy men, reciting from a brittle, yellow scroll. The old man's eyes darkened as he saw them, and for a second Ash wondered if he might be one of Ujba's informants.

He pulled his sister along. "Hurry up, Lucks."

Neatly stacked piles of logs began to fill the alleys. They wove through more and more of these man-high bundles, heading deeper into the labyrinth, deeper into the gray phantoms of smoke that drifted on to the path leading to Manikarnika ghat.

The place of burning.

A line waited beside a small stall, nothing more than a canvas awning held up by two wooden poles. Inside, a small boy cried as a barber skillfully scraped the hair off the child's head using a razor. A river of foam and hair ran along the open gutter, forming a black thicket over the half-blocked drain. Ash caught the sweet scent of sandalwood, of incense, and of burning wood.

They stopped just as the alley opened on to a landing beside the river. A thick cloud of smoke swooped over Ash, stinging his eyes and blocking his lungs. He backed away, coughing.

He found himself overlooking a funeral. The wide, flat stone platform was smeared with soot from centuries of fires, and in the center was a pyre. The sticks had been piled in neat stacks to a man's height, making a high bed. On this lay a body, blackened by the raging flames, the skin already burned away. Ash stared at the skull that gazed upward in the blazing light. The dry logs crackled and snapped and popped. A wall of fire swung side to side, fiercely hot on his face and bare skin. Men chanted ancient prayers as a soul soared heavenward in the black smoke. Beyond the flames Ash saw the river, glistening with thousands of reflections of this burning man. It was as if the river itself contained the images of all the cremations it had seen since Time began.

"Where's Dad?" asked Lucky. She was hopping up and down with excitement, searching over the heads for a glimpse of him.

"He'll be here." The men were just hazy silhouettes and Ash couldn't make them out; the light and heat from the flames were too intense.

But after ten minutes, Ash started worrying. Dad should have arrived by now. Where was he? If only Ash had taken John's cell, he could have called again. Had something happened?

Down in the river, the dark waters rippled as a pilgrim descended waist-deep. The man took a deep breath and, palms pressed together, plunged underneath. In a few seconds he came back up, took another breath, and went under again.

Out of the corner of his eye, Ash caught sight of what looked like a floating log, just visible on the edge of the firelight. It must have rolled free from some other funeral pyre. When he looked back up, the log was gone — floated off down the river, most likely.

There was a splash as the pilgrim came back up. He coughed and loudly cleared his throat, whispered another prayer, then went under a third time.

Ash watched the bubbles of his breath rise and pop on the surface of the water. The river was still, the color of dark green marble. Ash idly scratched his thumb and looked down at it, feeling a slight tingle.

The bubbles stopped.

Ash shivered. Something was wrong, way wrong.

"Get up, Lucks."

The water did not stir, but a stain began to spread across the surface, just where the pilgrim had dived under, the water turning darker than it had been.

Lucky sprang to her feet. "Do you see Dad?"

A figure emerged out of the Ganges. Thick, dark, crusty scales covered his round head, heaviest over his brow. His shoulders were double-door wide, and water ran in sparkling rivulets between the deep crevasses of his muscles. His long arms swung as he strode up the steps. There was no sign of the pilgrim, other than the bloody, fresh gristle hanging from the teeth that jutted out at all angles from the man's — the rakshasa's — long, crocodile snout.

"Mayar," whispered Ash. But how had he known they would be here?

It didn't matter. Rishi had warned him to stay in the Lalgur, but Ash had thought he'd known better. Now they were both going to pay for his stupidity.

"Lucky, run," he said. "Back to the Lalgur. Quickly!"

People screamed. One man ran at Mayar, but he swung his sledgehammer of a fist and the man's skull shattered. The crocodile rakshasa stepped over the body without a glance.

"Run!" Ash turned, hand in hand with Lucky as they fled. They had to get back into the old city. The place was a labyrinth and some of the alleys would be too narrow for Mayar.

The ground shook as Mayar pounded up the steps behind them. The funeral pyre blocked his way, and Ash thought he had a few more seconds, but Mayar just barged straight through the blazing logs. The wood crackled and the air roared as he trod on the crumbling, blackened corpse. It crumbled like a charcoal stick.

If they could just get into the alleys —

"Hello, sweetie."

Jackie sat hunched on top of a column, her mane fanned by the flames rising off the fires. Her torn clothes ran like streamers from her massive pelt-covered thighs, and a tail swished back and forth as she stared at Ash and Lucky, her long tongue dripping with greedy hunger. She bunched up her legs, then launched herself across the ghat, howling maniacally.

Ash pushed Lucky ahead of him. Fear and the screaming demons destroyed any thought of a plan. They just ran. He heard Jackie's snarl and Mayar's wall-shaking roar. Heavy feet thundered on the flagstones behind them.

Ash threw himself down lanes and scrambled over a cart that had been left across one of the alleys. He crashed over a group of sleeping pilgrims, scuttling on his hands and knees over the mass of limbs and shouting men. Lucky, far lighter on her feet than Ash, was already way ahead and disappearing down the unlit lanes.

Ash's foot slipped on something as he charged deeper into the maze. Jackie's wild, bone-chilling cackle echoed behind him, and he expected her claws to tear open his back at any second. No alley was wider than six feet and none ran straight for long. Red lamps and small fires glowed in the darkness behind the silhouettes of the destitute and outcast of the city.

A dog snapped at his toes and Ash had to jump to get past. It was still yapping as he disappeared down a side alley.

Lucky — where was she? Ash ran blind, fingers outstretched and probing the darkness. His breath came in short, desperate gasps, as though the old city was trying to smother him. The narrow cobbled lanes turned in all directions, and Ash's legs burned as he rounded another corner into a dead end.

He twisted the nearest door handle but the door was locked. That dog was still barking somewhere behind him. Then it growled, becoming dangerous and aggressive. But then there was a yelp, a snap, a crunch, and no more barks.

Ash searched the walls. If he couldn't go back, sideways, or forward, he would have to go up. He looked at the drainpipe rising thirty feet up the outside of a tumbled-down temple. The pipe passed through a net of loose wires; the old city was powered by exposed cable strung along the streets, then carried up farther, disappearing into the darkness beyond. It didn't look good, but he knew he had no choice.

Somewhere behind him, claws scratched along the flagstones.

Totally stupid.

Ash tightened his hold on the drainpipe and hoisted himself up. The pipe shook and leaned away from the wall. John had told him he regularly scrabbled up such drainpipes — how hard could it be? But then John was half his body weight, even after all the exercise Ash had been doing.

Ridiculously stupid.

Arms and legs wrapped around the clay pipe, Ash slowly shimmied upward. The rough surface of the pipe scraped against his skin, rubbing his belly raw.

"Insanely stupid," he muttered. Any second now he'd fall and split open his skull. No need to be killed by demons, he'd do the job himself. Serve him right for being an idiot.

The cables brushed against his back, and Ash hoped he wasn't about to be electrocuted. But the cables seemed dead, and he found gaps in the walls and loose cement to dig his toes into and push himself the last few feet. With a grunt he heaved himself over the low parapet, dropping on to the flat roof. Holding his breath and willing his heart to quieten, he heard a deep, threatening growl.

The drainpipe rattled, then tore off the wall and smashed.

After a few seconds a door shattered. Ash heard muffled

screams from downstairs and the sickening sound of flesh tearing.

A rakshasa was coming up the stairs.

He jumped up, ran to the edge of the building, and stopped dead. There was a gap between this roof and the next.

Parkour. He'd seen it on YouTube: running and jumping and diving over walls, balconies, from roof to roof. He'd tried it once with a few mates but ended up limping home with two bleeding shins after failing to clear a park bench. And now this.

Ash peered over the edge. On the ground he wouldn't think twice. It was probably a couple of yards to the other roof — he couldn't be sure in the dark. But it wasn't the gap that bothered him — it was the height.

There was a growl from nearby, and he realized the height wasn't as much of a problem as the rakshasa right behind him.

A fist crunched the door. Ash stared as a long crack opened up along the wood. The second punch tore it off its hinges and hurled it across the roof. Mayar, his face and jaws dripping with blood, gave a rumbling, low laugh. He pointed a claw at the arrowhead dangling from Ash's throat.

"The aastra, boy, and I'll make your death quick."

Ash licked his lips. He settled his bare feet on the stone, letting his toes get a firm grip.

Then he ran. And jumped.

CHAPTER EIGHTEEN

The wind roared in Ash's ears as he sailed through the night. For a moment, he saw the city lights shining brightly on the surface of the black river. The chants of the priests echoed like lullabies, and the sharp coldness of the river breeze caressed his body. His skin was electric with adrenaline, his fingers and toes tingling as he peered down. A man stared up from the street below, aghast —

Ash landed with a thud, skidding a yard or so before stopping.

"Oh, wow," he said. "I *totally* made it!"

He had to tell himself that because otherwise he wasn't sure he'd believe it. He should be a street pizza.

He looked back and realized the gap was a lot bigger than he'd first thought. It was a total miracle he'd done it. He saw Mayar slam his fist at the far wall in frustration, knocking off a pile of bricks. No way was he making that jump; he was just too big and cumbersome.

"Hey, Mayar," shouted Ash. "Maybe next time!"

Ash glanced over the edge. No sign of Lucks or Jackie. His sister was small and fast; she was probably back at the Lalgur already. Ash spotted the stairs in the corner of the roof. He'd head back and —

Across the alley, Mayar laughed. It rumbled up from his belly and he clapped his hands. And when Mayar laughed, it was time to be afraid.

A shadow passed across the moon, and a black shape high in the sky gave a blood-chilling scream.

Ash gazed up. "My God."

The shape took form as it hung silhouetted against the moon. Its long wings curved over it like a sickle, and its bony body was pallid and thin. Instead of feet, a pair of curved talons swung below its frame, each claw as bright as steel. Its bald head was distorted by a long beak and a thick necklace of feathers.

Jat rose higher and slowed his ascent to pause, for a moment, among the stars. Then he folded in his wings and dived with an ear-piercing shriek.

Ash dropped down to the roof of the adjacent building. The old city was packed tight. The houses had been rebuilt and modified so many times over the centuries that many of the roofs merged together. The inhabitants slept up on them during the summer, and Ash saw people pointing at the monster as it swooped down. He hopped on to a cluster of beds, using the springy web of rope mattresses to shoot himself across the next gap, wider than the first.

As he landed on the roof opposite, talons grazed his shoulder, and Ash fell badly. He stumbled back up to his feet, knocking over a small table laden with a china tea set. The entire thing shattered and an old woman yelled. "What do you think you're doing, you hoodlum? Police! Police!"

Ash grabbed her and dived to the floor as Jat's talons sliced the air right behind him.

"Stay down," Ash hissed. Then he sprang up and grabbed the tea tray, flinging it like a Frisbee.

It shot across the short gap in a flash of silver. Jat yelled as the tray sliced his forehead. But it didn't stop him from flying forward again and slamming his fists into Ash's chest, hurling the boy off his feet.

Ash's chest was on fire. He lay dazed as the rakshasa glided on to the floor.

Get up.

Ash's arms were lead-heavy. Jat's long talons clicked on the concrete roof as he approached. His huge wings swung back and forth, blowing dust over Ash. A sharp pain stabbed through Ash's lungs as he tried to breathe.

Get up or die.

The roof was crisscrossed with laundry. Sheets flapped in the breeze, saris, shirts, shrouds. Jat cut a white bedsheet in two with a quick slash of his curved fingernail. He had to duck to pass under the web of clotheslines. The billowing walls of cloth created a series of corridors across the roof.

Ash got up. This was it — no more running. He couldn't escape across the roof: Jat was too fast. He couldn't flee through the street, not with Mayar and Jackie lurking in the alleys.

Jat pushed another long flowing sheet aside with a hiss. His eyes fell on the arrowhead around Ash's neck and he leaned over, flexing his long fingers eagerly.

"The aastra, give it to me. Now!" A multicolored sari flapped in Jat's face. He ripped it off with a jerk, tearing it to ribbons. "The aastra!"

He jabbed forward, but Ash ducked under one of the large bedsheets. He weaved in and out of the washing as Jat turned and swiped at him. The rakshasa's wings, each over fifteen feet wide, became tangled in the lines and wrapped up in the drying sari. Jat tried to barge through the web of cables, but it only made things worse. He looked like a mummy risen from his sarcophagus, with long, torn strips of fabric trailing off his body and limbs.

Ash dived and ducked, playing a deadly game of hide-and-seek. Jat ripped the material off his face and leaped forward, ignoring the cables that now bound his shoulders and neck.

Ash's feet touched the edge of the roof. Glancing back, he saw the opposite building was higher than this one. There was nowhere left to jump.

And Jat knew it. "I'm going to eat your eyes, boy," he said, smacking his lips. "Mayar and Jackie can fight over the rest, but your eyes are mine."

Ash raised his fists, tightening his fingers until the knuckles hurt. Jat wriggled closer, freeing his arms. The cables slipped higher up his shoulder, around his neck.

He launched forward and Ash gasped as Jat rammed into him. They tumbled backward, Ash grabbing the rakshasa's arms as they dropped down the side of the building. His eyes locked on Jat's, who grinned at him with murderous glee.

Then the fall ended with a jerk and a snap as the cable around the rakshasa's throat tightened into a noose. Jat bounced up and down like a puppet, Ash still desperately hanging on, a few yards above the stony ground.

Ash stretched, then let go. He landed with a thud. Leaning against the wall, he sucked in breath, each gasp sending hot needles through his battered lungs. But he was alive. He was alive and the demon was dead.

Jat's lifeless body swayed on the end of the cable. His neck hung crooked and his bloodshot eyes bulged, like two big, round tomatoes ready to pop. The creature's face was red and swollen, and its long tongue flapped. This was what death looked like. Ugly.

The air turned foggy, and Ash's sweat turned to ice. He sank to the ground, his body wracked with pain. The aastra burned against his skin and he tore it off. He held it in his hand as the gold glowed and hissed against his palm. The pain raced up through his arm like a million biting ants under his skin.

What was happening to him?

Ash stared at the swinging corpse, the rakshasa he'd just killed.

Shadows coalesced, crossing the wall, creeping toward Jat's body. The shadow, now a single, moving form, had many arms. Bony fingers reached across the crumbling bricks toward Jat. The head turned, and a long, eager tongue licked the rakshasa's face, savoring the taste of freshly dead, warm flesh. There was a rattle of bones.

Ash curled up as another wave of agony ripped through him. Howls echoed around him. The other rakshasas were coming. They wanted the aastra, and the moment they had it, his life was over. He couldn't let that happen; he had to hide it.

Ash crawled to a small street shrine — a statue at the corner of the building. It was a crude lump of stone, so painted over that all the original features had been lost. Ash shoved the aastra behind it, hiding it from view.

He stumbled away a few paces, but the pain was too great. He felt as if his bones were covered in molten lead. Ash's head swam with delirium, and he collapsed.

Seconds or minutes or hours later, nails dug into his shoulders and he was raised off the ground. Dangling in the air, Ash met Mayar's blazing reptilian gaze.

"The aastra, boy. Give it to me." The demon's breath was suffocating, filled with the stink of rotting meat. He shook Ash. "Where is it?" Mayar began to press his hands together, crushing Ash between them.

"Don't kill him," said Jackie. Ash watched her approach, more or less human now, but still with a grinning mouth too full of canine teeth. "At least not yet."

Mayar tossed Ash against the wall. The impact punched all air from his lungs and should have broken every bone in his body, but he just slumped to the ground, all his strength exhausted.

Jackie stood over him, pushing his face up toward her with a bare foot. The long toenails scratched his cheek.

"Bring him," she said. "Lord Savage is waiting."

CHAPTER NINETEEN

"*Lord Rama is waiting,*" *says Lakshmana.*

Rama sways, blinking away the dizziness that suddenly came upon him. He glances around, aware that rakshasas are present, and meets the gaze of Mayar, one of Ravana's most loyal warriors.

Lakshmana steps between them and points downward. "On your knees, demon."

Mayar, his hate undisguised, slowly lowers himself to the ground. Hands, still scarlet with the blood of Rama's kin, plant themselves down as the rakshasa bows before him.

Behind Mayar kneel the other rakshasa generals, the other princes, kings, and maharajahs of the demon nations, all humbled, all preparing to surrender to Rama.

Their hatred, impotent though it is, is undiminished. And they should hate him. With blood and bronze swords, with the aid of the gods, the rakshasa armies have been destroyed. Yesterday these rakshasas ruled the world, while humanity was merely a race of slaves. Now these mighty princes and grand monsters are vagabonds, their lands and palaces destroyed, their great king dead. Without Ravana, the demons are powerless.

The rule of the rakshasas has come to an end; now is the age of Mankind.

"Is that all of them?" asks Rama. He looks out across the demon lords. There are so many, and though defeated, the fire of rebellion still burns in their eyes.

Lakshmana frowns. "No, my lord. One fights on."

"Take me to him."

"Her, Rama," says Lakshmana. "It is Ravana's daughter."

The chariot rattles over the battlefield. Lakshmana handles it with his natural lightness and the horses respond to the merest hints from his reins. Rama stands beside him, surveying his new kingdom.

Funeral smoke blackens the sky, hiding the sun, or perhaps it is ashamed to shine upon such slaughter. The only light comes from the huge pyres. They cover the black earth. The dead, bodies mangled and bloodless, lie like fields of corpse flesh. Kings are burned alongside peasants, demons beside mortals. There are no causes, no flags and warring nations among them; they all belong to one country now. Yama, the land of the dead.

Ravana was master of the ten sorceries, the greatest of all Demonkind. Some of the demons have refused to believe their king could be killed, least of all by a mere mortal.

Is it any surprise some have not surrendered?

But he knows Ravana is dead, destroyed by the Vishnu-aastra. Rama looks down at his hand, at the thumb that drew the bowstring that launched the divine weapon. Why does it still ache?

"There," says Lakshmana, pulling the reins. The chariot rolls to a halt.

There is a hill. It is surrounded by a wall and beyond that wall waits Rama's army. Men, weary to exhaustion, sit on the bloodied battlefield, clutching their weapons and tending to their wounded. Neela, Rama's best friend and most loyal general, slaps his hand on Rama's shoulder.

"You look tired, Your Highness." He grins.

"Where is she?"

"Look beyond the wall."

The soldiers part silently as Rama approaches. They say nothing. It is too early for stories, epic poems, and grand feasts. Not before their friends, their brothers, their fathers and sons have been cremated and sent into the afterlife.

Do they blame him? Rama wonders. They fought and died for him, and how can he ever repay them? There is not enough gold in the world.

The wall is not of stone or timber, but of flesh. Neela scratches the back of his neck. "She built this wall herself. Each man, slaughtered by her." He grips Rama's arm and there is quiet fury in his eyes. "Kill her, Your Highness. She is Ravana's daughter. A hundred thousand dead men cry for her blood."

"Trust me, my friend."

Rama climbs. His hands slip on cold skin, on torn bodies and mortar made of flesh and blood. By the time he reaches the top, he looks as though he's swam through a river of blood.

And so I have.

She stands there, waiting for him. Her armor is black and grimy with dried blood. Her helmet has been discarded so Rama can see her face. She is young, and her hair is long and black, loose and fluttering in the breeze. Her pallid skin is lightened by the green fire in her eyes. Her fangs are partially extended. She smiles and unravels her weapon, made of four long razor-sharp strips of metal — curling blades that work as whips and swords. Not for nothing is it called the urumi, *the serpent sword. A true master can dismember a man with a single flick, and given the limbless corpses in the wall, she is clearly a master. It is true what they say about her: She was born to end men's lives.*

She bows her head. "Lord Rama."

Rama too bows. Then he stands straight and meets the girl's gaze. "Your Royal Highness."

"You are unarmed," she says.

"The war is over."

The urumi quivers. Rama knows he's easily within striking distance.

"The others have surrendered," he says. "Your brothers are dead. As is your great father."

She flinches. "Ravana is dead. So it is true."

"The war has cost us all, Parvati. Why continue? You would be honored in our court."

Her shoulders are slumped. "I was born for one purpose, Rama. You know that."

"You are not just your father's daughter." Rama looks at the slaughter around him. The countless men this young woman has

killed. "You had two parents. Your mother was a kind, beautiful woman. I mourn her passing."

"My father brought me up to believe humans were weak, beneath contempt."

"It is a terrible thing to hate one's mother, when all she did was love you." Rama steps forward. "Come with me, Parvati."

The serpent sword, the urumi, clatters to the ground.

CHAPTER TWENTY

Ash breathed in deeply — the soft, sugary fragrance of jasmine, lemon, and freshly clipped mint. Cool air drifted over him, a low whisper of wind that was the only disturbance of the silence and peace.

Eyes closed and senses not fully awake, he lay caressed in soft cotton. It rustled like leaves as he turned in his bed. He slid his palm over the flat, smooth mattress, smelling the freshness of it, the scent of the soap, and feeling the residual heat where his body had just lain.

Ash opened his eyes and took another deep breath.

The air was clear of the damp mustiness of the Lalgur. The lingering odor of too many bodies in too cramped a space was also missing. Nearby was a table upon which stood a large vase filled with flowers, flooding the room with their perfume. The windows were open but covered with deep red gauze curtains that billowed in the breeze, diffusing the morning light into a soft pink glow.

Another dream of Rama — or vision or memory. Ash didn't know what it was, but he knew it was true. Even now, Mayar's fury made him shiver, reaching out over the thousands of years since Ravana's death. How the demons hated Rama. His victory meant the ascension of Humankind. Once mighty rulers, the rakshasas became scavengers, lost and leaderless, serving people like Savage. And he'd seen Parvati, back in her demon days. He had some idea of the torment she'd suffered being the demon king's daughter.

But he wasn't in the battlefield now. Ash sat up. His tattered rags were gone, replaced by a pair of light cotton trousers and a loose shirt, both brilliant ivory white. The collar and cuffs bore embroidered patterns in shimmering silk thread.

He looked at his feet. They were clean. Even the grime that had worked its way deep under the nails after weeks of running barefoot was gone. He checked his hands. They didn't just look clean, but manicured. His hair had been washed and oiled, slicked back over his head rather than fizzing and spiking everywhere like usual.

What's going on?

"You're awake at last."

A woman rose from a chair. He hadn't seen her because she had been hidden behind the floating curtains. She stood before him in the light.

It was the tall, beautiful Indian woman with the web-patterned sari from Savage's party, the one with the spider-style hair. Now she wore a white outfit similar to his, but covered with red spiderweb embroidery. As she came closer, Ash saw that this time her skin wasn't plastered with makeup, and she wasn't wearing glasses.

Her eyes were black. Not just the pupils, but all black. Her forehead was cut with a row of scars, four across, and there was a scar on each cheek. These must be what she'd been hiding under the powder.

The scars opened and six more black, shining orbs stared at Ash.

The woman had eight eyes. Like a spider.

"Come," she said. "It's time for breakfast."

Ash gulped. He'd thought, hoped, that Savage just had the three rakshasas: Jackie, Mayar, and Jat. Scratch that, two: Jat was dead. But Savage obviously had a lot more where the vulture demon had come from.

The woman snapped her fingers and motioned toward the door.

Where's Lucky?

Maybe she'd made it back to the Lalgur. Ash couldn't remember anything after he'd been caught by Mayar.

Please let Lucky be okay. He didn't care what happened to him as long as his sister was safe.

Ash stood up, trying hard to cover his nervousness. He looked down at his palm, remembering the searing pain, the agonizing energies surging through him the night before. It should be black and burned, but the skin was unblemished.

Something had awakened the aastra.

What on earth had happened? Rishi said that an aastra made by the fire god, Agni, would be activated — awakened — by fire. Ash thought back to last night. He'd been near that huge funeral pyre, felt the heat on his skin. Was it an Agni-aastra? Somehow that didn't seem right. The aastra hadn't reacted until much later. The pain had come on suddenly —

When Jat had died.

It hit him hard: The aastra was activated by death. The pain he'd felt, the energies that had wracked his body, must be death energies absorbed from Jat by the aastra.

Now Ash knew exactly whose aastra it was. It had been *her* shadow he'd watched creep across the wall to claim the dead demon. He'd seen her hideous, red-tongued, skeletal statue as they'd drifted along the river with Rishi. The sadhu had warned Ash then what the goddess wanted.

What she loves most is death.

Kali. The goddess of death. The aastra was hers.

Ash licked his dry lips, the one external sign of his fear, then followed the spider-woman.

The door led into a long hallway. Cobwebs hung from the corners and fat black spiders sat in the deep recesses, their multitude of eyes glistening. They crept along the wall, following him.

The windows had been bricked up a long time ago, and the furniture was covered in a fuzzy layer of dust. Portraits lined the walls, hidden beneath a century or two of dirt.

Despite the grime, the gaze of one portrait, the first and largest, caught Ash's attention. Savage looked down at him full height from the long-ago past, one hand on the tiger-headed cane, the other holding the stem of a poppy. It had been poppies, and the opium they produced, that had made Savage's first fortune, selling the drug to the Chinese in the nineteenth century.

The aristocrat's hair was pale blond and shoulder length, loose and roguish. In the background Ash glimpsed a set of manacles on a table, a reminder that Savage had been a slaver as well as a drug dealer. His skin was blanched white, without any sign of color or life. He could just as well have been a corpse but for the fire blazing in his blue eyes. They were bright with power and arrogance.

Ash looked along the line of portraits. There were ten at least, all from different time periods. The most recent showed Savage in the uniform of a British army officer from World War II. His hair was gray, his back stooped, his hand again resting on his tiger cane. He looked about sixty or seventy, even though he was really over two hundred. But his eyes still held their cold, ruthless light.

"Why has no one's guessed he was the same man?" Ash asked the spider-woman. Now, with the portraits all lined up, it was obvious.

"Lord Savage traveled widely. Africa. The Far East. The Americas. He stays away for decades, so when he returns, no one is around who might remember him. At least, no one who isn't in the same business as him."

Ash paused. "Why do you serve him? You're a rakshasa. Why do you follow a human?"

"Lord Savage is far more than human." She smiled, and Ash's skin crept as though one of those spiders was on his back. "And he gives us what we want."

Light broke into the hallway as she opened the double doors at the end. Ash stepped out on to one of the pavilions on the edge of the Savage Fortress, overlooking the Ganges. A trio of small row boats bobbed just where he'd arrived with his uncle and aunt for the party that first night, a lifetime ago.

Above him the sky was a brooding gray, heavy with storm clouds. Shining blades of lightning flickered on the horizon. The wind out here, up on the high battlements, was strong and sharp. The monsoon was coming.

They approached a white silk gazebo. The cloth walls had been pulled back and tied to four supporting posts, and a table had been laid with delicate china. There were three seats and two people at the table.

The first was Mayar, back in human form. He stood, arms folded across his chest, eyes reflecting nothing but demonic anger. He ground his jaws together, and Ash's nerves jumped as the teeth slid across each other like scraping razors.

The second sat on a wrought-iron chair. Dressed in a slim-fitting white suit, he waited, hands lightly placed on the silver cutlery.

"Come, my boy." He raised his hand, and Mayar drew back one of the other two chairs. "You must be starving. I've had a full English breakfast prepared. Thought you might appreciate some home cooking." He reached over, picked up a narrow-necked china teapot, and held it poised over Ash's cup.

"Some tea?" asked Lord Alexander Savage.

CHAPTER TWENTY-ONE

Ash stood there, facing the man responsible for murdering his uncle and aunt. Every muscle locked; it was the only way to stop himself from ripping out Savage's eyes. Mayar leaned closer, as if sensing Ash's rage, eager for him to try. He just wanted an excuse to kill Ash, and Ash was about to give it to him.

No. Ash couldn't take on Mayar. Or Savage.

Maybe he was just a coward. Standing up to Hakim was one thing, but these guys, like Mayar, had been killing since time began. They were a whole different league of bad. He should attack Savage, even if it meant Mayar would kill him before he'd touched a hair on the man's head. That's what a hero would do, wasn't it?

But Ash wasn't that sort of hero. He wasn't any sort of hero.

"Sit down, Ash. It's getting cold," said Savage.

Ash sat.

In silence he watched the English lord pour out his tea. The flesh hung off Savage's fingers, and his skin seemed as brittle as autumn leaves, wrinkled, dry, crisscrossed with cracks. Cancerous black melanomas covered his hairless scalp. The cracks extended to his face, encrusted with blood where they'd dripped through the peeling, torn skin. Each facial movement stretched the thin tissue, opening up more tears and weeping scars.

How had Savage known about the meeting? He'd laid the trap and Ash had thrown himself straight into it.

"What have you done with my dad?"

"Nothing. Absolutely nothing." Savage raised his hand in a moment of realization. "Ah, you want to know why we were waiting at the ghat. Simple, really. I am an adult and you are a child. Did you ever play chess with your father? Or any adult?"

Ash grimaced. Of course he had. He'd played his father loads of times, but never won.

Savage recognized the defeat from his slumped shoulders. "Yes. And what did you learn? That adults beat children. It's what we're best at."

He continued, "When I heard about your relatives' tragic accident, I called your parents with the bad news that you were missing. I offered my assistance in trying to find you, assistance that was gratefully received. They even sent me photos of you both for the posters I had put up. Of course your father came straight over here to help." Savage sipped his tea. "I knew you'd contact your parents sooner or later. And there is no magic to tapping a phone, so I heard everything your mother told your father. Last night I merely had him drugged so he wouldn't keep your appointment and sent my rakshasas instead. They've been most eager to see you again."

So simple. And like a stupid kid, he'd fallen for it.

"Mayar's a little upset. Jat was a close friend of his." Savage cut into a fried egg. His movements were feeble, and he barely had the strength to lift the silver fork to his lips. Yolk splashed over his chin as he chewed. "And you, Ash, killed him."

"But he'll return. Be reincarnated at some point." Ash looked at Mayar. "Won't he?"

Mayar's snarl made the china cups shiver on their saucers. Savage raised his hand and the big demon backed off. "Alas, not in this case," Savage said. "There is a single thing in the universe that even the rakshasas fear. She is the ultimate force of destruction."

"Kali."

"Kali. You were wearing the Kali-aastra when you killed Jat. It is as though she did the deed herself, and there is no coming back from the black goddess, not for rakshasas. It is, how you say, game over."

This was all about the aastra. Why did Savage need it?

To open the Iron Gates.

What had Uncle Vik said about that Harappan city out in Rajasthan? The city would have libraries, temples, tombs. All with treasure. But that treasure was gold and knowledge. Savage was rich enough already, so he didn't need more gold. It was knowledge he was after. Were the Iron Gates guarding some great magical library?

"You want scrolls, don't you? To learn the other sorceries? Is that it?"

Savage laughed. "You think you can learn the ten sorceries from textbooks?" He shook his head. "No, Ash, I am not searching for *something*, but *someone*. A guru to teach me the last few forms of magic."

But only one being knew all ten sorceries.

"Ravana," Ash breathed.

Savage wanted to be able to alter reality, time itself. He wanted to turn back the clock and become once again young, strong, and beautiful. But only Ravana knew how to do that. Everything came back to Ravana.

"Didn't Rama kill Ravana?" Ash said.

Savage's eyes widened, then a slow smile cracked his face. A drop of blood fell from his chin on to the white tablecloth as the skin stretched.

"Rama *merely* killed him," replied the Englishman.

Ash rubbed his thumb, thinking about Rama, his first dream. Rama had held two aastras, one from Vishnu and the other from Kali. He knew that now. Only Kali offered utter destruction. Only Kali guaranteed total annihilation.

But Rama had fired the Vishnu-aastra. And that meant . . .

"Ravana can be reborn." He whispered it, appalled by what it meant. The demon king could come back.

The excavated city had palaces, libraries, temples, and tombs. *Tombs.*

Royal tombs were for the great and powerful. For ancient kings.

For demon kings.

"You want the aastra to open Ravana's tomb."

Savage nodded. "Did you know he forged his own body? Of gold and bronze and metals dragged out of the very deepest bowels of the earth? No flesh could contain his power. Look at me. Look at how my body withers and decays with just the weakest of spells. Now imagine that power, magnified a million times. Demons are naturally magical, but Ravana was in an entirely different league. He cannot be reborn into simple flesh."

"So Rama put his golden body in the tomb."

"And sealed it with iron gates. The iron prevents the spirit of Ravana from reentering the only vessel that can contain it. But once the tomb is open . . ."

Savage laughed — or it should have been a laugh. Instead it sounded like he was coughing up a lung. But Ash wouldn't be that lucky.

"Ironic, isn't it?" said Savage. "That Kali herself, the goddess born to kill demons, will be the one who releases the greatest demon of them all? Kali is the destroyer. Of mortals, of demons, of cities, of nations, of *everything*. So I will use the destructive powers of the Kali-aastra to smash open the Iron Gates. Imagine how generous Ravana will be to the one who frees him."

"You don't know what you're doing." Ash glared. "Are you totally insane? What sort of world will it be with Ravana free?"

Ash knew; he'd seen the Carnival of Flesh, the things Ravana did to humans just for his amusement. He thought back to Parvati, and the way she'd talked about her mother, who was made into a monster just to lift Ravana's boredom.

"I imagine for the likes of you it will become a living hell," said Savage. "But I will be young again, immortal, and second only to Ravana in power. It will be fun." He glanced across the table. "I'd put that down if I were you. It is quite blunt."

Ash looked. He was gripping the butter knife in his trembling hand. He put it down, but it was hard forcing his fingers to open.

"That's it?" he said. "Just so you can be twenty again and have a full head of hair? All this misery, just to cure your baldness? Haven't you lived long enough?"

"It can never be enough." Savage's eyes darkened. The Englishman's voice was low and brittle. "To gain what little power I have, I made deals, bargains, with creatures more terrible than any rakshasa. When I die, they will want payment in full."

"So what is waiting for you?" asked Ash.

"You cannot imagine, even in your darkest nightmares."

"Well, you're not getting the aastra," said Ash. "That tomb will stay closed for all of eternity." Thank God he'd hidden it.

The Englishman scowled. "Do you know how many decades I've been searching for Ravana's tomb and the key to open it? The fortunes I've spent? What would you give to wield the power of a god? Anything, I'm sure," Savage said, more to himself than to Ash. "I discovered the tomb last year. But I was still searching for the means to open it."

"The Kali-aastra."

"Exactly. You see, it had been found after Ravana's defeat by a priest who recognized it for what it was. Such things cannot easily disappear. The scrolls your uncle was translating described where the priest had placed the aastra, in a shrine, awaiting a hero to claim it. Instead an ignorant, stupid boy finds it by pure dumb luck. I can almost hear the gods laughing at me." Savage twisted his napkin, wringing it as tightly as he could. "They'll not be laughing once I have freed Ravana." His gaze locked on to Ash's. "Tell me where the aastra is."

"Or what? You'll kill me?" Ash didn't doubt it. He breathed lightly, his heart fluttering like a panicked sparrow's. But he knew he could not let Savage get his hands on the aastra.

Savage shook his head. "I won't kill you." The door at the far end of the pavilion opened. He tapped the edge of his cup. "Makdi, if you'd be so kind."

The spider-woman poured him some more tea.

"Bring more toast. Our other guest will be wanting breakfast," he said.

Jackie came out of a door, pulling someone behind her — a young girl in a long white dress.

Oh, no.

All courage ran out of Ash like water.

They had Lucky.

CHAPTER TWENTY-TWO

"Have you ever been on safari?" Savage moved his teaspoon around the cup, the silver chiming musically against the thin china.

Ash smiled at his sister as she sat down. He wanted to encourage her, but tears flooded his eyes and the smile threatened to become a sob.

"Lucks, are you okay?" he asked.

Lucky stared at him, pale and her eyes red and exhausted. She didn't look like she'd slept at all. "I'm . . . fine," she whispered.

He'd tried so hard — tried and failed. Chest heaving, he moved his hand across the table toward his sister. Their fingers just touched before Jackie pulled Lucky back against her chair. Lucky sat, head bowed down to her chest. She looked small and fragile under Jackie's shadow.

"Have you seen how jackals hunt?" Savage said.

A low chuckle came from Jackie. Ash glared at her as she put her hand on Lucky's shoulder. His sister flinched.

"Don't you dare hurt her," Ash said. Jackie didn't even raise an eyebrow. The rakshasa knew his threats were empty. "She hasn't done anything."

Savage continued, "They hamstring the prey. It's usually a calf, one that's young and soft. One that won't put up a fight." He glanced at Lucky. "Eat up, my dear. Those eggs are fresh."

"Leave her alone," Ash whispered, but all his fight was gone.

"The calf just lies there, eyes rolling madly, can't get up, can't defend itself. Then the jackals go in. Not for the throat, or the chest. Not for the quick kill. They tear open its belly. Nuzzle inside, get all the soft, juicy bits. All the time they're doing it, eating the calf from within, it's still bleating and its eyes are staring around everywhere, desperately hoping someone will save it." Savage sipped the tea. "Can you imagine the pain? Being devoured while you're still alive? I'm sure it's quite dreadful."

Ash closed his eyes to stop the giddiness. He gulped the damp air, hoping he wouldn't puke. He was imagining it right now.

"Then, with its heartbeat weakening, the calf gives up. The hope fades and the last look it has, in those innocent big brown eyes, is one of despair. Hopelessness. Complete defeat." He set the cup down on the saucer. "Do you know that feeling, Ash?"

Ash looked up. Hot tears rolled freely now.

"Please don't hurt her," he begged.

Savage sighed. "Yes, I think you do." He dabbed his mouth clean. "Where is the aastra?"

"Don't tell him, Ash!" Lucky cried.

What could Ash do? If he gave Savage the aastra, then Ravana was free and that meant terror and nightmares for the world. But this was his sister. She'd done nothing wrong. Ash pushed his fists against his eyes.

"Wait," Ash said. "I'll make you a deal." He met Savage's gaze. "My life for hers."

"No! I'm not scared." Lucky struggled to get up, but Jackie's hands pressed down on her shoulders.

"You would die for your sister, I admire that. But that is not part of the deal. If you tell me where the aastra is, I will have you and Lucky on the first flight back to England. First class."

"You're lying. You'll kill us both."

"Why would I do that? You will be unharmed as long as you give me the aastra. You have my word as a gentleman."

"How can I trust your word?"

"You have no choice." Savage raised his finger and Mayar moved his chair back. The Englishman stood unsteadily; he needed Mayar's arm to support him. He was so old, so frail, he'd crumble with a sneeze. If Ash could delay things, then maybe Savage would die first. He didn't look like he'd last five more days.

But Savage wasn't going to give him five minutes. "You're trying my patience, boy," he said.

Jackie sniggered and smacked her lips.

Ash gave up. "I hid it behind the statue," he said. "In the street where you found me."

Savage half-turned to Mayar. "You know it?"

"Yes, Master."

Savage nodded. "Then go."

Mayar bowed and went swiftly. Savage addressed Jackie and

the spider-woman, Makdi. "Take our two guests and put them somewhere safe, and apart."

"But I told you where the aastra is," said Ash.

"We shall see." He took up his tiger cane. "If you're lying to me, I will be most disappointed. I will feed your sister to my demons, and she will die slowly and in agony and you will watch. You have my word on that as well. . . ." He smiled. "As a gentleman."

CHAPTER TWENTY-THREE

Makdi snapped her fingers once Savage had gone.

"Come," she said.

Ash rose. He moved mechanically, just following orders. Lucky sniffed, trying to be brave, but her eyes were so wide with terror the whites were visible all around the irises. Jackie still rested her hands on her shoulders, and the jackal demon's nails were thick enough to slice Lucky to the bone.

"I'll come and get you, Lucks," Ash said. "I . . . I promise. I will."

Jackie chuckled.

He stopped and faced his sister. "You believe me, don't you?"

They looked at each other, and Lucky's hopelessness cut his soul. She knew there was nothing he could do. They both knew it. But Lucky nodded.

"Yes, Ash." Her voice almost broke.

She doesn't believe me. Why should she?

I can't do anything.

Makdi led him to a small, heavy door set deep in a wall recess. She lit an old-fashioned brass oil lamp and pushed Ash down a narrow spiral staircase. The air became more humid the deeper they descended, still and stale. Down and down they went.

"Where are you taking me?" Ash asked.

"Somewhere safe."

The steps opened into a small chamber with a domed ceiling, barely high enough to stand up in. Moldy straw covered the floor, and the room was empty but for a bucket with a long length of frayed rope attached to the handle. The woman scraped back the straw, revealing a large iron grille. The bars were thicker than Ash's fingers, and rusty, but solid. Peering through the grille, Ash could make out a large pit. He had seen one of these chambers in the Tower of London. It was called an oubliette. Prisoners were put in them to be forgotten.

"No," said Ash. He backed up, trying to get on to the steps, but Makdi blocked him. Ash grabbed her arm and tried to pull her aside.

A lump moved under her sleeve, and a pair of spindly, hairy legs touched the bare skin of her wrist. Then another pair of long legs protruded, followed by the bloated black body of an enormous spider. It crept over her hand and Ash let go. The spider jumped and scuttled up his arm.

"Don't scream," whispered the woman. "You might startle Charlotte."

Charlotte the spider perched herself on Ash's collar, tapping her front legs on his bare neck. Ash didn't scream. He didn't breathe. Only his eyes moved, looking sideways at the black monstrosity.

"No, please, I won't cause any trouble." Anything but putting him down there. The spider crept higher, and Ash felt the individual hairs of its legs tickle his throat. He stood perfectly still.

Makdi lifted up one side of the heavy iron grille. The hinges screamed and flakes of rust shook loose from the bars.

"Bye-bye," she said casually.

She pushed Ash backward.

Ash dropped a few yards then hit the ground, landing awkwardly. He tried to get back up but cried out in pain as he put his weight on his left foot. His ankle throbbed.

"Please, don't leave me!" he shouted.

Makdi crouched over the edge of the pit. She looked down at him with sullen indifference, like he was some kind of science experiment. Was that how rakshasas really saw humans? She held out her hand.

Charlotte, sitting a foot or so from Ash, ran to the wall of the pit and through the grille. It crept onto Makdi's palm and she stroked it before tucking the spider into her pocket.

The grille slammed down and the light faded until it was the barest glow. Then that too disappeared, and Ash was abandoned in the bowels of the Savage Fortress.

Time stopped down there in the dark. It could only be measured by Ash's thudding heartbeat, too fast and too loud. He sat with his knees tucked under his chin, arms wrapped around himself, and didn't let go. If he did, he would dissolve into the blackness. Eyes closed, eyes open, it didn't make any difference.

No escape. No escape.

He didn't even try. What was the point? Savage had Lucky.

Ash groaned, shivering there in the lowest dungeons of the palace. Water plonked into a small puddle somewhere else in the cell.

Scritch, scritch, scritch.

Something ran over his feet. Things scuttled over the bare stone. The sound of their scurrying made Ash's skin crawl. He heard the sharp, eager squeak of rats and recoiled as a long, leathery tail brushed his hand. A tongue licked his ankle.

Ash wept, great rib-shaking sobs that echoed off the walls so it seemed the cell itself was crying.

I can't do this.

But he could, he had to. He got up and, arms outstretched, limped to the edge of the cell. Water dripped down from somewhere and the walls felt spotted with spongy moss. There were crevasses in the rock, and for a second Ash thought they might lead out of the cell, but none went deeper or wider than his arm.

He tried to climb the walls, but it was hopeless; the stone was too slick.

Here, alone, with time going nowhere, Ash was in perfect hell.

"Please . . ."

He knelt down and leaned forward until his forehead touched the ground, praying Savage would take pity on him and let him go. But Savage and the rest of the world had forgotten him.

Ash curled up. He buried his head against his chest, covering it with his arms. There he lay.

And there he stayed.

CHAPTER TWENTY-FOUR

The sharp, hot bite woke him. Needle-pointed teeth dug into the swollen flesh of his ankle, and a slimy tongue lapped at the wound.

Ash snapped his other foot into the rat. The rodent squealed and thumped against the wall. Ash pressed his hand down on the bite, warm blood covering his foot. It burned worse than the sprained ankle.

Then Ash cried as the animal sank its teeth deep into his fingers before scurrying away, pulling off skin as it ran. It wasn't scared of him.

He glared around, but it was still utterly dark. He wasn't sure if he was awake or dreaming.

The rat darted at him again and Ash kicked out wildly, but the vermin still managed to bite his toe, hanging on for an extra second or two before fleeing. More rodent feet skittered along the flagstones, splashing in and out of the puddles. How many were there?

A loud hiss rose from somewhere in the cell, followed by a sharp squeak. Claws scrabbled on the floor as the rat fought frantically, its cries rising in fear. Then bones crunched and all was silent.

Ash backed away, pressing himself against the wall. What *else* was down here?

A weak orange glow spread across the chamber above his cell. A silhouette appeared, standing on the grille and peering down. In one hand was a silver-topped cane, in the other a lamp.

"Making new friends?" asked Savage.

Ash stared. Was he about to be set free? Did Savage have the aastra? He swallowed a bitter lump of dread.

"Where's Lucky?"

"Quite safe. For now."

"Please let me out. I won't do anything."

Savage smiled. A thread of blood ran down his cheek and fell. The bead of red splashed on Ash's shoulder, staining the white material with a crimson spot. "I know you won't. Down there."

"If you're not going to free me, why did you come?" There was iron in Ash's voice. He didn't know where it had come from. Maybe he had found his dormant anger because he had nothing left to lose. "Surely you're not afraid of me?"

"Afraid? Why should I be afraid of you?"

"You tell me."

Ash had stolen the aastra. He'd hidden from Savage for weeks. He'd killed Jat. Savage had had to resort to threatening a ten-year-old girl to get what he wanted, to beat Ash. Ash met the man's gaze and — he didn't know why — smiled.

"You're just a boy," snapped Savage. "And this is the real world. In this world, children lose. Always."

The lamp clattered on the floor, and the footsteps retreated back up the steps and away. Ash stood staring up at the amber light spilling some weak illumination down into the pit.

"What a windbag."

Ash turned. Someone had spoken. Someone in the cell with him.

"Hello?" he asked.

"Savage always did love the sound of his own voice."

"Who's there?" he asked, brow furrowed as he peered into the gloom around him. He was sure the voice had come from somewhere to his left. And it sounded familiar.

Impossible. I'm going insane.

Ash gave a harsh, cracked laugh. Insane. It hadn't taken long.

"I'm glad you find all of this so funny," said Parvati as she stepped out of the darkness. She gazed up at the grille above them.

"Parvati?" Ash whispered. He stared, not daring to blink in case she vanished. She looked like she was dressed in a skin-tight suit of shimmering green and black scales, but then he realized it was her skin; she was halfway between human and serpent. "What are you doing here?"

Parvati flexed her long, elegant fingers, cracking each one methodically.

"Saving the day," she said. "As usual."

CHAPTER TWENTY-FIVE

Parvati looked dangerously demonic in the semidarkness, just like in his dream: the daughter of Ravana, ready for battle. The scales formed a high collar around her neck, but a few rose to her face, flecking her cheeks with pale green. Her eyes were long sloping slits, larger than a human's and bisected by her pupils. She brushed her fingers through her hair, shaking it loose. As she did so, her face subtly transformed, becoming more round, more human.

"Good to see you too," she said.

Ash blinked and forced a smile. "I'm sorry. I'm in a state of shock."

"Get over it."

He grabbed her arm. "Where's Lucky?"

Parvati frowned. "I've just spent half the night wriggling through the rocks beneath the palace to find you. She's not down here in the dungeons, that's for sure."

"Then where is she?" Ash looked up.

"First things first. Let's get out of here and grab the aastra before Savage does something stupid with it."

"Like free Ravana."

Parvati turned quickly. "What?" She paused, trying to make sense of his words, then shook her head. "Ravana's dead. I saw him die."

"And he's coming back. Savage intends to free him. That's why Savage wants the aastra. It's the key to unlocking your father's tomb."

"I . . . I don't believe you," said Parvati. But she didn't sound too sure.

"Let's get out and I'll tell you." Ash pointed at the grille. "Anyway, he doesn't have it yet. But he knows where it is."

"How?" said Parvati. "You had one simple job: Keep the aastra safe. Have you any idea what will happen if Savage gets his hands on it?" She slapped her forehead. "What is it about you mortals? Are your lives so short you don't worry about the long-term consequences of your actions?"

"I'm thirteen. I'm not meant to think long term about anything." Ash threw his hands up. "They were going to kill Lucky. What else could I do?"

"Your job was to protect the aastra. I don't care about your sister."

"No. But that's because you're a monster." He stared hard, unflinching. Daring her.

Her gaze lingered on his. "One disaster at a time," she said. She drew her hands over her head, molding her skull smooth. Her black hair sank under the skin and she lowered herself to the floor. She pressed her arms to her side and, legs together, transformed back into a cobra. It took just a few seconds.

She slithered into a crack in the rock. Ash watched the tail flick sharply before it too vanished into the hole.

A minute later the grille creaked and began to rise. Parvati, human again but scaled, tossed down the end of a rope.

Ash took it. Ten feet to climb. Once, not long ago, he would have found it impossible, not even standing on the shoulders of his classmates in the gym. Then he'd have complained and sweated and dangled like a fool. The teacher would have despaired, given up on him, and sent him off to the showers.

That's what Savage was trying to do, get him to give up.

"Children lose. Always."

Not this time, Savage.

Ash used his feet as well as his hands. The rope swung and he struggled to hang on, but eventually he got steady and, hand over hand, worked his way up. Breathing hard, he ignored the sharp pain shooting up his leg from the injured ankle. He was not going to be left down here.

He hooked one elbow then the other over the pit edge, so his legs dangled in the air. Then Parvati grabbed his collar and hauled him out.

"Come on," she said. "We're leaving."

"No. We're going to find my sister first."

"Be sensible, Ash. The palace is crawling with Savage's servants." She checked the stairs leading back up. "We've got to get the aastra."

"We've got to find Lucky."

"Listen to me . . ." But Ash wasn't moving. Parvati gave up. "Fine. Whatever."

Ash tore his sleeve off and used it to bandage his ankle,

double-knotting the fabric and pulling it as tight as he could. Then he put his weight on it. The pain was a dull pulse rather than like someone was shoving broken glass into his flesh. It would do for now.

Parvati led the way up the spiral stairs. Every few steps she stopped and Ash held his breath, his ears straining for any slight sound. Then she'd nod and they'd continue up.

"You know the layout?" asked Ash.

"I have been here before." Parvati stopped at the closed door at the top of the stairs. "But it was a while ago. The old maharajah had a harem built, women's quarters, where his queens lived. Lucky may well be there."

"Is it near?"

"No."

Parvati pushed open the door. They were back on the battlements overlooking the river. The tide was in, so the water lapped at the walls. He'd been in the dungeon for at least one day. The moon was high, its reflection shivering on the oil-black waters.

Parvati pointed to the opposite side of the palace. "The harem."

Ash almost missed it. It sat in the shadow of the main building, flickering candles illuminating the lattice windows from within. Someone was inside.

They crept along the high walls. Ash's heart was triple-timing. Any second now he expected to bump into one of Savage's demons. But the night was quiet; no one seemed to be stirring in the palace. Was that a good or bad sign? His nerves were shredded after his imprisonment. The cool wind, charged with the promise of rain and thunder, brought him out in goose bumps. He had to clench his teeth to stop them from chattering.

"Why didn't you bring help?" he asked. Even if Rishi wasn't around, there was Ujba, Hakim even. They would love all this ninja stuff, wouldn't they?

Parvati scoffed. "After your idiotic stunt? Why would anyone risk their necks because of your stupidity? You were told to stay at the Lalgur."

"Then why are you here?"

She flicked her head. "Because I thought you had the aastra. Don't mistake this for anything sentimental or heroic. As you said, I am a monster. Monsters can't be heroes, can they?"

If she could have seen him, she'd know he was blushing. Parvati was saving him and he could at least be grateful. But he couldn't find a way of saying it. He'd thank her once they'd found Lucky.

What was it about Parvati? He was distracted by the way her skin shone in the moonlight, by the sleekness of her limbs, the raven-wing blackness of her hair. He couldn't help but look at her. She crept under his skin.

Stairs took them down to the central courtyard. The last time Ash had been here, the space had been covered with tents and filled with guests, food, and music. Now the only sounds were the cicadas chirping in the lone tree in the corner and the distant rumble of thunder.

Ash saw the corridor that led down to the water gate and the river. Parvati looked at it.

She's thinking about going through it. To the river and freedom. Why not? He didn't have the aastra. She could take a boat and be back in Varanasi in an hour.

But Parvati turned away from the corridor and carried on, to help him save his sister.

"Thanks," said Ash.

Parvati was startled. She stared at him as though he'd just suffered some mental breakdown. Then she softened. "My pleasure."

They skirted the edge of the courtyard. If they stuck to the shadows under the balcony, they could reach the harem without being in the open.

"I thought Savage would take better care of his home." Parvati brushed a thick curtain of cobwebs aside with her arm.

"Maybe he can't get the staff."

A nest of spiders poured out of a cranny in the ceiling. The webs around them fluttered as more and more spiders scuttled down.

Ash glanced ahead. Through the darkness he saw the curved trunks of the elephant statues that guarded the doorway leading into the main palace building.

"Wait," he said.

"Just look at my hair." Parvati picked at the strands of cobweb that had tied themselves to her long black locks.

The spiders were an army now. They fell off the ceiling like a black waterfall, dozens, even hundreds of them, just dropping to the ground.

"I've got a bad feeling about this," Ash said.

Parvati hissed and her deadly fangs extended, ready to attack.

The spiders formed a lump on the ground ahead of them. The shape rippled and grew. The tangle of limbs melded together to create a pair of slim arms. They were dense at first with spiny black hairs, but these faded as the limbs took on human dimensions.

The spiders were a solid mass now, and Ash stepped back as the last of them merged into the body and Makdi stood up. Her face was broken by her eight big round eyes, and instead of a jaw she had a pair of hairy mandibles, each ending with a venomous fang. Her body was now fat and swollen. A pair of human arms stuck out at her shoulders, but jutting from her ribs were four long, bony spider legs, two on each side, all spiky with coarse black hair. They ended in stubby human fingers.

Ash spun around, alerted by a clicking sound. Climbing down the walls was a man — a sort of man. His upper torso was covered in black armor, like heavy plates of knobbly skin, and he had a pair of pincers instead of arms. His lower abdomen carried three pairs of insectoid legs, and arching above his back was a huge scorpion's tail, a bulbous sting mounted on its tip. Still other creatures crept across the courtyard toward them, men and women with tails and twitching rodent noses and whiskers.

A match was struck, and a figure came alive in the glow of

its small, weak flame. The match moved to a lamp — Ash heard the scrape of glass as the lamp lid was raised. The flame suddenly bloomed.

"Parvati, my dear. How kind of you to visit."

Savage leaned against one of the elephant statues and put the lamp on its head. Jackie was a few paces behind him.

"Have you missed me?" asked Savage.

"Still not dead?" Parvati's fangs were long and wet with poison. "Come here and let me fix that."

Ash stepped back, but where could they go? Jackie positioned herself in front of her master, and the spider-woman stepped closer. With them both protecting Savage and at least another dozen rakshasas around them, Ash and Parvati had run out of options.

"Just give me the girl and I'll let you live," said Parvati.

"Parvati, you should be here beside me," Savage said. "Like in the good old days."

"You mean back when you betrayed me? No thanks."

Ash and Parvati retreated toward the corridor and the water gate. The other demons formed a semicircle around them, but no one made the first move. Ash remembered that Parvati's venom was lethal to all living things — including demons.

The rakshasas' circle tightened around them like a noose.

"You can't take us all," growled Jackie. "Not alone."

"She isn't alone," said a voice from behind Ash.

Rishi stepped up beside him, and Ash could have wept with relief. The sadhu had his staff ready, sweeping it slowly in a wide arc. The rakshasas shuffled back. The air about the old man hummed, just like it had when he'd flattened the Humvee.

"What a gallant party," said Savage. "Cowardly boy, self-hating demon princess, and meddling old fool. The years have not been kind to you, Rishi."

"Have you looked in a mirror lately?" replied the sadhu. His eyes never shifted from the horde before them, but he spoke to Ash. "To the boat, boy."

"I'm not leaving without my sister."

"Then we're not leaving at all," said Parvati. "In case you hadn't noticed, we're outnumbered twenty to two."

"I can fight too," Ash snapped. Hadn't he spent the last few weeks learning? He'd help them.

Parvati snorted. "Er, no, you really can't."

"Enough!" Savage slammed his cane hard on the stone, the sharp crack bringing his demons to attention. He pointed the tiger cane straight at Ash. "Just kill them," he said.

"Lucky!" Ash shouted. The harem was just there! If he could get to it, he'd save his sister. "Lucky!"

Ash's feet were whipped out from under him. He tried to get up, but thick white cobwebs bound his legs. Makdi leaped through the air and he stared in frozen terror at her big black eyes and the pair of fangs jutting out of her jaw. He tore at the webbing around his feet, but thick clumps stuck to his fingers. He wasn't going to make it.

Then Parvati collided with the spider-woman in a blur of scales and long, spindly legs. Rishi, his staff in one hand, dragged Ash up. His eyes shone blue, as if minute lightning storms raged within the pupils. All around him the air shivered and electric arcs ran over his skin, sending tingling waves through Ash.

Makdi screamed. Her arms and her too many limbs shook violently.

"Come on, boy!" Rishi shoved him down the corridor toward the water.

"I've got to get Lucky!"

Rishi charged into the fray, swinging and jabbing with his staff. Wherever he struck, demons were hurled backward. But as each one fell, two more entered the battle.

Parvati pushed Makdi off her and stood up. She smiled at Rishi.

Then she collapsed.

Ash saw a pair of puncture wounds on her arm, the skin around them already turning black. The spider-woman and Parvati must have bitten each other at exactly the same moment. The spider-woman was clearly dead, while Parvati lay there, pale and twitching. Alive, but only just.

Ash ran forward but was blocked by one of the scorpion-men. He dived sideways just as the sting slammed into the ground where he'd been standing.

"The boat! Get to the boat!" shouted Rishi.

There was no way Ash could abandon Lucky, but as he looked around the battle, he knew they only had seconds. Parvati was unconscious, and Rishi's blows lacked the power and the electric speed they'd had earlier. His strength was fading fast. The rakshasas sensed victory.

A hero would fight on. Deep down, Ash knew he should be prepared to fight and die if necessary to save his sister and friends, but maybe he'd be more use to Lucky if he stayed alive. That way he'd be able to come back and rescue her later.

He wrapped his arms around Parvati and lifted her up, then ran down the corridor as Rishi swung his stick wildly, forcing the demons back.

Ash burst through the water gate and suddenly he was splashing knee-deep in the river. A single shallow-bellied boat bobbed nearby, tied to a post, and Ash hauled Parvati into it. It had to be Rishi's; he could see the old man's shoulder bag lying under the seat. Ash's hand slipped the knot and his feet dug into the sandy floor of the river as, heart pounding, he pushed the boat out.

Parvati moaned. Semi-delirious, she lay in the boat, cradling her injured arm. Ash gave another heave and the current took hold. He dragged himself up into the boat and grabbed an oar. Then he started half-paddling, half-pushing the boat farther out.

Rishi bounded toward him, hopping like a sprightly monkey through the water. "Don't wait for me, boy!"

Figures paused at the water gate, now a good one or two hundred feet behind them. A few waded into the water up to their knees, but then stopped, the distance between them and the boat too great.

They're not chasing us. They're letting us go.

The boat scraped on a submerged sand bank in the middle of the river. Chest heaving and limbs aching, Ash dropped the oar and checked Parvati. Her breath was shallow but steady.

Lights lined the upper battlements of the Savage Fortress. The lights shone on the water's surface too, spots of gold trembling the waves. Still no one gave chase.

Ash watched Rishi swim toward him — not so easy with his stick in one hand. The wake formed a wide triangle behind the old holy man, the small waves bouncing into a complex pattern as a second V-shaped ripple overlapped it.

A second?

Ash glanced back up at the fortress. Why was no one chasing them?

The waves rocked up and down roughly now, increasingly disturbed.

Ash put his hands on the oar.

"Hurry up, Rishi!" he shouted.

The old man shook the water from his ears. He waved at Ash.

Ash leapt into the water, gripping the oar in both hands like a baseball bat.

"Rishi!"

The water trembled, and Rishi went under.

CHAPTER TWENTY-SIX

"Rishi!"

Ash searched for some movement, but there was nothing. He waded toward where he'd seen Rishi disappear. Maybe if he —

Then an immense, demonic crocodile, almost twenty feet long, leaped high out of the water. Rishi, his arm trapped in the monster's jaws, screamed. For a second they hung suspended, poised in the air, almost as though the crocodile was balancing on the tip of its tail. Then it languidly pivoted, twisting its head, and they slammed down flat into the water.

The river foamed and churned but Ash couldn't see anything.

"Rishi!"

After what seemed like an eternity Rishi burst out, gasping. He blinked as he saw Ash. An inarticulate cry rose from his throat, which gave way to spasmodic coughing.

Ash tossed the oar aside and pulled the old man toward the sandbank. It was only when he was back at the boat that he was able to take a good look at the sadhu.

Mayar had torn off Rishi's arm. Blood poured from the holy man's ruined shoulder and teeth marks punctured his chest, each wide and deep. His torso was awash with scarlet.

Ash cradled the spindly old man against him. Each time Rishi breathed, red bubbles frothed across his chest.

"I'll save you," said Ash. He'd get Rishi in the boat. Somehow he'd save him. Somehow.

"Turning into a hero, are we?" muttered Rishi. "You always do. Sooner or later."

Ash squeezed the old man tightly. If he hung on, then so would Rishi. "I'll save you," he said again. The words were useless, but he couldn't think of anything else to say.

"Don't be afraid, Ashoka." Blood ran from Rishi's lips. "It's only death."

Then his chest sank and did not rise again. Rishi's eyes closed and his body relaxed as his spirit fled to the lands of the dead.

"You'll be back," whispered Ash.

Mayar's head broke the lapping ripples. Ash watched as the long snout sank back into his face. The neck shrunk and the demon rose out of the water, walking as a human onto the sandbank.

That was why they hadn't been chased. Mayar had been waiting for them in the river all along.

Cold hard rage gripped Ash's chest, as tight as nails digging into his heart. His blood pounded like a massive drum, filling his head with pain. He hugged Rishi against him, trying to contain the agony shooting through his body. He gritted his teeth but couldn't hold in the scream.

What was happening to him? He'd felt like this when Jat had died, only this was a thousand times stronger.

He bit down so hard he thought his teeth would shatter at any second. Then a final shock wave exploded along his spine, burning every nerve. Ash's eyes snapped open just as Mayar joined him on the sandbank.

"Jat was my best friend," growled Mayar. "This won't be quick."

Ash let Rishi slip to the ground as he stood up. The world seemed filled with floating lights, like a million fireflies. He swayed on unsteady feet, waiting for the sprinkling lights to disappear, but they didn't. Instead they settled like glowing dust over Mayar.

What was he seeing? The lights coalesced at different points. Some of them were faint and barely visible, others shining brightly. They seemed to change location second by second as Mayar moved. It was like a sparkling map covered the rakshasa. Could anyone else see this, or only Ash?

Ash stumbled back until he hit the boat and had nowhere left to run.

Mayar grabbed him by the throat.

"This is going to hurt. Scream as much as you want," said the demon. "I like it when they scream."

Ash made his left hand into a fist. He couldn't take his eyes off the spot glowing halfway along Mayar's jaw. The brightness was almost blinding.

"What are you looking at, boy?" snarled Mayar.

Ash swung his fist into that glowing point on the jaw. Mayar screamed as bone, teeth, and blood erupted from his mouth, and Ash fell to the ground as red spittle sprayed his face.

Ash stared at his clenched fist. Mayar's jawbone had shattered like a dry, rotten twig. He gazed at Mayar, at the confusion in the demon's eyes. Mayar held his broken jaw with one hand. Then he gave a gargling cry of rage and swiped his free arm at Ash's neck. Each finger ended with a long curved claw, each one easily capable of tearing open Ash's windpipe.

But Ash jabbed his fingers into another glowing spot, this time by Mayar's elbow. Mayar cried out again as his arm went limp. It dropped to his side, fingers twitching and useless. He backed away, terrified.

Ash advanced, watching the ever-evolving pattern of lights glide over Mayar's body. Energy roared along Ash's veins, boiling the blood within and filling him with fire. His heartbeat echoed through him, each beat sending a brand-new surge of strength to his limbs and muscles.

The fire consumed him and he knew that he wanted to let it all out. He wanted to rip Mayar to pieces. He wanted to wash himself in the rakshasa's blood.

Ash threw back his head and roared, pouring out all his rage and anger at the world. The clouds shook with fear.

Mayar hurled himself into the water and dived under. Ash glared at the river, scanning the surface for movement.

He would not be denied. He wanted to kill.

A moan from behind made him look around.

A rakshasa lay in the boat.

Her body sparkled with light. There were so many ways to break her. So many ways to kill her. Kill the rakshasa — Parvati.

Ash faltered. Her name was Parvati.

Parvati was his friend. She'd saved him. He didn't want to kill her.

He slumped into the water, and the cold wetness against his face brought him to his senses.

Ash ached, suddenly weak. He watched the ripple of water head toward the Savage Fortress and saw Mayar stumble out, dragged by the other rakshasas.

Ash's gaze rose toward the battlements. Savage stood up on the wall; there was no mistaking him. A small child was beside him. Lucky.

Savage raised his right hand.

Even from this distance it shone, a bright golden light shimmering off its polished metal surface.

Savage had the aastra.

CHAPTER TWENTY-SEVEN

The waters lapped against the boat, rocking it gently like a baby's cradle. Ash, exhausted, slumped down beside the unconscious Parvati. Her skin was cold.

He watched the Ganges take the old man. Rishi's hair spread out over the water's surface as he floated for a moment before his body turned sideways and disappeared.

They drifted off the sandbank, carried by the slow current, carried away from Varanasi. Ash gazed across the river at the Savage Fortress. Leaden weariness dragged at his heart.

"Lucky . . ."

He'd failed.

The clouds loomed over them, dark gray and heavy.

Ash closed his eyes.

Sunlight — warm, bright, and new — woke Ash. The boat was still. He got up and saw they'd drifted into the bank alongside some small dried-out fields. A cluster of huts stood in a circle about a mile away. Smoke rose from a campfire to fade into the blue sky.

Parvati murmured. She was in her complete human form, with no scales at all. The wound on her arm had faded to a small dark blemish, and while she looked pale, she didn't have that sallow, sick tinge to her skin anymore.

Her eyes snapped open. Her pupils pulsed, then narrowed into a pair of pencil-thin slits.

"Rishi?"

Ash shook his head. "I'm sorry."

Parvati sat up and inspected her arm. "What happened?"

"Mayar got him. And Savage got the aastra."

She gazed at the water rippling against the boat. "Rishi's been dead before," she said quietly. She looked up abruptly. "Do you have any good news?"

"I know the aastra is Kali's."

"A Kali-aastra? That doesn't fall into the 'good news' category."

Ash began to explain what had happened. He told her about breakfast with Savage and the Englishman's belief that Ravana was ready to be freed from his prison.

"But how?" asked Parvati. "Ravana was destroyed. I was there."

"Rama used a Vishnu-aastra to kill Ravana. But he knew Ravana would be reborn, so he imprisoned his body within the Iron Gates," said Ash. "Savage intends to use the Kali-aastra to smash the gates open and let Ravana's spirit reunite with his body."

Parvati went pale as he talked and, just for a moment, he saw her tremble. He had thought she wasn't scared of anything.

He described getting her on the boat and she asked him a few things, but then he realized something truly important.

The cobra scales that had covered her like armor had disappeared.

Totally disappeared.

He tried to keep his mind on the story and his gaze on her face, but — oh, God — he couldn't help it, inch by inch his gaze fell. Ash could just make out the faintest outline of scales beneath her skin, down her neck, on her shoulders . . .

"Look at me when I'm talking to you," snapped Parvati.

"I am looking at you." Ash bit his tongue, but a moment too late. "Er, I didn't mean it like that. I meant, sorry, what were you saying?"

"Give me your shirt before your eyes pop out."

Ash handed it over and heard Parvati muttering about "hormonal teenage boys" as she slipped it over her head. It fit her like a short dress — okay for now. At least he could focus on what she was saying.

"How did we get away?" Parvati asked.

Ash looked at his hand — the hand that had shattered Mayar's jaw.

"I don't know," he said. That was the honest truth. "I really don't know."

Had the Kali-aastra given him all that power? But Savage had the arrowhead now. Could it have somehow transferred power over that distance, from the palace to Ash down in the river? He scratched his hand, confused. There was so much he didn't understand.

"What's that?" asked Parvati, pointing to something in the bottom of the boat.

Rishi's bag. Ash had forgotten it was lying under the seat. He opened it.

A wooden begging bowl. A necklace made of sandalwood beads. A small purse and a map.

Parvati took the map and opened it up. It was a large-scale map of part of the Thar Desert, out in Rajasthan.

She smiled. "Now this is what I call good news."

Rishi had marked a crude series of lines and blocks on what appeared to be an empty patch of desert. Ash recognized the layout. His uncle had dozens of these maps scattered around the bungalow. It was the outline of a Harappan city, but on a scale far beyond anything Uncle Vik had ever worked on. This must have been the civilization's capital.

Where they'd buried Ravana.

Ash opened the purse and shook its contents onto his palm.

"Cool," he said.

Dozens of gems sparkled in the morning light in a kaleidoscope of brilliant colors: diamonds, rubies, sapphires. He'd thought Rishi had given Ujba a big rock, but there was a ruby in here the size of an egg.

"We need to move," said Parvati. She folded the map and placed it back in the bag.

"We need to get back to the Fortress," said Ash. "We've got to get my sister."

Parvati shook her head. "Do you honestly think Savage is there now that he has the aastra? No, he'll be on his way to my father's tomb by now." She waved the map. "This is where we'll find him."

They walked in silence to the edge of the village. A goat, tethered to a stick, nibbled at a cast-off shoe. A woman dressed in a threadbare sari squatted over a small fire, cooking chapattis.

Ash's stomach rumbled. When was the last time he'd eaten? He honestly couldn't remember.

The woman smiled at them, motioning for them to join her. She scooped up a round ball of dough and expertly rolled it out on a flat, flour-dusted stone. Then she flicked the disc on to the pan where it hissed and cooked.

"While you're getting breakfast," said Parvati, "ask her if she's got something proper to wear."

"That was probably the most expensive breakfast in history," said Ash. "I could've bought an island with that ruby."

Parvati straightened her sunglasses. She was wearing a knee-length tunic, trousers, and a headscarf, all faded black. The outfit suited her. "They're only stones, Ash."

They hitched a lift on a truck heading back to Varanasi. Hot wind blasted them as the truck did its rounds, bouncing in and out of the potholes as it collected farmers and their produce for the city's Saturday market. Ash sat on top of a cage of live chickens, which had been packed so tightly that all they could do was squawk and blink. Parvati sat beside him, headscarf covering most of her face to keep out the dust, and the attention of the other passengers.

As the truck drew closer to the city, Ash's heart filled with dread. He closed his eyes, drifting back to that dream, that vision he'd had when he first found the arrowhead, where he'd fought the giant golden warrior. Ravana had carved his way through armies, laughing. No mortal weapon could harm him.

And what would he bring? Pure horror. The things Ash had seen in his visions would become real. The Carnival of Flesh, a rambling monstrosity of whole populations, melted into a gigantic mass of screaming mouths and tormented souls. Humans driven beyond madness by the mere presence of the demon king.

But then he thought of his second vision and what Parvati was capable of. She'd built a wall out of the best warriors in Rama's army. If he was going to get Lucky back, he could ask for no better backup.

Backup? Who was he kidding? This was Parvati's show. Ash looked at her. Could her venom kill the demon king? She was the only chance they had.

I'm so useless, he thought.

He'd escaped, though, hadn't he? He'd punched Mayar in the face. A thrill ran through him. Wow. He'd done that. He'd broken the demon's jaw, and the big, bad crocodile had fled, tail between his legs.

How had he done it? It didn't make sense.

"What I don't get," Ash said, "is that I awakened the aastra when I killed Jat. I felt its power burning through me. But then nothing happened after that. When I woke up the next day, I felt completely normal. I thought the aastra gave you permanent superpowers or something."

"Remember the rat? I killed it and then you punched out Hakim. Now that should never have happened, should it?"

"What do you mean?"

"Come on, Ash. He's way better than you and yet you kicked his butt."

"Maybe I'm better than you think."

"You're better than you were, but — how can I put this delicately? That's still not very good."

"You're saying it was the aastra, right?"

"Right. The rat's death powered the aastra, just a little. Enough for you to beat Hakim."

He didn't like it, but she was right. That was why he'd beaten Mayar. Rishi's death had charged the aastra with power. But one thing still didn't make sense: Savage had had the aastra by then.

Parvati continued. "Little energy is released in killing something like a rat. Not enough to really awaken the aastra. Kali will not give you her power unless you kill someone important. The greater the death, the greater the power of the aastra."

"So what constitutes a 'great death'? Killing an elephant?"

"It's not a question of size, but value. It would have to be someone who means a lot to you personally. Either someone you truly hated or truly loved. For the aastra to be made powerful enough to kill someone like Ravana, it would have to be a very great, very important, death indeed. A huge sacrifice."

So that was it. Ash's dream made sense now. He'd wondered why Lakshmana had taken off his armor, telling Rama to strike. Rama could only kill Ravana if he charged the aastra by sacrificing his own brother. Nothing else would have been enough to destroy the demon king forever.

But Rama couldn't bring himself to do it, so he had used a less powerful aastra — enough to destroy the demon king, but not enough to prevent him being reincarnated and returning. That's why Rama and the gods had trapped Ravana behind the Iron Gates. The demon king must have spent the last four and a half thousand years planning his revenge, waiting for the day someone would open the gates again. Because they had been sealed by the gods, only the power of a god would open them again.

And that's where the aastra came into it. *Oh, no.*

Ash gazed out over the dry fields. "Savage is going to kill my sister. Use her death to power the Kali-aastra."

"Maybe," said Parvati, but she didn't seem convinced. "The Kali-aastra exposes the weakness of all things and gives you the power to exploit those weaknesses. If it was fully charged, it would show you how to stop a man's heartbeat with a tap, or demolish a castle wall with a mere kick. It is the ultimate force of annihilation."

Like the way he'd taken out Mayar. Those lights had shown him where to strike and do unbelievable amounts of damage.

"And Savage has got it. How do we stop him?"

"Let me worry about that. You've done enough already."

Ash flinched under the insult, but didn't say anything.

"We're here." She shuffled to the edge of the truck.

They'd hit the Grand Trunk Road, one of the main arteries into Varanasi. The clouds were darker and heavier than before;

the rains were imminent. Soon all of north India would be awash with the annual torrential downpour. The streets would flood and the rain would fall so hard and heavy it would hurt. But right now it was being preceded by a cool sea wind straight in from the Indian Ocean.

They jumped off while the truck was still stuck in traffic, well outside of the old city. The hustle and bustle was still as bad, the noise brain-numbing as cars, horns, cattle, and thousands of people went about their business, like any normal day. No one gave Ash or Parvati a second glance.

"This is where we go our separate ways," said Parvati as she brushed off the worst of the dust.

"What?"

Parvati stopped. She looked at Ash and sighed. "You've got a good heart, Ash, but I'm going after Savage. It'll be better if you stay here."

"Where it's safe, you mean?"

"Where I don't have to keep looking out for you."

Her words cut him all the more because they were true.

"I can help."

"How?"

Hot shame flushed his cheeks. Ash stared at her, furious, but Parvati didn't budge. She stood there, arms crossed, her cool gaze unflinching. She wasn't scared of him.

Nobody was.

"In case you've forgotten," said Ash, "Savage has my sister."

"And you want to rescue her. I understand, but the question remains: How?"

"How are you going to kill Savage?"

She pointed at Rishi's sack. "The map. I know where Savage is. He can't have more than a few hours' head start. I'm going to find him and bury my fangs in his neck. Something I should have done a hundred years ago."

"You make it sound simple."

"Killing *is* simple. For me."

Ash's eyes narrowed. "And your plans, they've always gone perfectly? No hiccups? No unforeseen circumstances?"

"There are always unforeseen circumstances."

"So you don't know if you might need me?"

Parvati scowled. "Fine. Come along. But I'm not waiting for you."

"And if we're too late? And Ravana's free? What then?" Ash asked, even though his throat tightened around the question.

"Then we die, Ash. We all die."

CHAPTER TWENTY-EIGHT

They walked into the departures terminal of the local airport. The vast hall echoed with thousands of unhappy voices. There were no lines to the check-ins, just a heaving mass of humanity. An *angry* mass. People jostled and argued as surly security guards tried vainly to keep them in order. Luggage lay scattered and abandoned everywhere. Overhead, rusty fans groaned but did nothing to lift the stifling heat generated by the volatile crowd.

"Flights to Jaisalmer have all been canceled," said Ash, inspecting the old clapper board overhead. Not just Jaisalmer, but Bikaner, Jodhpur, all of Rajasthan. He headed toward a guy in an Air India uniform. The man was using his clipboard as a shield to hold off the irate crowd.

"I am very sorry, ladies and gentlemen," the man said, "but all planes are grounded until we have confirmation from Delhi."

Ash barged forward, pushing people aside, and grabbed the guy's arm. "What's going on?" he asked.

The man glared down at him. "Riots across Rajasthan. All the cities are in chaos. Some say bands of criminals are rampaging across the desert. Some say it is terrorists from

Pakistan. No one knows, though, so no flights until we get the all clear."

Ash went back to Parvati. "Do you think we're too late? That Ravana's free?"

Parvati shook her head. "This wave of madness precedes my father's awakening. When people start eating one another, then we know he's arrived. Right now, it's only the rakshasas gathering at his tomb."

"Great. So we'll be facing an army of demons. Could today *be* any better?" Ash looked up at the long list of canceled flights. "How are we going to get there?"

"Follow me."

They made their way out of the main hall and into a labyrinth of offices behind. The rooms were old-fashioned partitions of dark wood and frosted glass. Signs in Hindi and English proclaimed the names of small independent airlines.

"This is the one," said Parvati as she knocked on a door labeled MAHARAJAH AIR and went straight in, not bothering to wait for a reply.

A man lay across the table, a handkerchief over his face. Cotton wool was stuffed in his hairy ears. His khaki trousers were oil-stained and his shirt wore breakfast and possibly yesterday's dinner. A thin black tie hung loose around his stubbled jowls. Along one wall stood a line of wooden filing cabinets over which was a yellowing poster of Princess Diana and Prince Charles. An air-conditioning unit rattled above their heads, its filter black with grime.

"Get up, Jimmy." Parvati nudged the sleeping man.

The man spluttered and lifted a corner of the handkerchief. His small, puffy eyes peeked out and darted from face to face.

"I'm off duty," he muttered, then let the handkerchief fall back.

Parvati lifted up the side of the desk and the man swore as the entire contents — a small desk fan, the telephone, books, and he himself — slid off. He just managed to avoid falling on his backside, but the rest of the gear crashed over the bare concrete floor.

The man's wide black mustache bristled as his face darkened. Then he recognized Parvati and laughed. Even from where Ash was standing, he could smell the alcohol.

"My princess." He glanced over their shoulders out into the corridor. "No Rishi?"

"No. Not anymore."

The man paused and scratched under his chin. "Then what can I do for you?"

"Take us to Jaisalmer."

"Jaisalmer's out of bounds. Good grief, all of Rajasthan is out of bounds."

"Never stopped you before, has it?" Parvati held out her hand.

It was another big diamond from Rishi's stash.

The man picked up the gem and turned it in the light, admiring the reflected beams that filled the room. "No, I suppose not."

"And we're leaving now. Understood?" said Parvati. She looked around. "Oh, and my gear? You still have it?"

Jimmy clapped his hands and wrestled open a locker. "Of course."

Inside was a large canvas bag. It looked heavy. Jimmy lifted it up and dropped it on the desk with a crash. Then he fished out a pair of green-tinted aviator Ray-Bans and a baseball cap. "This way."

"What gear?" Ash asked Parvati as he lifted the bag on to his shoulder. His back bowed under the weight.

"Fashion accessories," Parvati said.

They emerged on to the tarmac. The ground shimmered in the heat, and the air was thick with the smell of fuel, sharp and sweet. Jimmy pointed past a line of empty luggage trolleys to a hangar plastered with dozens of old and faded advertising boards. Among them was Maharajah Air, the ad's colors bleached out but still bearing the outline of a gaudy jeweled crown.

Maharajah Air comprised one plane. Jimmy went off to speak to air control, taking a fistful of gems to pay the "emergency departure tax." Ash approached the aircraft warily. The hangar was unlit, but even in the gloom, his first impressions did not fill him with confidence.

"It's ancient," he said.

"It's a classic," said Parvati.

"A classic piece of junk."

The wings bore rotund propellers and the windows were minute portholes. The paint finish was streaked and patched, and an odd odor hung around the whole plane, musty, like a grandmother's armchair.

"I'm sure he wouldn't fly it if it wasn't safe," said Parvati doubtfully.

Jimmy returned and pulled down the door-steps. He handed them a brown paper bag.

"In-flight catering." He winked. "Only the best for my passengers."

Inside the bag were broken shortbread cookies. Ash took it and climbed into the plane.

The interior had been stripped to almost nothing. There were columns of seats down either side, six in total, but the central aisle was clear except for webbing that formed a carpet. Buckles and straps dangled loose from the fuselage, and near the back sat two large steel trunks, firmly screwed to the floor. A thin cotton curtain separated the passengers from the cockpit. Jimmy cleaned his aviators and drew out a packet of cigarettes. He ran his fingers through his hair before flipping his baseball cap back on.

"Like Tom Cruise?" Jimmy asked. "From *Top Gun,* yes?"

"Who? Oh, yes. Just like him," said Ash. The seats were missing their belts, and he wasn't surprised. If it came down to it, seat belts weren't going to make much difference on this plane.

Glued to the top of the control panel was a plastic statue of Ganesha, a plump pink boy with an elephant's head, the patron god of travelers. Jimmy touched it and whispered a prayer. Ash really hoped the gods were paying attention to this one. They were going to need all the help they could get.

"What if I need to, you know, go?" Ash asked.

"Just stick your pee-pee out the window." Jimmy set his Ray-Bans in place. "But remember to point it downwind."

Two men in blue overalls sweated and struggled against the

huge steel hangar doors. The screeching of metal as the doors rolled apart was deafening. A blast of light broke along the windows. Jimmy pulled on his headset and began his preflight checks, occasionally tapping his cigarette ash onto the floor. With a loud cough and a tremble, the engines started up and the propellers whirred into life. The plane rolled out into the sun, its body humming.

Ash watched the ground rushing beneath them as the plane bumped its way down the runway. The engines' drone increased in pitch and then the plane surged upward, pushing him into his seat with its sluggish power. He kept his eyes on the scene below, the dense cluster of houses and the endless fields of temples. The Ganges sparkled beneath them as the plane banked westward.

He and Parvati were going to Rajasthan to fight an army of rakshasas, a black magician, and possibly the demon king himself. Just the two of them. As missions went, this was beyond stupid — it was suicidal.

But Lucky was in Rajasthan too. And Ash was going to get her back.

He gripped the armrests as the plane juddered through the clouds. But soon the monotonous humming of the engines and the sheer exhaustion of the last few days began to make his eyelids droop. Even as sleep came on, he wondered if this was the last night he'd ever get. Tomorrow he would either save Lucky, or he would be dead.

CHAPTER TWENTY-NINE

"He is dead," says Rama. "Ravana is dead."

He leans forward on his throne and stares at the priest. The others in the court fall silent.

"Ravana is *only* dead," says the priest. "That is not enough. What prevents his rebirth? Nothing."

"I used the aastra."

"Of Vishnu. We gave you the Kali-aastra for a reason, Your Majesty."

The priests of Vishnu murmur angrily. One of the saffron-wearing monks stands up and shouts, "Are you saying that Vishnu's gift was not powerful enough?"

The priest in front of Rama smiles. "That is exactly what I'm saying."

The court erupts. The monks barge forward and Rama's soldiers cross their spears to protect the black-clad man in the center of the hall. Lakshmana, ever ready at Rama's side, puts his hand on his sword hilt, and Rama sees the rage in his younger brother's eyes. To insult Vishnu here? It is blasphemy.

Rama worships Vishnu. Some say he is an avatar of the god — Vishnu in mortal form. How else could Ravana have been defeated?

They say out in the markets and in the fields. Rama cannot be a mortal man; he must be a god.

But the priest standing before the throne cares little for Rama's devotion. He is a follower of Kali.

Rama observes the silent priest. The man is gaunt, skeletal, and there is cold, deadly power lurking behind his black eyes. His robes are plain cotton, but his prayer beads are of bone. Rama wonders of which animal. In spite of the man's thin frame, his hands are large and his fingers look powerful. The priests of Kali are said to strangle their enemies.

Rama stands and the court falls silent. He walks toward the window, gazing out over his city of Ayodhya.

They are rebuilding. After years of war, he sees hope in the faces of his people. Men sing as they hammer beams together, and children run in the streets, laughing and crying as they chase a poor scurrying dog. Carpenters, builders, farmers, and craftsmen from all over the world have come here to reconstruct his war-torn nation. Rama smells the warm bread rising from the bakery at the wall of his palace.

If Ravana returns, then this will be for nothing.

"I have heard there is a metal that resists magic," Rama says.

Lakshmana nods. "Iron."

"Then we will imprison the demon king."

The Kali-priest raises an eyebrow. "An iron prison?"

One of the Vishnu-priests comes forward. He bows low. "My brothers tell me that the metal would prevent Ravana's spirit from returning to his body. It is a most elegant solution, Your Majesty."

Rama looks at the map on the wall. The map, a mosaic of crystals, marks the boundaries of his kingdom. There are the cities, the white-capped mountains, and the wide seas. And to the west is the desert. There are allied kingdoms there too, but sacrifices must be made.

"We shall build it in secret," says Rama. "Then destroy any mark or memory of it. Men cannot search for what they do not know."

The Vishnu-priest bows again. "We shall summon the gods to seal it. The tomb will be unbreakable."

"What of the Kali-aastra?" interrupts the black-robed priest. "What have you done with it?"

Rama hesitates. He left it in the battlefield. But it is one arrow among millions. It is lost forever.

"I used it to destroy one of Ravana's generals," says Rama. "That was why I could not use it against the demon king himself. It had already been shot."

The ebony eyes of the Kali-priest search Rama's face. But if the priest thinks he is lying, he does not say. It is unwise to call a king a liar in his own palace. The Kali-priest bows and retreats.

Rama turns to the Vishnu-priest. "Gather your most powerful magicians. When the tomb is complete, I want the entire city buried and lost. Make sure it is hidden beneath the sands for all of eternity."

CHAPTER THIRTY

"I hope you didn't have any relatives in Rajasthan," said Jimmy, peering out of the window.

They'd flown over the city of Jaisalmer and continued west, deep into the Thar Desert. Dozens of villages blazed below them, forming a pattern of golden dots across the black landscape. Dense columns of smoke rose in a swirling mass above them. Distant lighting flashed among the massive clouds that gathered in from the horizon.

"The gods are angry," said Ash.

"No," Parvati replied, removing her sunglasses to stare out of the small porthole window. "They are afraid."

They're not the only ones.

Ash could barely speak, his mouth was so dry. The feeling had built as the hours had passed. He was in over his head. Out there were demons, monsters, and chaos. How could they hope to fight them all? How had it come to this? Just a few weeks ago his biggest worry was low battery power on his Nintendo DS. Parvati looked cool and collected. Ash, on the other hand, wanted to be violently sick.

"Is now a bad time to mention I'm risk intolerant?" said Ash.

Parvati twisted around. "What?"

"Risk intolerant. It's a real condition," said Ash. "My doctor said I should avoid all situations involving mortal danger and acts of heroism. They're really bad for my health."

"Yes, now is a bad time to mention it." She shifted back into her seat. "So don't."

Farther to the west, on the horizon, the sky glowed orange. Parvati tapped Jimmy's shoulder and pointed. "That's where we're going."

Ash knew that there were no cities this far west, so the intense light could only mean one thing: Savage's excavations. And Ravana.

He thought back to his dream. Rama's plan had worked, almost. It had taken over four thousand years for someone to find Ravana's tomb. Countless historians and archaeologists, like Uncle Vik, had spent their entire lives trying to find out how and why an entire civilization, the most advanced of its age, had disappeared so completely.

And now Ash knew. The Harappans had imprisoned Ravana and wanted to leave no trace of him, or themselves. They had *chosen* extinction. They'd given up their entire way of existence. Huge cities left to ruin, all their culture, their language, abandoned. All their greatest achievements allowed to fade away.

He searched the burning horizon. Lucky was somewhere out there. Did she know he was coming? Or had she given up all hope? Ash couldn't bear the idea of losing her. He'd been brought up knowing it was his job to look after her. At times he'd seen it as a burden and a chore, but now he knew it was his honor. Lucky was a great sister; they were as close as any siblings could be. If anything happened to Lucky, he didn't know what he'd do.

And if he couldn't be brave for himself, he had to be brave for her.

It didn't take long to cover the last fifty miles, but the night caught up quickly. The fires were denser now and Ash realized that some of them were torches: a procession. Like a nest of snakes, long lines of fires wove their way across the dark desert toward the ancient city of Ravana.

Ash watched large, winged creatures glide below them across the smoking fires. They were too large to be normal birds, even vultures. He saw wild packs of jackal-human hybrids hunting through the villages, feasting and tearing at those who'd been too slow or weak to flee. Monstrous serpents, their fangs catching the firelight and their scales glimmering with ever-changing colors, slithered across the sands, leaving half-devoured corpses in their wake.

And this was just the beginning.

Parvati pointed to an area below, one dark and empty. "Land there," she said, comparing Rishi's map to the landscape below. "We'll walk the last few miles."

Ash, up in the cockpit now, gazed out at the flame-lit black buildings and strange, ruined towers that stood half-buried in the sands.

"You sure you want to do this?" asked Jimmy. "Looks like a very bad idea to me."

"No one's asking you to come," said Parvati.

"Good, I wasn't planning to," said Jimmy with a resigned sigh, then drew the control column down. "May the gods be with you."

The gods? Ash looked down at the endless stream of monsters marching toward their master. They looked ready to burn the world.

If the gods had any sense, they'd be a long way from here.

The plane bounced on the rocky earth and the engine screamed as it went into reverse. The fuselage vibrated like a washing machine. It felt like the plane was going to shake itself apart. After all this, it would be such a stupid way to go — in a plane crash. Then the plane slowed, the engines quietened, and they rolled forward and stopped.

Parvati kicked open the door and tossed out her canvas bag. She jumped down and moved away from the buzzing propellers. Ash hopped out next.

"Do you want me to wait?" shouted Jimmy over the rumbling propeller engines.

"Do you want to?" asked Parvati.

"No!" He laughed.

Parvati tossed the bag of gems into the plane.

"What'd you do that for?" Ash shouted over the roaring propellers. "We could have saved those for the future!"

Parvati looked toward the far fires. "You think you've got a future?"

Jimmy gave a final wave and pulled the door shut. The engines rose to an ear-piercing pitch as the plane slowly turned, plowing up clouds of sand. Ash and Parvati watched it through narrowed eyes as it began to accelerate. It hopped once, twice, then jumped into the air, dipped, and finally rose. Within a few minutes the only thing Ash could see was the red taillight. Then that too was eaten up in the clouds.

Parvati unzipped her bag and pulled out weapons, one by one: two pairs of swords, a dagger, and a steel whip made up of four long, flexible strips of steel coming out of a standard sword handle.

"The urumi," said Ash. He picked it up and then flinched. Blood dripped from his finger where the edge of one of the lashes had cut it.

"You know what it is?" said Parvati. She carefully wound the six-foot-long steel around her waist — on top of her sash to prevent the metal from cutting her skin — then held it in place with the hilt.

"The serpent sword," said Ash. "I saw one in a dream once."

"Strange dream."

"You were in it too."

Parvati laughed. "I'm sure I was."

"No, you don't understand. It wasn't like that at all." What was with Parvati? Did she think he was interested in her? *As if.* But he still blushed. "Forget it."

Ash looked at the weapons, all razor sharp and ready for use. He tried one of the swords and drew half the blade from the scabbard. The cold steel edge was mirror-bright.

"Take it," said Parvati.

He put it back down. "What we need is a nuke."

"I knew I'd forgotten something," she said. She'd ditched

her sunglasses and loosened the knot in her hair. The long, silky black tresses blew in the wind as she inspected the weapons. "This might suit you better." She handed him a punch dagger. "Let's go."

Ash followed her gaze to the distant horizon. The fear that had been bubbling away deep in his guts now boiled into terror. His legs wobbled, and his skin was coated in cold sweat.

"Ash? What's wrong?"

"I feel sick."

"Best get it out of your system." Parvati pointed to a rock. "Vomit over there if you want."

Ash bent over, gasping and trying to dislodge the lump of dread in his throat. His head pounded hard, like his brain was pulsing away within, ready to burst.

Oh, God, how had it come to this? Now, more than ever, he just wanted to go home. He thought of his friends, laughing and belching and crowded around the video-game console with their bargain buckets of KFC. He thought about Gemma. All those years of being in the same class, of sitting next to her in math, and he'd never asked her out. If he wasn't even brave enough to speak to a girl, how on earth was he going to face down a rakshasa king?

All those things he'd done, or not done. His life flashed before his eyes, and it didn't take long. He'd achieved so little, thinking it was going to go on and on. And it wasn't. It was going to end tonight, right here.

Slowly he straightened and met Parvati's gaze. She watched him curiously.

"You don't feel fear, do you?" he asked.

She blinked her slow, reptilian blink. "What is it you're afraid of?"

"What else? Death."

"No. You're afraid of what you'll miss, being dead."

"Yeah, that too." He looked around, lost. "I'm not even fourteen. I've never kissed a girl. Haven't been to first base, let alone anywhere beyond that. Not one decent kiss, and here I am, trying to save the world!"

"Look, I'll kiss you if it's so important," said Parvati, flicking her hair out of her face. "But then can we get a move on, please?"

"Stop right there," said Ash. "A charity kiss wouldn't count. Anyway, knowing my luck, you'd bite my tongue and kill me."

Parvati shrugged and began walking. Ash, after a moment, hurried up and fell into step beside her. She looked at him out of the corner of her eye.

"We could hold hands, if you like," she said.

"Just shut up, Parvati."

CHAPTER THIRTY-ONE

"This would be so much simpler if Rama had used the Kali-aastra like he was told to," said Ash. "Then we wouldn't be in this mess."

"He couldn't kill his brother," Parvati replied. "Would you kill Lucky, if it meant destroying Ravana?"

"No. Never."

"Well, then," said Parvati. "Only humans feel love. It is what we demons hate most about you." Her brow creased in pain. "You don't know how lucky you are." She whispered the last sentence with such longing.

So that was why she so wanted to be human. He hadn't understood why, until now. Parvati was beautiful, super-fast, super-cool — and immortal, yet there was something missing. She couldn't feel love. How must it feel to live through all those centuries alone? To be feared by those you wanted to be close to?

Ash coughed and moved the conversation along. "What would have happened if Rama *had* fired the Kali-aastra at Ravana?"

"He would have become a thing of Kali. The perfect killer. Eventually he would have turned into a monster more terrible than the ones he fought."

"Great. Then how are we going to beat Savage?"

"Leave that to me."

"He must have a thousand rakshasas surrounding him by now. You can't take them all."

"I won't need to. We just need to get in close. Who'll notice another rakshasa among all of my father's followers?" Parvati ran her tongue over her fangs. Each was only half-extended. Her hands rested comfortably on the hilt of the urumi.

She truly was born to end men's lives.

If only he had an ounce of her courage. If only his heart wasn't panicking like a terrified fox being chased by hounds. If only his skin was as cool and dry as hers, not hot and slick with sweat and fear. The rumbling thunder above him made him shiver. Gods and monsters. This was their war, and he was neither.

Ash laughed. "You know what? I just realized something. I'm the sidekick, aren't I?"

"What?"

He pointed at her. "You. Batman. Cool. Hard as nails." He pointed to himself. "Me. Robin. I get to wear green shorts. No one is cool in green shorts. Just not possible."

Parvati frowned. "Let's just hope you're not a red shirt."

Ash had seen enough episodes of *Star Trek* to know anyone in a red shirt was a phaser magnet. "Wow, I never figured you for a Trekkie. Popular among rakshasas, is it?"

"You'd be surprised."

Ash fell a few paces behind. Parvati strode over the cracked and uneven earth without faltering, while he stubbed his toe and tripped over every unseen rock. But he followed her, step by step. Ever closer to Ravana. Ever closer to his sister.

I'm coming, Lucky. No matter what else, I keep my promises.

They marched silently across the desert. The wind hurled dense clouds of skin-cutting sand at them, forcing them to fight for every step.

Thunder rattled overhead and the sky glowed with lightning. They held hands as they battled against the encroaching storm. Ash's skin itched with the building charge of power. The gods waited.

Parvati drew him under a rocky outcrop. She tugged down the scarf she'd wrapped across her face.

"This is your last chance, Ash. Stay here until it's over," she shouted, even though she was only a handsbreadth away.

Ash, throat too parched to reply, just shook his head. Parvati gave a brief nod. She gripped his arms and stared deep into his eyes.

"Stay focused. My father's realm was one of pure chaos. You'll see things that will . . . disturb you."

Coughing out sand, Ash managed to speak. "Like what?"

"Whatever you can imagine, it will be worse. He can, he will, alter reality to suit his whims," she said. "He can turn the skies to flame, the rain to blood, and twist everything you see, feel, even think. No mortal mind can cope. He will change the world into one of ever-evolving madness."

"Why?"

"Because he is Ravana. Because he can. Because he thinks he is more powerful than the gods, and he intends to prove it. He will not bow to any law. It is the way of all kings. They make the rules; they don't follow them."

"It's insane."

"Yes, it is. And don't forget it. If you give in to his insanity, you will be lost forever."

"I'm not afraid."

"There's a thin line between bravery and stupidity." Parvati's eyes glistened. "Can you guess which side you're on?"

The storm abated as they came to the outskirts of Savage's excavations. They passed an abandoned campsite where tents, pulled loose from their pegs, flapped crazily in the winds and the door of a cabin banged and clattered against its frame. Lines of cars, all bearing the Savage logo, stood parked in neat rows, covered in sand and grit.

"Where are all the workers?" asked Ash. There were the dying embers of campfires, pots and pans. Sacks of rice and boxes of fruit had been blown over, disgorging their contents over the rocky ground. The workforce must have been in the hundreds.

"There," said Parvati, pointing ahead.

As they approached the excavated ruins, Ash gazed at a city unlike anything he'd ever seen. The flat ground ahead was covered with a neat lattice of trenches and low walls. Mud bricks outlined the buildings and streets of a city that had died over four thousand years ago. Ragged lines of sand lay blown across the flagstones, leaving undecipherable patterns.

But the city was alive. People, mostly men, haunted the doorways, the streets and alleys, brandishing torches. They still wore torn remnants of uniforms, their badges decorated with the poppies and swords of the Savage family crest. But they walked, crawled, slithered. Some had their bodies twisted backward, their limbs at odd angles. Some lay curled up, sobbing. Some moaned and others screamed, nothing more than tormented things, driven insane by their transformations.

"These people worked here, didn't they?" asked Ash. "What's happened to them?"

"The Iron Gates are weakening. The Kali-aastra must be near. My father's magic is already seeping out, transforming the world," said Parvati, keeping them both hidden in the shadows of a partially fallen wall. "This is only the beginning. Once he's free, this will seem like a garden, a paradise, in comparison."

Animals snarled and crept along the shadowy paths, some with two heads, others skinless but alive, their bodies turned inside out so their guts and arteries hung loose in the dust. The smell was a miasma of putrid gases and hot, rotting offal. The biting wind couldn't lift it — it hung over the city like a foul fog.

Ash gripped his punch dagger tighter. Otherwise it would have shaken like a tree branch. He had clamped his mouth shut to stop himself from puking. He stepped on something that slithered under his foot and squealed. He didn't look. Lucky was somewhere in this place. If he did nothing else, he had to get her out.

Two long lines of blazing bonfires stood along either side of what must once have been the royal avenue. Ash and Parvati headed toward the center of the city. Closer up, Ash realized they were funeral pyres. Even through the near-blinding flames, he could see human bodies twisted in torment, their limbs chained. So that was what had happened to the rest of the workers: They'd been thrown on to the blazing logs while still alive.

Ash could barely bring himself to move forward. He looked up at Parvati. Her ivory fangs were fully extended and oily with venom.

"Don't let that happen to me, okay?" he said. "If you know what I mean."

"You won't feel a thing," Parvati promised. She would finish him off. Better that than suffer the fate of those poor souls.

Screams, chants, and cries echoed all around as the damned called up to the heavens. The clouds above them trembled. Wind roared through the streets, carrying clouds of dust.

"So this is hell," whispered Ash.

He felt a rush of air and pulled Parvati hard up against the side of a building. They just got into the shadows as a creature landed on top of a nearby wall.

The monster squatted, chewing some lump of meat. Its beak was black and slick with gristle, its scaled head decorated with globules of blood. The talons on its feet scratched the hard mud bricks. The wings, dark and shiny, looked like those of a giant crow, and it clutched something in its claws.

Ash held his breath, squeezing Parvati's hand. He watched the demon tear strips of flesh off the thing in its claws, cracking bones to get at the marrow and tossing back its head to gulp down the morsels. Then with a snap of its beak, it dropped the meal, spread out its wings, and, with a triumphant cry, leaped skyward.

Ash let out a puff of breath and released Parvati. His gaze fell on the thing the crow-rakshasa had been eating.

A hand.

"There are patrols everywhere." Parvati scanned the sky. "Above ground, on it, and no doubt below too. Savage isn't taking any chances."

She was right. Closer to the city center, Ash saw lumbering creatures barging their way through the mutated humans, scanning them and attacking at random. They tossed one man back and forth between them, his body flying and cartwheeling through the air.

"What are we going to do?" Ash asked.

"What else?" Parvati unhooked the serpent sword. She shook out the coils and the steel edges hissed against each other.

"Wait," said Ash. There had to be a better way of finding Savage than wandering aimlessly around the excavations. Ash searched his memory. All the Harappan cities had been designed the same way; he had heard his uncle talk about it. This one, the city chosen to be Ravana's tomb, was on a far larger scale, but seemed to have the standard layout. They were in what archaeologists called the Lower City, the residential district for the main, or common, population. The houses here were basic, two or three stories high, and all built on a grid system. This wasn't where they'd find Ravana. The tomb would be nearer the heart, where the more important buildings stood.

"He's up in the citadel," said Ash.

He pointed up the main road to the heart of the city. At its end was the huge central square, featureless but for a single black building. The square itself was surrounded by a deep moat and could only be reached by a single bridge.

Between it and them were ten thousand demons.

Parvati followed his gaze, and her serpent sword twitched, eager for battle. Ash had seen her fight: She was death incarnate, wrapped in the body of a teenage girl with cobra eyes. Still, despite four and a half thousand years of fighting experience, even she couldn't beat these odds.

What they needed was a diversion.

"I know what you're thinking," she said. "You're thinking this needs someone to do something brave, bold, and stupid."

"That's me," said Ash. "Just promise me you'll save Lucky."

Parvati's pupils dilated, then narrowed into the thinnest of slivers. "You're going to die," she said. "You know that, don't you?"

Ash nodded once, unable to speak. He tried to smile, to act as though it was no big deal. If he were really brave, he'd make some cool joke and not stand there, trembling with fear, his throat as dry as ash.

"Just give me ten minutes to get closer to the tomb. Then create your diversion." Parvati put her hand on his cheek, her palm cool and dry. "I'll save her, I promise."

"Then get a move on before I change my mind."

She kissed him.

It took his breath away, his heart quickening as her lips pressed against his. When she stepped back, the soft touch lingered and there was just the faintest scent, like grass after the rains, old but still fresh and ever renewed.

His first, and last, kiss.

Parvati tied her hair up into a knot, getting it out of her eyes, and retreated into the shadows. "Good-bye, Ash," she said. The darkness thickened around her. "We will meet again."

Then she was gone. Ash heard the softest of footfalls and the scrape of blade against blade, then nothing.

Perhaps they would meet again.

But not in this lifetime.

CHAPTER THIRTY-TWO

Fingers locked around the dagger hilt, Ash wiped the tears from his eyes.

His father had told him stories of the ancient warriors called the Rajputs. Rajasthan was named after them. When they'd faced certain defeat, the men had dressed in their finest robes and adorned themselves with their brightest jewels. Then they would charge the enemy, fighting, knowing they would be slaughtered but never hesitating, never surrendering. Like true heroes.

But Ash was no ancient hero. A month ago he was having his lunch money stolen by the school bullies.

Today is a good day to die. That's what the Rajput warriors would say.

But it was never a good day to die.

He wanted to live, wanted it so badly that he shuffled backward, ashamed of his cowardice but unable to prevent it. He wanted to live! Surely Parvati could kill Savage without him? Maybe he'd underestimated her. She'd save Lucky and bring her here. He'd just wait on this spot. Safe.

No. If he stayed, Parvati would fail, Savage would win, and Lucky would die. If he stayed here, Ravana would be freed.

Look after your sister.

He could do that. He *would* do that.

How long had it been since Parvati left? He wasn't sure. It must be ten minutes by now. If he waited any longer, he might never find the courage to act. This was it. He had to create a diversion — now.

Ash crept forward, keeping himself in the shadows. The hideous servants of Ravana didn't notice him. They screamed and wailed and danced, celebrating the imminent coming of their king, but he pushed his way through, eyes on the citadel ahead. Ash turned a corner and tripped over two crouching figures.

"I'm so sorry," Ash said as he trod on a thick, leathery tail.

Two rat rakshasas glared at him as they squatted over their meal, a small mangy dog. One pushed Ash back, hard.

"Away, fool," snapped one. "We're having dinner."

Ash stepped away. He needed to get a lot closer to the citadel if he was going to create a diversion that might work. Cold sweat crept down his back. Time was running out. He looked for an empty alley.

"Hold."

One of the rat demons, the dog's hind leg still in its hand, came up to him. It sniffed at his feet, then stood, smelling around his throat. Its pink eyes came close up to Ash's.

"Why aren't you changed, like the other mortals?" it asked.

Ash swallowed. He needed to think of something *really* clever. "I am. It's just on the inside. *Completely* changed."

The rat widened its jaws to give Ash an extremely close-up view of its crooked yellow teeth. It clearly didn't believe Ash's cunning lie. And it wasn't going to let him get away.

"I'm really sorry about this," said Ash, and he rammed his dagger into the rat's belly.

The cut bit deep and blood gushed out. The second rat leaped at Ash and the two of them fell. Ash lost his grip on his weapon, so he punched the rat's long nose as it snapped its yellow, crooked teeth at his fingers. Its tail twitched and encircled Ash's leg. This was a brawl, no skill or style, just the two biting, punching, and kicking each other. The rat screamed as Ash pulled out a handful of whiskers. Then he kneed the monster between the legs and the rat groaned and let go.

Ash picked up his dagger as more creatures approached. He was panting hard from the scuffle and blinded with sweat, but he struck out at any who got too close.

"Fight, then! What are you afraid of?" he roared.

A high-pitched cackle Ash recognized echoed from the alleys. A rakshasa bounded out of the crumbling walls and houses, her thick red mane quivering in the wind. She landed a few yards from him, crouched on all fours, grinning, her amber eyes wide with delight.

"My dear, sweet boy," said Jackie. "How good of you to join us."

Ash pointed the dagger at her. "Come on, then." Funny, he wasn't scared. Now that he'd made the decision to fight, he felt strangely calm. All he wanted to do, before Jackie tore him limb from limb, was to wipe that ugly grin off her face.

But before he could strike, she pounced, knocking him flat on his back and smashing all the air out of him. Ash jabbed with the dagger but Jackie cuffed it out of his hand. Ash was almost suffocated by the stench of decaying meat hanging around her.

"Savage is waiting," she cackled. "He knew you'd come. Stupid human."

She head-butted him and Ash's neck almost snapped. Black spots swelled in front of his eyes and his limbs gave up. He stared at her, dimly aware of the monster leaning back to head-butt him again.

The next blow didn't hurt at all. But that was because Ash was already unconscious.

CHAPTER THIRTY-THREE

Senses swimming, body limp, Ash was dragged through the city. Dimly he made out the grotesque faces of rakshasas glaring at him with undisguised hate.

They came to the royal avenue, lined by burning pyres and monsters. The path rose upward and Ash blinked away the dull, wavering confusion in his head. He needed to focus.

The road was arrow straight and led to a bridge about ten yards long and two wide, crossing over to the central square. There was no railing, and Ash peered over the side as they crossed it. One slip, and he'd tumble a hundred feet or more down into a dry, empty moat that surrounded the central square, which was vast, flat, and marked by just one feature.

A huge cube of black iron.

Ravana's prison.

It had to be at least fifty feet wide and high. Set into the front of the cube were a pair of gates, two high panels that groaned as though the metal itself was being tortured by what lay within. The air around the building shimmered with a heat haze, distorting the cube so it looked unearthly — not quite solid, not quite real.

Jackie forced him onto the square and Ash collapsed in front of the iron building. He had to dig his nails into the carvings that covered its surface to hoist himself up. The metal was warm, pulsing with heat. Ash sensed the hatred radiating from within it.

The gates bore ornate scenes of warriors and strange creatures, half-man and half-beast. Rakshasas. There was no spare patch of wall that wasn't filled with bloodshed. The battlefield seemed endless. Undecipherable runes lined the top and bottom of the walls, no doubt the story of the great war between Man- and Demonkind. In the heart of the slaughter stood an immense warrior, decorated with gold leaf, the one bright spot on the dark iron canvas. He stood upon a mountain of corpses, a sword in each hand. He could not be touched or harmed, though his armored body bristled with arrows and swords. Each sweep of his weapons tore apart bodies, and armies turned to dust under his gaze.

Where is Parvati?

The prison of Ravana shimmered and the metal moaned. The trapped demon king was stirring within, his power already corrupting the country with his madness. This close, a few feet away from his spirit, Ash could barely stop himself from screaming.

"Beautiful, isn't he?"

Ash blinked and turned toward the speaker. Light distorted around the cube, colors quivered and fractured, and he could make out a cluster of figures beside the prison, but nothing more. Then one approached him, coalescing into a single, solid form.

Savage. He had changed, and for the worse. He was bent double, a crooked, wrinkled thing, his head sunk low on his chest and his spine curved and humped. But his eyes still shone with insane desire. He turned his deformed head, smiling at Ash. Only his black magic and immense willpower was keeping him alive. He leaned heavily on his cane, and Ash glimpsed something in his other hand, something silver and gold.

"Ash!"

He recognized the voice instantly and sobbed with joy as he saw the small girl held by Mayar.

"Lucky?"

She ran into his arms. They hung on to each other, and Ash could feel her heartbeat, as light and fast as a sparrow's.

"You okay?" he asked.

"I am now you're here." She smiled weakly, wiping away her tears.

Ash smoothed her hair away from her face. "I promised."

"I didn't believe you. I'm sorry." Lucky trembled against him. "I'm sorry, Ash. I'm so sorry."

"Me too. I'm sorry I dragged you into this mess." He ran his fingers through her tangled black hair. "It'll be okay, Lucky. I promise."

"How terribly touching. You came all this way by yourself?" Savage peered across the city, searching with his nearly blind eyes. "Where's Parvati?"

"Dead. The spider-woman's poison was too much."

Jackie handed Savage the punch dagger. "Then this was your rescue plan? To barge in here, with this piece of cutlery?"

He tossed the dagger away. "My, my, you do suffer from delusions of grandeur."

Ash stood up and faced Savage. Now, with Lucky here and Parvati on her way, he wasn't afraid. He had Savage's attention; he had to delay the Englishman as long as possible. Parvati was coming. She had to be.

"Delusional?" said Ash. "I got this far, didn't I? I escaped the fortress and beat your demons."

Savage leered. "True, but I still ended up with this."

He revealed the object hidden behind his back: the aastra. The golden arrowhead had been fixed to the end of a slim silver shaft so it looked like an arrow again. The fletching was mother of pearl and rippled with color. It was too heavy to be used as an arrow, but it would serve perfectly well as a dagger; the arrowhead was easily sharp enough.

Savage gazed down at the weapon. "A great death. That's all I need now to awaken the aastra. Once it is awakened, I'll use it to smash open the gates, and my lord, Ravana, will be free." He touched the iron reverentially, like it was the holiest of shrines. "He will make me immortal. Young again. Beautiful again. Safe from death, forever."

Where's Parvati?

She was meant to be here. Now was the perfect time for a last-minute rescue. But as he searched the rakshasas beyond the moat, he couldn't see her. Maybe she'd met some rakshasa tougher than her after all. There was always a last-minute rescue in the stories. But this was real life, and maybe in real life, the bad guys won.

It came to him, only now, when it was too late. He'd thought Savage would sacrifice Lucky to awaken the aastra. He remembered Parvati hadn't sounded so sure. To open the Iron Gates, a great death was needed, and Lucky was not a "great death." Not for Savage.

"It's me you want, isn't it?" said Ash.

"At last, the penny drops." Savage pointed the aastra at him. "Yes, I need *you*. The eternal warrior. Yours will be the great death."

Lucky looked at Savage, then back at Ash. "No!"

Savage continued, "I wondered why Rishi was so interested in you: a weak, cowardly, and quite useless child. But then, despite everything I threw at you, you not only survived, you prospered. Jat's death could have been mere chance. But escaping my fortress? Defeating Mayar? That was not chance, that was destiny."

Ash looked at Lucky. He smiled at her, though he could hardly see through his tears. "I'm sorry, Lucks. It's the only way."

She dug her fingers into his arms, shaking her head. "No . . ."

"Lucks, think about it. I have to do this." She was his sister and he had to get her out of here; nothing else mattered. He brushed her hair from her face. Parvati would be here soon, he was sure of it, but maybe not in time to save him. He faced Savage.

"Me for her. You let her go."

Savage's eyes narrowed. "You're in no position to negotiate. You are powerless."

"I don't know," said Ash. "I did kill Jat, and I gave Mayar one heck of a toothache."

Mayar growled and thumped his foot forward, arms flexing. Drool dribbled off his bandaged jaw, and his upper teeth overhung the lower like a ledge. "You little runt, I'll rip your —"

"Easy, Mayar," said Savage. He peered at Ash, then nodded. "I will let the girl go. Once the ritual is complete."

"Your word on that?" Ash asked. "As an English gentleman?"

"My word, as an English gentleman."

Ash knew Savage was lying, but it didn't matter. All he needed was to delay things long enough for Parvati to turn up.

Savage snapped his fingers. "Hold him, Mayar."

Mayar hesitated. "I . . ."

What was wrong? Then Ash realized. Mayar was scared. Of him.

"What are you afraid of?" said Savage. "He's just an ordinary boy."

An ordinary boy who had beaten up a rakshasa. Ash's heart quickened as he met the demon's reptilian gaze.

"You act like he has the aastra. He doesn't," Savage said impatiently. "Hold him."

Mayar shook himself. Snarling, he reached forward and grabbed Ash, twisting his arms sharply behind his back. Ash bit down but couldn't help crying out. Still, his eyes blazed defiantly.

"You've changed, boy," said Savage. "Once you were plump,

spoiled, and weak in body and soul. Now? Now there's something inside you. Seeing you here, I'm convinced you are an eternal warrior. Your death will awaken the aastra. You should feel honored."

"Let him go!" Lucky pummeled the crocodile's legs, but she might as well have been trying to batter an oak tree. Jackie laughed and pulled her back.

Ash tried to ignore the agonizing creaking of his joints as he was lifted up to balance on his toes. But, strangely, the pain was sharpest in his hand — his left hand. He clenched it, and the pain doubled as he touched his thumb. Where he'd cut himself with the aastra. Where the splinter had entered.

There's something inside you. That was what Savage had just said. He meant Ash had changed, become tougher, more determined, but that wasn't all of it.

Ash's gaze fell on the aastra Savage held a few inches from his chest. The golden arrowhead shone brightly, with the two edges that formed the needle-sharp point smooth but for the slightest imperfection — a sliver missing.

The sliver that had gone into his thumb. The tip of the arrowhead.

Because Ash had held the arrowhead at the time of Jat's death, he'd thought the power inside him was coming from that. But when Rishi had died, the aastra had been nowhere near him. Instead, Rishi's death energies had passed into the splinter of metal in Ash. A part of the aastra was within him. That was why he'd defeated Mayar.

The Kali-aastra. It all made sense now.

Sweat poured off him. Black waves of oblivion threatened as Mayar twisted his arm to almost breaking point, but Ash fought back. He needed to keep focused! He could do nothing but defy Savage. Every second's delay was another second given to Parvati.

He stared at the golden arrowhead, the Kali-aastra. He stared so hard its golden light filled his vision. Savage ran his wrinkled thumb along the edge.

"Shame there's a bit missing," he whispered. "Only the smallest piece, and you have to look really closely to notice it. It's still sharp enough to do the job, but I'll have to really twist it in. Really work it into your heart. Won't be easy. Won't be quick."

Ash pressed his forefinger against his thumb. The tip was still in there, somewhere.

Savage drew the flat of the cold arrowhead down Ash's chest. Ash gasped as he felt the sharp prod of metal over his heart.

Charged with the power of a god. That was what Rishi had told him that morning on the boat.

Savage scratched Ash's skin. A sharp, hot pain, and then a thin line of blood ran down his chest.

What would you give to wield the power of a god?

"No! Please don't hurt him!" That was his sister's voice, but she sounded far away. She was far away from where he was going.

What would you give?

What pleases Kali most is death.

Savage handed his tiger cane to Jackie and took the aastra in both hands. "Good-bye, Ashoka Mistry." He pressed the point against Ash's bleeding chest, dragging it lower until it was in the center of his stomach.

Then Ash screamed as Savage drove the golden arrowhead into his belly, and a shockwave, hotter than lava, burst through him. Savage twisted the shaft, then ripped the arrow back out. Ash sagged in Mayar's grip. Savage held the arrow before him, the arrowhead thickly covered in blood. His blood.

What pleases her most is death. A great death.

"Kali . . ." whispered Ash with the last of his strength. "I'm yours."

Mayar released him. Ash fell a hundred miles, a hundred years it seemed, before he hit the ground. He tried to raise himself but nothing worked. He lay there, his cheek against the stones.

"Thank you, Ash," said Savage. "I couldn't have done it without you." He smeared the blood over Ash's cheeks. "Stomach wounds are fatal, but not instantly. I really do want you to see this, so don't die quite yet."

Ash's eyesight was already fading into blurry grays and blacks. He'd thought, hoped, that his own death would awaken the aastra in him, enough to give him some strength, some way to strike back the way he did against Mayar. But as his blood began to spread across the flagstone and his energy faded, Ash knew he'd been wrong. He'd lost, and Savage had won.

Savage joined his two rakshasas. "We have a god to awake."

He faced the gates and raised his arms, the bloody aastra in his hand. The skies shook and the earth rumbled and groaned, and the buildings around the central prison cracked and swayed.

"My lord," whispered Savage.

He struck the golden arrowhead against the black iron.

The gates began to melt like wax against a blazing fire. Even from where Ash lay, just hanging on to life, he could see the iron twist and deform. Faces, beautiful and evil, leered. Divinely carved women rose to the surface of the metal and transformed into screeching harpies, full of fangs and wicked claws.

Savage leaned against the prison, pushing the arrowhead deeper within.

A lightning bolt exploded out of the gates. Sparks flew in all directions, and demons screamed as they were struck and instantly vaporized. Another bolt burst out, then another. The cube began to roar and blaze with white-hot energy. Wild arcs of electricity shot across the moat, demolishing buildings, burning the living.

"My master," said Savage.

"My slave."

The voice was metal, grinding, ear-piercing, and it filled the city. Howls and screams from the rakshasas drowned out the thunder. Their god was coming.

"Come to me and receive your gift, most loyal of my creatures."

"Master?"

The gates melted for good, revealing a tunnel in the solid cube of iron. Though his eyes were dim, Ash made out tall spikes of cooled iron forming a labyrinth of stalactites. Some looked like limbs — human, beast, others a combination of both. The hole ate the light so that beyond a few steps was utter darkness.

Savage took a step into the passage and the floor bubbled and hissed. Flames licked his boots, but he continued farther in.

The tunnel sealed up behind him.

All was silence. The only sound Ash heard was his own panting breath. But each gasp was shorter, weaker than the one before. Mayar loomed over him and nudged him with his scaly toe.

"He's finished," the crocodile demon said.

"Get rid of him, then," replied Jackie. She took Lucky's hand. "Come with me, sweetie. We'll have a bite, shall we?"

Mayar grinned and pushed Ash to the edge of the platform. Ash tried to hang on, to bury his nails in the thin cracks, but his strength was gone. He dangled over the edge of the moat.

Mayar waved at him. "See you in hell, boy." He gave Ash a final shove.

Ash fell.

CHAPTER THIRTY-FOUR

Ash tumbled down, bouncing against the walls. Eventually he crashed to a halt on the dusty stone at the bottom of the moat.

It wasn't happening to him. Just his body. He was slipping away from his mortal flesh. Darkness crept around him, drawing his spirit down. Oblivion summoned him like a dark, deep ocean, silent and all surrounding. He was sinking deeper, and it wasn't so bad.

This was death.

Eyes dull, he stared up at the sky, a black heaving mass of clouds split by lightning. But the thunder he heard now was nothing more than the last few beats of his heart.

The thunder became faint; beat by beat it weakened. Then it stopped. Ash let out a final sigh, and the silence was complete.

The ocean took him.

CHAPTER THIRTY-FIVE

The formless dark begins to take shape. Ash watches as it tears apart the veil between the lands of the living and the dead. A figure strides toward him. Black she is, and bejeweled with skulls. Her red eyes blaze down and her tongue, long and bloody, licks his face with hunger.

The goddess of death herself has come for him.

She stands over him, her ten arms outspread, serpents woven through her bloody tresses, and she stamps her foot. The earth shakes, and Ash's body jumps.

Kali steps over him and stamps again.

A second shock runs through Ash's body.

Kali dances, and with each footstep and pounding leap Ash is jolted again and again. The sky swirls with storms as she slashes with her bright swords and screams at the heavens.

Pain rises through him. The dead should not feel pain.

It starts in his thumb, then splits, sending tidal waves of pure energy through him. It splits again and again as the Kali-aastra divides over and over, multiplying until it has pierced his every atom.

Then Kali leaps high, higher than before. The earth shatters as she crashes down and the final impact rips through Ash.

The pounding continues even as the goddess fades.

The pounding comes from his own heart, beating again, beating to the dance of Kali.

CHAPTER THIRTY-SIX

Rain splashed on his face, moistening his dry lips. Stinging wind whipped across his skin. Hot, living pain sparked within his muscles. He opened his eyes and stared unblinking as lightning flashed across the black clouds.

Ash gasped as air rushed back into his lungs, and he roared at his rebirth.

CHAPTER THIRTY-SEVEN

Quivering, Ash tried to get up, forcing his limbs into action. A groan escaped his lips as he stood. He pressed his hands against his stomach, feeling the wound seal up, and watched as the rain washed the blood away. Already the bottom of the moat was filling with puddles, growing bigger, deeper by the second.

The monsoon had finally come. Fat, heavy drops of rain pummeled him, and thunder roared among the swirling clouds.

His heart battered against his ribs, threatening to burst out. Electric power shot through him, charging every sinew. Every sense tingled: His skin felt like it was being pricked by a million needles, and he could smell the faintest odors. Water. Sweat. Blood. Fear and joy. Sounds echoed, his ears picking up the distant cries of the rakshasas, the scuttling insects beneath the city, even the silent dead. By giving the aastra the great death it needed, Ash had awakened both pieces: the arrowhead and the splinter. The immense energies in the aastra had been enough to restart his heart and repair the arrow wound, bringing him back to life.

But what have I become?

A thing of Kali.

Ash had been reborn for a reason. Savage had opened the Iron Gates.

He had to get back to the main square.

He stumbled toward the long, thin legs of the bridge. The old stone of its supports was pitted and cracked. Heart pumping on overdrive, he climbed, inch by inch, not thinking about anything else as he moved upward. The rain and winds threatened to rip him from the stone supports, and more than once he stopped. Below him were the waters of the rapidly filling moat and above, thunder and lightning.

Then a new sound rose above the thunder.

Laughter. So full of fury and contempt it was like spit in his face.

Ash shook the water from his eyes and glared up at the top of the bridge. He ached all over, and his skin was red and raw from being scraped along the rough brick as he'd climbed. But he had to get to the top.

The laughter continued, deeper, more defiant. It seemed to dare the lightning bolts to strike.

Cold, drenched, so exhausted he wanted to puke, Ash reached the top of the bridge support. The bridge was above him, but the support column was a foot narrower than the bridge road itself, so he was tucked underneath it. He reached out for the road, fingers creeping into the brickwork to find some purchase. Rain poured like a waterfall over the edge.

Ash wedged his fingertips into a small groove and swung out into the open air, dangling a hundred feet over the dark waters beneath him. The blackness below spun in hypnotic, chaotic circles and spirals, pulling him down into oblivion. He wouldn't feel a thing.

But he hadn't come back from the dead just to get splattered. Ash gritted his teeth and with his other hand grabbed on to the wet, slippery stone of the road. He hauled himself upward, his fury feeding him with power until he'd finally wormed his way up on to the bridge. He looked toward the end of the bridge. There waited the vast hordes of rakshasas, none daring to step on to it. Blinding columns of white fire shot into the sky. Over the grumbling winds he heard wild, demonic cries of celebration.

But one voice, heavy as lead, rumbled beneath the shrill screams of the rakshasas. It was the sound of huge slabs of stone grinding over each other beneath deep oceans. It was the noise of a being ancient and afraid of nothing: not man, nor demons, nor gods. He had shaken the heavens once before and almost eaten the world. Now Ravana was free again, and the only thing that stood between him and the destruction of all reality was Ash.

He was Kali's now. He'd chosen his path and there was no going back. His heart beat to the dance of Kali, now and forever.

This was his destiny, his karma. The world would burn with a billion funeral pyres if he failed. Ash stepped forward, closer to the prison of the demon king.

CHAPTER THIRTY-EIGHT

Deep cracks covered the black cube, and supernova-bright beams of light shot out from the tears in its walls. The Iron Gates were nothing more than black lumps of molten metal.

Ash covered his eyes as he approached. Against the white inferno he could make out hazy silhouettes. Mayar stood, arms outstretched in greeting. Jackie, down on her knees, howled, Lucky trapped in her arms. His sister was alive, mute with terror.

But where was Savage?

The ground trembled and the light from within the cube dulled. The sound of screaming iron died, leaving just a rolling echo, and the burning air was hard to breathe. The prison gave a final cry before it melted away completely. Red-hot streams of metal trickled across the flagstones, spouting patches of flame.

But where the prison had been, there was now a figure.

He was over twenty feet tall and forged of solid gold. Huge slabs of muscle slid under his glowing, flame-wreathed skin. He looked like he could crush mountains. A golden mane of hair fell loose on his shoulders. Upon his forehead, radiating with intense white light, was a brand made of a circle of ten skulls. He blinked, and his eyes were as dark and as fathomless as the night.

All was silent now, even the wind. The demon king stood and gazed upon his followers, summoned here to serve him once more after four and a half millennia.

They were his army and he their general. They were his subjects and he their king.

Ravana spread out his mighty arms and the demon nations roared with joy.

CHAPTER THIRTY-NINE

Jackie and Mayar were on their knees. A hush fell over the city again as all the rakshasas gazed in awe at their returned king.

The rain pelted down, hissing like a thousand serpents as it struck Ravana's blazing skin.

"Come forward," said Ravana. His voice was the thunder of war drums, echoing across the battlefields.

Someone lay on the ground among the bubbling metal. He slowly stood up, then strode out of the flames, unharmed. The only mark on his ivory-white skin was a large brand on his chest, five skulls arranged in a circle. Each skull glowed as though it had been painted on with phosphorous. He drew his blond hair away from his face with his slim, delicate fingers. He looked about twenty, even less.

Savage, but not Savage. If Ash hadn't seen the portrait, he'd never have imagined this man and the one who'd destroyed his life were the same.

Then Savage opened his eyes. The cold blue had gone, and in its place were two orbs of complete, mesmerizing blackness.

Savage stepped into the smoke rising from a flaming puddle of iron. The soles of his feet caught fire. Flames licked his lower legs and the ribbons of fire wrapped themselves around him, cooling and transforming into cloth, so within seconds he was robed in a suit of burning brightness.

He knelt before the golden demon king.

"My lord and master."

"My loyal slave," said Ravana. *"Is your reward to your satisfaction?"*

Exhausted, terrified beyond measure, Lucky was still on her hands and knees, held down by Jackie. But then she turned and her eyes met Ash's. Suddenly her face lit up with joy. She blinked at him, her eyes filled with tears, clearly unable to believe what she was seeing.

"Ash!" she shouted.

Then they all looked toward him, Savage, Mayar, and Jackie. Each stared, dumbstruck to see him standing, breathing, alive. Savage's handsome face twisted with rage.

Ash stretched out his hand. "I just want my sister." He closed his eyes and swayed, momentarily dizzy from the bright lights.

Mayar laughed. "The boy's delirious, Master. Let me kill him properly."

"Do it," snapped Savage.

Mayar's heavy footsteps made the entire structure tremble. Battered by the storm and rain, the bricks on the edge cracked and a few tumbled down.

"Out . . ." Ash winced, his eyes aching suddenly. ". . . Out of my way, demon."

Mayar gave a throaty half-growl, half-chuckle. "Afraid,

boy?" He stopped and spread his arms wide, blocking Ash from getting past him. "Good. First I'll tear your arms off, then your legs. I'm going to eat you alive. There'll be no coming back this time."

Ash couldn't retreat; there was an army of rakshasas behind him. None had dared step on to the bridge, but there was no way they were going to let him escape.

Bright lights flared in Ash's eyes, sending spikes of icy pain through his sockets into the back of his head. The pain tingled down his spine and into every point of his body, pouring out of his fingertips and toes.

He'd never felt so alive.

Glowing points of light appeared over the demon's body. They varied in brightness, most intense over his vital organs and along his arteries. Ash knew exactly where to strike to do the most damage.

This was true marma-adi, the true death touch. This was Kali's gift to him.

Ash's hands curled into fists.

Mayar stepped forward. He was five or six yards from Ash. There was no way past him, no way back. The only way was through him.

"Jackie and I will feast on your sister. Sugar and spice, that's what little girls are made of." Mayar smacked his lips. "Delicious."

Ash bit his lip so hard that blood swelled in his mouth. He gazed back at the yellow eyes of the crocodile demon. "Stand aside, rakshasa."

Mayar roared and Ash charged, arm stiff in front of him, fingers out like a spearpoint, aimed at the bright, glowing center of the rakshasa.

He closed his eyes as he smashed into a wall of leathery skin, bone, and muscle, but he didn't stop. There was a moment when he thought he'd drown or suffocate — he was trapped — then he surged forward and tore through a barrier of flesh to air and wind on the other side.

His eyelids were sticky, and he blinked slowly, watching the threads of blood cling to his eyelashes. He was covered in torn bits of flesh and splinters of bone.

The gurgle made him turn. Mayar swayed, then dropped to his knees. There was a gaping hole in his torso. Torn arteries and veins poured back into the empty space.

Ash had charged straight through him.

Ash's skin tingled with electricity. Strength surged through every muscle as he drew in Mayar's death energies. He felt power crackle down to his very fingertips.

Mayar tried to gasp, but he had no lungs now. His jaws just clicked one final time as he dropped on to his face. Jackie screamed. Savage gaped at the mess that had been Mayar with slack-jawed amazement.

But Ravana clapped. His mouth split into a grin of razor-sharp teeth, and he slammed his palms together, filling the city with the clamor of clashing metal. It sounded like armies fighting with swords and shields.

"Very good, boy. Very good." He waved Ash forward. "And I thought the gods were too afraid to send anyone."

Ash looked at Lucky, but she stared back at him, confused. There was hope there too, and fear. A terrible fear. His sister had never been afraid of him before.

More terrifying than the monsters. Parvati had warned him this might happen if he drew on the power of Kali.

Savage too retreated, Jackie beside him. Only Ravana stood immobile. He tilted his boulder-size head and gazed down at Ash.

"Which god sent you?"

"No god. A goddess." The rain loosened the blood and guts over Ash, and rivulets of red washed over his skin. Wherever he stepped, he left behind a trail of blood.

"Kali, of course." Ravana smiled and spread out his arms. He turned slowly. *"What do you see, servant of Kali?"*

Ash wiped the remaining blood from his eyes. Ravana glowed, but it was the demonic heat and fire of his soul that filled the dark night. He stared hard, searching the rakshasa for those glittering spots of vulnerability. But he saw nothing. Not a single point of light to attack or exploit.

Ravana had no weakness.

CHAPTER FORTY

The ground shook with each step as Ravana approached Ash.

"You are a destroyer, like me," said the demon king. *"Serve me and we shall eat the world. I will teach you all the ways of terror and violence."*

He couldn't be defeated. He was Ravana, and Ash, despite the powers he had, was just a thirteen-year-old schoolboy.

Ravana smiled. *"Think hard. I make my offer only once."* He hissed, and the air flickered with flames. How could such a beautiful face have such a hideous smile?

Ash fought for control. Ravana's heat washed over him, but he couldn't retreat.

"I am here to kill you," said Ash.

"You are a fool." Ravana shook his head. *"So be it."*

Ravana slammed his foot and the ground exploded. Ash leaped sideways as deep crevasses tore across the square. Chunks of masonry flew like shrapnel in all directions and tiny slivers of stone sliced Ash's skin. He catapulted himself dozens of yards, landing in a light-soled crouch. Ravana bellowed and a hurricane blast of heat swept across the ground, turning the flagstones red.

Ash picked up a chunk of fractured stone, its edge sharp and jagged, and hurled it at Ravana. The stone exploded into dust as it shattered against the demon king's exposed throat. It didn't even leave a scratch.

Ravana responded with a backhand blow that sent Ash tumbling through the air. The demon laughed as Ash hit the ground, battered and semiconscious.

Ravana stomped over. He pressed his huge foot down on Ash's chest, slowly increasing the pressure and crushing the life out of him.

"Did you really think you had a chance? Against me?" said Ravana as he crushed Ash. *"I, who brought terror to the gates of Heaven?"* He pressed down harder. *"Time to die, boy."*

Ash felt his ribs crack. Waves of agony lashed over him, and he almost passed out.

Then Ravana howled and Ash was free. The demon king stumbled backward. Black clouds still swam across Ash's sight, yet he glimpsed a figure on the demon king's back.

Parvati held on to Ravana's shoulder, her fangs buried in his neck, pumping her venom into his bloodstream. Ravana tried to shake her off, but she wouldn't let go. There was a long, ragged cut across her shoulders, splattering her back with blood. Ash could see how pale and exhausted she was, how battered and bloody, but she hung on grimly. Then Ravana slammed his open hand across her head and she flew off. Parvati slid across the broken ground and lay there, still and limp.

Glittering golden blood flowed from the puncture wounds. Growling, Ravana darted forward and grabbed Ash by the throat. He raised him off his feet and hissed his fetid breath across the boy's face.

"You could not hope to defeat me, boy," whispered Ravana. *"Who should I kill first? My treacherous daughter? No, I know."* He leered at Lucky. *"Your sweet sister."*

There.

A glowing spot had appeared on Ravana's neck. Parvati had forced open a chink in his golden skin with her fangs: two small holes, little larger than pinpricks, just to the side of his jugular. The light shone weakly, but it was all he had.

Ash stiffened his neck muscles, trying to resist the vice-like pressure crushing his throat. He focused all his remaining strength down into his hand, along his palm, and into his thumb — the thumb where that tiny, deadly splinter had entered.

"Or perhaps I should change her?" Ravana continued. *"Transform her with my gift of madness? Corrupt her mind and body so death would be a release . . . one I will deny her. Imagine how it will hurt."*

"What, like this?"

Ash jabbed his thumb into the small, blazing white point just beside Ravana's windpipe. His thumb tore into the flesh like paper, and his hand was flooded with golden blood.

Ravana dropped him and stumbled back, clutching his neck. *"No. No!"*

A constellation of lights burst to life over Ravana. Ash saw the points, glowing brighter every passing second along his arteries, in his joints, above his heart. The demon king was weakening.

Ash stepped up to the swaying giant. The lights grew brightest in the spot over his heart. He saw himself reflected in the bright metal of Ravana's skin. Covered in gore, eyes bright and grim, face gaunt, he looked like death. Their eyes met and there was a glimmer of fear in the demon king's black gaze, perhaps for the first time in his existence.

"No," growled Ravana. *"It's not possible. Not without the Kali-aastra."*

Ash drew back his fist.

"I *am* the Kali-aastra."

His blow shattered the golden chest, and a thunderous cry burst from Ravana. Ash's arm slid in up to his elbow. His fingers gripped the demon's heart, and he tore it out in a flood of golden blood.

Ravana's death bellow knocked him off his feet, creating winds like a hurricane. Ash stumbled back, heart still in his hand. He squeezed, and the pulsing muscle burst.

Ravana stumbled and swayed upright, hands covering the gaping wound in his chest and hole in his neck, trying to staunch the river of sparkling gold pouring out. The color began to fade from his skin, turning gray and lifeless. He lowered himself to his knees and fixed his gaze on Ash. His body turned into a lifeless statue of cold dust.

Ash drew back his fist, ready to deliver one final blow, to make the thing explode into a cloud of nothingness. But he stopped.

The rain was forming black craters in what was left of the demon king. Thin streams of water mixed with the ash and ran off the body, leaving grooves and alleys through the new statue as they descended. The wind whipped away its outer layers in long and winding ribbons. Moment by moment, the elements broke the demon king down into a billion specks of dust and gray water that dribbled away down the cracks in the ground. Soon there was just a malformed lump of ash, like the remains of a funeral pyre.

Ravana was dead. Forever.

Ash's heart swelled as he absorbed the death energies of the demon king, a thousand times greater than Mayar's. His body seemed to expand, swell, until it felt as if it would tear apart. His bones screamed in agony, and his sinews and veins burned with furious power.

He stood there swaying as the last tremors passed deep into his soul, becoming part of him. Then his eyes snapped open.

Ravana and Mayar were gone, but there were yet more to kill.

Two down, two more to go.

Ash searched the platform and saw Savage backing away, Jackie retreating with him across the bridge. Glittering golden lights covered both of them. Ash shivered with supernatural might.

"Ash!"

Ash spun around at his sister's cry. She was stumbling toward him against the howling winds, trying to cover her eyes against the sands and biting rain. He struggled to his feet and Lucky ran into his arms.

On the edge of the city, tidal waves of sand rose, battering the walls and demolishing the buildings. The central platform they were standing on tilted. The corner smashed apart, and large stone slabs tumbled into the moat. The bridge bowed, then shattered. But as Ash peered through the blinding rain, he caught a glimpse of Savage barging his way through the terrified mass of demons, Jackie beside him. They'd made it over the moat and were trying to escape from the city. If he ran now, he could still get them before they disappeared.

"Ash! Come on!" Lucky screamed.

Ash grabbed Lucky's arm. He'd come here to save her and that was all that mattered. Except —

"Parvati, where's Parvati?"

Suddenly he saw her, lying on the ground, and ran over to her. Her eyelids flickered.

She saw him and winced. "What happened?" she asked.

The ground trembled and jagged tears in the earth appeared, spewing lava. Ash lifted her up. "I'm not quite sure," he said. "But I think I've just saved the world."

"You're going to be pretty insufferable from now on, aren't you?" Parvati slung her arm over his shoulder. She could barely walk, so Ash had to support her.

"Yes. Totally."

They grabbed Lucky, and the three of them ran to the edge of the demolished bridge. The vast central square that formed the heart of the city was crumbling around them. More huge chunks of stone cracked and shattered, falling down into the moat. Lava hissed as it reacted with the moat waters, sending up thick curtains of steam.

There was a thirty-foot-wide gap to the other side.

"Parvati, I can't carry you both across like this," said Ash. The entire citadel was collapsing.

Parvati nodded. She twisted herself and became a cobra.

Ash slung her around his neck and swept his sister into his arms.

Ash closed his eyes, directing his superhuman energies into his limbs, making his heart quicken and legs surge with more and more power. He didn't know how much would be left, if anything, but he didn't care. They had this one chance.

Ash ran. Each step was longer and faster, and his speed increased a hundredfold as he hit the edge of the tilting square and launched himself high into the air.

Up and up they rose, Lucky with her arms tight around his neck, eyes closed, and Parvati wound around him. As they flew over into the gap, Ash glimpsed the demons crowding the alleyways and streets ahead of them, clambering over each other as they fled from the crumbling city.

Then Ash was in the storm, the city gone. Wind and rain lashed him and he almost seemed to pause in midair, lightning bursting around him. Then he lowered his head and dived down, piercing the black clouds.

Ash slammed down into the roof of a building, shattering the flagstones under his feet and sending tremors through the house. They were at the edge of the old city. The desert lay before them, hidden in the rising sandstorm. He dropped Lucky as the cobra wriggled off his neck and transformed back into Parvati. Together they tumbled down the steps from the roof and into the chaos of the streets.

Rakshasas ran in screaming terror down the narrow alleys and flooded lanes. The sky swirled with rain and sand, a sharp, corrosive mix that stung their skin and scratched their eyes. The rumble of thunder was deafening, and the winds ripped down walls and scooped up bodies, carrying them up into the black sky.

The gods had waited and now unleashed their full wrath on the city of demons.

"That way! That way!" screamed Parvati. She pointed toward a cluster of large rocks on the outskirts of the city. They stumbled out into the desert, and after a short while all three collapsed, exhausted, among the large sandstone boulders. Parvati and Lucky squeezed themselves into a low alcove under one of the boulders, getting out of the skin-ripping sandstorm. But before he crawled in behind them, Ash looked back. A huge cloud of sand rose high over the city like a giant tornado. Lightning flashed within its vortex and the rumble deepened. Then there was a single, ear-splitting roar as the earth opened up, and the city of Ravana vanished back beneath the sands.

CHAPTER FORTY-ONE

The ground trembled and shook loose the curtain of sand that covered Ash. He lay curled up under the edge of the boulder, his body protecting the sleeping forms of Lucky and Parvati. A loud, angry buzzing filled the air.

Rakshasas?

The buzzing grew louder. He turned his shoulders, shaking off more sand. A shaft of bright sunlight pierced the crack between the underside of the boulder and the wedge of hard-packed sand that had blown up against it.

Ash rolled out of the crevice and rose to his feet.

There was nothing but empty desert. Dust devils whirled across the flat expanse, and snaking dunes hissed as the wind caressed them.

All gone. The city. The rakshasas. Ravana.

And Savage?

Ash turned toward the buzzing. A plane rolled across the desert. The paint had been scoured clean off, so the bare metal, aluminum bright, shone with blinding intensity. He could just make out the faded image of a crown on the tail fin.

The plane swiveled and came to a stop in front of him. The side passenger door opened.

Jimmy took off his sunglasses and looked around at the transformed landscape in amazement. Then he smiled at Ash. "Namaste."

"You came back?" asked Ash. "For us?"

"Alas, nothing so heroic. I didn't get five miles before the storms drove me down." He gestured to the horizon. "Spent the night praying to every god I could think of. Want a lift back?"

"We can't pay you."

Jimmy took a big blue sapphire out of his pocket. "I think this covers a return flight," he said. "First class."

"What does that mean, 'first class'?" Ash said.

Jimmy grinned and waved a paper bag. "The cookies aren't broken."

CHAPTER FORTY-TWO

"How do I look?" said Ash.

John shrugged. "Like an English."

A couple of days had passed, and India was returning to normal. The story out of Rajasthan was confusing, contradictory. Some people were blaming the riots on religious fanatics, others on terrorists. No one seemed too sure.

The journey back to Varanasi had taken ages. Jimmy had needed to make a stop on the way for repairs. When they'd got back to Varanasi, they returned to the Lalgur. Ujba had given them food and rest. He'd said little, but there was a calculating look in his eyes now whenever he spoke to Ash. Hakim too kept his distance. Ash wasn't the same boy they'd known before.

But now they were here, Ash and Lucky, Parvati and John, in the crowded lobby of the Best View Hotel. Ash put his finger in his shirt collar, loosening it. How had he ever felt comfortable in clothes like these?

He watched tourists arrive. A group of kids ran around the small courtyard, and families greeted each other with hugs and garlands of flowers. All normal, day-to-day life.

We came so close to all this ending.

"Where is he?" Ash said.

"It's not quite twelve o'clock," replied John. "You nervous?"

Nervous? After having saved the world? Why should he be nervous?

"Yes. Very."

They'd called Mum the moment they touched down, and here they were, waiting for their dad to take them home.

Home. Where was that? Ash had spent the last month dreaming of London — but now, it didn't feel like going home.

Lucky sipped on a bottle of Coke. She smiled up at him and tapped her foot impatiently, eyes on the elevator doors that her father would come through any minute now.

Parvati looked at Ash. She wore her blackest shades and gave him a weak smile.

John followed his gaze and nudged him. "Go say something to her."

"What?"

"How should I know? Something. Something nice."

With a deep sigh, Ash agreed.

"I'm going," he said as he reached her.

"Yes."

Ash scratched his thumb. "You'll be okay?"

"I've been okay for four thousand, five hundred, and fifteen years. Yes, I'll be okay."

"Great," he said. Ash stretched his collar again. In spite of the clothes he was wearing, the shirt, jacket, creased trousers, and polished boots, he didn't feel like "an English" anymore.

He wanted to stay. His heart told him so. India was where he belonged.

But there was more than that. Something he hadn't told the others. They'd seen him defeat the demon king and practically fly through the air, but since then Ash had tried to be normal, to act as if those superhuman abilities had gone. But he felt far from normal.

See Varanasi and die.

Pilgrims came here at the end of their lives, and their deaths fed him energy. He was absorbing it from all around him now. Each passing spirit made him stronger. Power waxed and waned within him. He didn't need to sleep anymore, nor eat or drink. Was he now more than human, or less than human?

What was he becoming?

"Are you okay?" asked Parvati.

"Why shouldn't I be?"

"Oh, I don't know. Maybe because you were resurrected by Kali. Maybe because you have the powers of a demon king in your heart. Nothing important, I'm sure."

"Things have changed, Parvati."

"And that's why you need to be careful."

Ash laughed. "With great power comes great responsibility, right? I learned that from Spider-Man."

"Do you take all your philosophy from comic books?"

"Doesn't everyone?"

Parvati gazed at him. Even with her eyes hidden behind dark glasses, Ash felt them penetrate his own. "Then let me tell you what I think," she said. "Power corrupts, and absolute power corrupts absolutely. It's a famous saying, but it's true. So watch yourself, Ashoka Mistry."

"He's still out there," said Ash. "I should stay and help you find him."

"Your job is done. You need to look after your sister. I'll deal with Savage."

Savage. The thought of him darkened Ash's mood.

"Easy, Ash," said Parvati.

Ash blinked, then smiled. "I'm good."

Parvati didn't look convinced. She'd been wary around him ever since that night. Sure, she smiled and was friendly, but the power balance had shifted, big time.

She put her cool hand against his cheek. "My hero."

Hero?

He didn't feel like a hero. He'd fought Savage and Ravana, but each time he'd been almost paralyzed by fear, ready to give up. But he hadn't. Maybe that was it: He'd never quit. He'd gone on even when he'd been terrified. Being heroic wasn't about being fearless; it was about conquering your fear and never giving up.

He just hoped he never, ever had to go through that again. Saving the world once was enough for anyone.

"I'm still me, Parvati. That hasn't changed."

"You just make sure you stay this way."

Suddenly Lucky screamed with joy and dashed into the arms of a man emerging from the elevator. There were tears streaming down his face.

"Dad," said Ash. His heart swelled to bursting and he

tingled all over. He couldn't believe it. After all they'd been through, there was his dad, and that was the most important thing in the world.

He saw the man's red-rimmed eyes and his unkempt black hair. He saw the ruffled clothes and the tiredness. He saw his father smile at Lucky as he swung her in the air.

And then Ash blinked as he saw the golden spots glow over his father's body. There, above his heart. There, on his neck, his lungs, along the arteries. The temples of his head. There were so many ways to kill. Ash closed his eyes.

The Kali-aastra. He could never forget it.

He took a deep breath and opened his eyes again. The glowing points had vanished, for now, and then their eyes met. His dad put Lucky down. The smile was soft, and he gave a slight nod. But Ash felt the joy radiating brightly from his father.

He was the Kali-aastra, but that was not the sum of him. He was Ash. He was thirteen and he missed home so very much. He was that man's son.

Ash turned to Parvati. "I have to go."

She leaned forward and put her warm, smooth lips against his. They lingered there and Ash felt a shiver run right through his body. In a good way. A very good way. He could get used to this.

"May the gods protect you, Ashoka Mistry," she whispered.

Ash smiled, unable to answer. He held her hand and, reluctantly, released it. Then he went to his father.

A shadow loomed across the ceiling, one only Ash could see. Arms, sinewy and shaking with bangles of bone, spread out to embrace him. He nodded to her in acceptance. She would protect him, of that he was sure. Protect him until she needed him next. He had given himself to her and he would never leave her. The black one. The slayer of demons.

Kali.

ABOUT THE AUTHOR

Sarwat Chadda is the author of the acclaimed young-adult novels *Devil's Kiss* and *Dark Goddess*. He was inspired to write this book by the "real" Savage Fortress — a maharajah's palace near Varanasi, India — as well as his long fascination with the goddess Kali and other awesome warriors of legend.

Sarwat lives in London, England with his family. Please visit his website at www.sarwatchadda.com.

Ash escaped the Savage Fortress...but can he survive the City of Death?

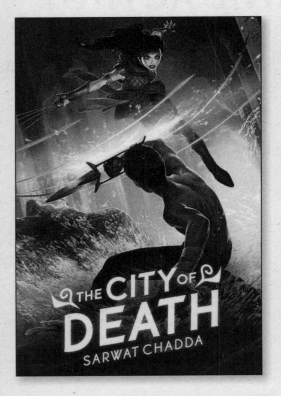

Praise for
The Savage Fortress

★ "Fast paced, exciting, and sometimes terrifying...Very hard to put down."
—*School Library Journal*, starred review

"Breathtaking... nonstop action."
—*Kirkus Reviews*

After Lord Savage steals one of the British Crown Jewels, Ash and Parvati team up to track him down... until Ash must fight the rakshasa princess herself.

■SCHOLASTIC
scholastic.com/savagefortress

Available in print and eBook editions

CHADDA